LITTLE AMANDA

There had been a strange change in ten-year-old Amanda Westerhays's behavior recently. She spent long hours in her room alone. Her parents hadn't seen her eat for weeks—except once, when she licked a plate full of blood that had dripped from a steak and laughed wildly. And just recently, she had threatened to cut little Davey Schwimmer's tongue off.

Then one day her teacher took a look in her lunch box. And as soon as he did, he slammed it shut. There in the lunch box was the severed head of a rat...

JORGE SARALEGUI

LAST RITES

CHARTER BOOKS, NEW YORK

LAST RITES

A Charter Book / published by arrangement with
the author

PRINTING HISTORY
Charter edition / November 1985

ISBN: 0-441-47185-4

Charter Books are published by The Berkley Publishing Group,
200 Madison Avenue, New York, New York 10016.
PRINTED IN THE UNITED STATES OF AMERICA

For Mary

LOURDES, 1882

THE FOOTSTEPS ECHOED in the darkness.

One by one the wall candles were lit by the man in the black cassock, illuminating the vaulted ceiling and all but the farthest corners of the cathedral. It was almost midnight, and the images on the stained-glass windows remained indistinct. This was just as well, he thought as the last candle was lit. For him the light revealed only an impending abyss.

He glanced at the altar cloth before disappearing into the sacristy: it was black, the color of the Requiem Mass.

No sooner had the man stepped out of sight than four tall, pale men wearing cloaks that covered hotel livery entered the cathedral from the back and positioned themselves at the four exits. They were followed by three couples dressed in elegant evening clothes who passed down the center aisle and sat in the front left pew.

The man who had lit the candles had now put on an archbishop's black funeral vestments. He was a dramatically handsome man of about fifty, but even as he cinched his knotted belt, there was more than a flash of discomfort in his features. It was as if something were gnawing at his insides. He bent over the small sacristy altar and kissed a gold, bejeweled cross and chain, then slipped it over his head. Next to it was the miter that symbolized authority over the Archdiocese of San Francisco. He held it in his hands for a few seconds before placing it on his head.

Moving to the sacristy door, he cracked it open and peered into the church. The sycophants have arrived, he noted, and he looked to the rear door, awaiting *her* appearance.

He had met her two years before, at one of the charity events the city's upper crust had instituted in a vain attempt to gloss over the recent Gold Rush past. It no longer struck him as strange that he, the archbishop of San Francisco, had become the lover of the madame of a grand hotel soon after, just as it was no surprise that many of the town's most powerful men had shared her bed. Fornication was only a blister on his charred soul, the first step down in what seemed an eternal descent.

Then the doors opened and another cloaked figure carrying a strangely wiggling bundle entered the church and strode down the center aisle. She followed ten feet behind.

Tonight she was wearing a white gown that exposed her back and the swell of her breasts. Silver clasps ringed both her wrists, but her throat was bare. The archbishop's gaze paused on the fragile tendons of her neck before settling on her face: the rippling black hair, the gaunt, ravenous cheekbones, lips so ripe they conjured the odor of slightly rotting fruit. These were lips that had requested crimes and ensured that those who heard obeyed. She was looking at him, acknowledging and possessing with eyes that blinded him with their darkness.

The servant preceding her moved past the rail and to the altar, placing the shifting contents of the bundle inside the tabernacle. The archbishop stepped out of the sacristy and greeted the woman at the foot of the altar.

"Lourdes," he whispered, and raised her hand to his lips. But she slipped it behind his neck and brought his head over to hers. The kiss was long, and their bodies, set as if posed, never moved; but he felt the oxygen escaping from his lungs, his head, his veins—she was sucking the life-force from him, giving him a delirious taste of death. When Lourdes broke away, it was not just a respite from passion: it was a reprieve from oblivion.

She laughed, the tinkling sound of glass he feared, and breathed his name: *Ambrose*. It sent shivers through him, made him smile while she fingered the cross on his chest, rendered him defenseless as she stole the cross from his neck and hung it between her breasts.

The three couples in the front row tittered, and Ambrose blushed. Lourdes was already moving toward the altar, and he reluctantly took a seat on the bench. He had been humiliated before, worse than this, but there was nothing he could do.

Lourdes opened the tabernacle door and reached inside with one hand. A weak, bleating cry rose in the air, and Ambrose closed his eyes, as if this gesture would shut out the sound.

The bundle lay on the altar, emitting the same pathetic trembling cries. Lourdes picked up the dagger from the altar, turned to face the pews, and raised the blade to eye level.

"Tonight we sacrifice a lamb." She paused. "The lamb of God."

One of the men in the pews grinned, but the others remained solemn. Lourdes turned back to the altar and began to unwrap the sacrifice. It cried out again, and Ambrose squeezed his lids tighter, seeing the lamb, the lamb of God, the Holy Infant, an innocent baby . . . and one long bleat, his eyes wide open now, as a double trail of blood seeped over the edge of the altar and into the black cloth.

He looked at the six people in the pew, saw them squirming with barely suppressed excitement, and wondered whether they really understood what was happening in his church. Then Lourdes faced the congregation once more. Light glinted off the cross on her chest and the chalice she raised above it.

"The blood of the lamb," she pronounced, and drained the goblet.

Ambrose moved quietly behind the altar and toward the sacristy as Lourdes refilled the chalice and the three couples knelt at the altar rail. They think this is a black mass, he mused: a tribute to the Devil. He shook his head.

The six communicants sipped from the chalice and, holding the blood in their mouths, turned to kiss their partners. The blood mixed, oozed down their throats. And before Lourdes had even replaced the chalice in the tabernacle, they were already ripping off their clothes, sinking to the floor, ready for what they had come for.

For them the blood was an excuse for the ritual, Ambrose thought, and the ritual was an aphrodisiac to their lust. His gaze shifted to Lourdes, who was coming toward him from the altar, even as the cloaked assistant stepped up to clean the mess. Her eyes claimed him again, telling him to undress. And he knew that, for her, the ritual was an excuse for the blood.

PART ONE

A GARLAND OF THORNS

Those who do not remember the past are condemned to repeat it.

—*George Santayana*

First Meeting

THE CORNER OF Mason and Ellis, drenched in San Francisco's rare September sun, glistened like the gold-paved streets Spanish explorers had died in search of four centuries before. Jessie Westerhays stepped into the light from the Cathedral Arts store, slipped on her sunglasses, and focused on the figure slumped over the hood of her Saab.

"Amanda," she said softly to her daughter, "take my hand."

A friend of Jessie's who was also a stained-glass artisan had recommended "a great little glass store in that sleazy area near Union Square." From the safety of her Presidio Heights home, she had forgotten how "sleazy" the neighborhood really was, and had brought Amanda along so that her fifth-grader could pick out some school clothes at Macy's. They had gone there earlier in the afternoon, and the new clothes were now in the trunk of the car, less than twenty feet from where they stood.

If anything happens, she thought, I'll never forgive myself—and reached out for her daughter's hand.

"Amanda . . . Amanda!"

Amanda never glanced at her mother's extended fingers. She was already moving toward the body on the car hood.

"If you don't mind, sir," Amanda began, enunciating each syllable with as much deference as she could muster. She got no further, because the derelict had turned around.

Dressed in rags that seemed only rips and smudges, he had road tar in his hair and tiny veins running in relief off the whites of his eyes and down his cheeks. As he lurched toward them, Jessie saw the dark stains he had left on the Saab's hood. They came from what was left of his bloody, lipless mouth.

Amanda recoiled, suddenly struck dumb, and Jessie placed her hands on her daughter's shoulders. The derelict's hand, covered with a fingerless mitten, stretched toward them briefly, and disappeared in the grip of a second man, who had arrived as if from nowhere. The man placed his free hand on the derelict's shoulder and directed him down the street, away from the women.

"Get in the car," Jessie ordered, and ignored her own command (along with Amanda) as she absorbed the scene. *I couldn't do that in a million years,* she admitted ruefully, and watched as the derelict vanished around a corner and their hero turned back toward them.

He was tall, she noted—almost as tall as her husband—with wavy brown hair and gray eyes that grew deeper and more subdued the closer he came.

"Thank you so much for helping," Jessie smiled, and surprised herself by not extending her hand. Was she so repelled by the incident that she couldn't even touch her benefactor's fingers?

She never answered her question, because the man's right hand was already picking up the suitcase he had apparently been carrying.

"I don't think he meant any harm," he shrugged. "The poor guy was probably in shock."

"Don't be so modest, mister," Amanda interjected with her most winning, knowing grin. "Somebody here almost had a stroke."

The man looked at Jessie as he laughed, then back at Amanda. "The name's Nick," he offered, and tousled her hair before nodding and moving away.

"What a hunk," Amanda opined as she got in the car.

"Amanda."

"And you didn't even introduce yourself," she added disgustedly.

So mother and child, having brushed with their fate and seen it as chance, locked their doors with a little more emphasis than usual.

•   •   •

After watching the woman's Saab blend into the traffic, Nick turned and surveyed the area he had decided to make his temporary home. Across the street, the stately Hilton sagged, a beached whale being slowly gnawed to death by the crabs from the Chez Paree, Frenchy's K&T bookstore, the Oriental spa. A grim little surprise, he thought, for some tourist from Illinois who books his family first-class into the armpit of the most beautiful city in America.

The armpit even had a nickname: the Tenderloin, a neighborhood flanked by Market Street and Chinatown, the Civic Center and the financial district. The Tenderloin housed the sleazier half of the city's strip joints and porno theaters, the uglier whores and the slower hustlers. It was also an area not too far from the grade school he would be teaching at, and an area where a cheap room could be found.

He hefted the bag in his hand; it had grown heavier with every step away from the Greyhound station. The *vacancy* sign swinging directly in front of him seemed as good a place to start inquiring for a room as any.

The hotel's name was La Casa de Dolores: he reread it several times and appraised the front of the building before slow, uncertain steps came down a stairway in response to the bell. There were no advertising bills slapped on the entrance, nor was there the familiar smell of urine. A sign outlining the basic policy of the house had long since faded into illegibility. Months later, when he reviewed all the events and seeming coincidences of that day in a chimeric effort to find the thread of design, he would remember that even as he had aimed the bleeding derelict in one direction, the Westerhays women had left him facing another.

The door was opened by a man whose age could be estimated only in terms of the twenty or more years he had obviously spent with a bottle. Most of his hair was gone, and what was left had the same murky, colorless sheen of his eyes. His nose, a furiously red pulp, provided the focal point of his face. Nick would have dismissed him as an exiting bum were it not for the tone of his voice.

"What can I do for you, young man?"

The words were clotted, even indistinct, but the sounds

carried a gentle note of self-mockery Nick couldn't avoid noticing. There was no present ambition, only a bemused re-
membrance of past purpose.

"Ah, looking for a room—one with a private bath."

The old man smiled but said nothing, and Nick felt the
mocking tone in his own voice.

"Money is no object, of course." Nick's grin flicked out.

"Of course."

He hadn't been wrong about him; this was no ordinary
derelict. "So do you have anything?"

"You're a student . . . or a teacher?"

Nick nodded.

"Please come in." He stepped aside so that Nick could enter.
"They call me 'the Doctor,'" he said, smiling. "That is, if they
call me anything at all."

Nick introduced himself and followed the Doctor through
a small, plain lobby and up a flight of stairs wide enough for
only a single-file ascent. The top of the stairway intersected
with the center of a hall periodically lit with old-fashioned gas
lamps; from the stairs, neither end was visible.

There were shapes littered along the hallway, indistinct even
from a distance of a few feet. But as the Doctor led him toward
the left, Nick realized that all the forms were men slumped on
chairs, some sleeping, some mumbling, some nodding at the
opposite wall.

"Meet," the Doctor said with a shaky sweep of his arm,
"your fellow roomers."

"Prospective fellow roomers," Nick corrected. They both
smiled, and moved on down the hall. The walls appeared to
be a faded violet in color, although with the insufficient lighting
Nick couldn't be sure. There were some dark spots on the
walls, as well as one old painting of a ballroom.

The Doctor paused by an open doorway, and Nick looked
in.

An old woman sat facing them, the first female roomer Nick
had seen. Her age, like the Doctor's, was impossible to esti-
mate; Nick could only be sure that she was the oldest person
he had ever seen. Her frame seemed to consist of nothing more
than loose skin and clothes attached to a huge, gem-studded
cross that hung from a chain over her chest. The sense of

museum-piece fragility about her extended from the strands of spider's web hair on her skull to the winter-twig fingers that held an album of photographs open on her lap.

"Would you like to see my pictures?"

The old woman smiled vacantly. As she spoke, Nick noticed that the skin around her mouth was scarred, not just wrinkled, and that most of her teeth were missing. Periodontoclasia, he reflected, remembering the term from his dentist mother: a loosening of the teeth, deterioration of the gums, discoloration of the lips.

"I'd love to," Nick answered broadly, and winked at the Doctor while he leaned over the old woman's shoulder.

There was one photograph on each page. The images were sepia toned, and faded with age. The one on the left showed a gowned woman moving through an archway, away from the camera. Four men wearing cloaks over what looked like hotel livery stood at attention to her right. The other photograph was a group shot: a long row of dignitaries in evening clothes broken up only by a dark man in a tunic and turban, and a tall, solemn cleric in a black cassock.

Nick noticed that the old woman held a finger under the image of a young, dark-haired woman near the center of the photograph. "That wouldn't be your likeness in younger days, would it, ma'am?"

"You could say that," came the meandering response. "This was her hotel once, in younger, better days. And it is my hotel now. I am Dolores."

Nick, caught off-guard, looked at the Doctor, and then back at the old woman. *La Casa de Dolores*. "I'm sorry, I didn't think—my name is Nicholas Van Lo."

"Thinking means little over the course of many years, Mr. Van Lo. You will come to realize that most of what happens to us *happens*—no matter what we think."

"Mr. Van Lo is a student or a teacher," the Doctor offered.

"A teacher just now—a fifth-grade class over at the John Swett School. Until recently I was working on a doctoral thesis, but that's neither here nor there."

"Quite right, Mr. Van Lo," Dolores responded. "I shall finish showing you the house. Would you mind pushing my chair?"

Only then did Nick realize that Dolores was sitting in a wheelchair. He moved behind her, took hold of the two grips, and responding to a slight motion of her head, wheeled down to the right. The Doctor, meanwhile, had disappeared.

While Nick pushed the wheelchair along the row of nooks and doors, Dolores spoke of the history of the house, and how it had deteriorated along with the rest of the Tenderloin since she had acquired it. Some film stars had stayed there on occasion as late as 1930.

She motioned for him to stop.

"This very room here . . . a beautiful actress lived in it once." She had settled there with her dachshund in 1931, not too long after her movie-star lover blew out his brains, Dolores went on. She had always been a big drinker, but once her career was on the skids, the bottles had grown more and more numerous. No one came to visit her, and she never went out; the only people who saw her were the delivery boys from the grocer and the bootlegger. The other tenants—people rented by the month then—eventually forgot her tarnished celebrity, eventually forgot her completely. They didn't remember until the smell reminded them.

It wasn't the only unpleasant odor the house ever bore and, truth to tell, it wasn't the worst. Perhaps the tenants resented her origins, or the rigid distance she had kept from them. Whatever their reasons, they contacted the Health Department and demanded that an inspector come and check on the situation.

The inspector came, ignored the protests of the staff, and knocked on the actress's door. When several raps drew no response, he obtained a pass key and opened it. The actress was lying on her bed, in the first stages of decomposition, "and the little dachshund—why there he was, eating her leg for dinner!"

Dolores let out a cackle that should have raised goosebumps on Nick's skin. He wondered why it didn't, why he was able to laugh with her, actually feel *warm* about the processing of an alcoholic actress into carrion. He decided it was the way Dolores told the story, making the survival of that dog a natural thing, something no one need feel ashamed to acknowledge.

"Don't tell that story to too many prospective boarders," Nick kidded.

"Only to the ones," she answered, staring straight into his eyes, "who will be living in her room." And she handed him the key to the door.

The room was innocuous enough, reminding him more of the dachshund than the more famous tenant. It was a high-ceilinged rectangle with aging woodwork around the door and the base of the walls. The walls were the inevitable pea-green and faded. The bed was large, soft, with a night table and lamp to the right. There was no writing desk, just a dresser with a chair in front and a dark spot above it on the wall.

"Is there a bathroom also?"

"The door on the left," Dolores answered. "The other one is a closet."

Nick opened the door and peered into the bathroom. It was small, the sink and the toilet running parallel to the tub. There was no shower nozzle, he noted.

"Looks fine to me. How much is the rent?"

"Fifty dollars a week, payable whenever it is convenient." She fixed one bird eye on him. "Do you see women often, Mr. Van Lo?"

The question caught him off-guard, like everything else had that evening. "I lived with my wife until just recently."

"Well then I am sure you will see them everywhere," she smiled, and Nick wondered how her destroyed mouth could manage it. "That is quite all right by me—we have no rules concerning visitors. Other roomers see other things. They will respect your fantasies. I would hope that you respect theirs."

There was a perfunctory knock on the door. It was the Doctor.

"The Doctor handles day-to-day affairs in this house. You will pay him the rent, compliments, and complaints." She motioned, and the Doctor started wheeling her out of the room. "I enjoyed our chat, Mr. Van Lo. Visit me in the evening and tell me how it goes with the children."

The door closed; the interview was over.

"I'll take it," Nick said to the far wall, and tossed his suitcase on the bed. When he found a permanent place, he would send for the rest of his belongings. For now there wasn't much to unpack. The few books nestled over a sweater came out first, to be stacked on the left side of the dresser; the photograph of his son he set down on the right.

So much to remember, he thought as he looked at the boy's clear face, and so much more to forget. But the sorting process could wait until the next day. Tonight, all of his memories insisted on sharing the room.

Second Chance

TOD WESTERHAYS ROSE from the couch to shut off the projector shortly after the last of *Kramer vs. Kramer*'s credits had rolled off the screen. Jessie, her mind still on the movie's dramatic conclusion, reached forward from her seat and brought Amanda back against her legs. Amanda took her mother's hand down from her shoulder and pressed it against her chest.

"Oh, damn," Tod cursed, glancing at his watch. "We just missed *Dallas!*"

Television, with its indiscriminate and sedating effects, had been banned from the Westerhays household for six years— ever since Amanda had entered nursery school. Even the advent of VCRs and affordable movie cassettes had failed to shake Jessie and Tod's conviction that Amanda would grow up the better for its absence; when his "two girls" wanted to see a particular movie that wasn't showing locally, Ted would borrow a 16-millimeter print and screen it for them on his old Bell & Howell projector.

After all, he would remind them each time, being the film critic of San Francisco's third-largest newspaper did have *some* advantages.

"Dad, why did the mother want to take the little boy away from his father after she left them?"

Amanda's movie questions were always directed at Tod; Jessie tended to get the ones concerning biology.

"Because it would have made for a very short movie, dear, if she hadn't," Tod cracked as he slipped the film reel into its case. "Apart from that, I guess she had a change of heart."

"That's not fair, Tod," Jessie protested. "She was entitled

to some time off by herself, so she could sort out her life. Who would *you* have awarded the child to?"

Tod smiled impishly. "I would have given Dustin Hoffman the kid's arms and legs, and Meryl Streep the sundered torso."

"So much for a little family discussion," Jessie grumbled, easing back on the couch. "You're impossible."

As Tod put away the projector, Jessie turned to her daughter. "It's time for bed, Mandy. School starts tomorrow morning."

Amanda had been thinking about how pretty her mother was, and how she wished she could cut off her braids and have a man's haircut too, when Jessie interrupted this reverie to remind her of her bedtime. How seriously she meant her response to be taken, therefore, was open to question—but her parents didn't know this.

"My name is *Amanda*. And I'd like to walk to school by myself this year."

Tod rolled his eyes at Jessie from the cabinet by the fireplace where he stood. "Now see what you've done."

"Lots of kids from around here walk to school by themselves, dad. Ask mom."

Mom qualified that statement. "I know for a fact that Lucy Matturro doesn't walk to school by herself."

"I meant *normal* ten-year-olds. Lucy Matturro doesn't tie her own shoes, either."

Tod decided to change tack. "It's not a matter of shoelaces. I don't think you'd get lost, and you have more sense than to step in front of a car. But John Swett isn't in the same neighborhood as the school you went to last year—"

"I didn't walk to that one, either."

"It was three miles away, Amanda," Jessie cut in. "Listen to your father."

Tod treaded out on thin ice: Jessie didn't like being reminded of what he was about to bring up. "Take, for example, what happened to you and your mother the other day, when that bum attacked you outside of the stained-glass store. I drive past your school all the time on my way to work, and I see plenty of characters on the street like that one. I wouldn't even want your mother walking around there at certain times."

Amanda's chin dropped to her chest, and her fingers listlessly twirled one long braid. "And you're always telling me to be *independent*."

Tod made eye contact with Jessie before responding. "Yes, and we mean it. That's why we're taking your request seriously. That means no snap judgments, no quick answers. Tell you what—run off to bed, and we'll give you a serious, adult answer in the morning. Deal?"

That was as far as she was going to get this evening, and Amanda knew it. "Deal," she answered, and put on her slippers. After kissing them both good-night, she climbed the stairs to her room.

When Tod heard the door to Amanda's bedroom close, he returned to the couch and sat next to Jessie. "Better rearing her than a future entry for Biggest Potato at the State Fair."

This was one of their private jokes; as usual, Tod brought it out at just the right time. They put their arms around each other, and looked across the comforting confines of their living room. It was Jessie's favorite part of her home, and she was largely responsible for its appearance. Apart from picking out the furniture, the design of the wallpaper that ran over the wainscoting, and the shade of white on the exposed walls, she had also stripped the paint off the fireplace, and carefully restored it to its original wood. All this, however, was just decorating. The bay windows were art. Over the years, panel by panel, she had removed the plate glass from the frames and replaced it with her own work: rich, multicolored, abstract patterns that altered themselves by the minute with the sun's progress across the sky.

Jessie loved this room, just as she loved their life. They had done a wonderful job so far, she thought, of *building*. Now it was time to face the fact that, in Amanda's case, the world outside those windows demanded to contribute.

"You know I was exaggerating about the school's neighborhood," Tod began. "It's certainly not the skid row I implied it was. The neighborhood's integrated, but other than that . . ."

Jessie knew he had exaggerated, but the blood trickling from that horrible man's lips was still fresh and wet in her mind.

"Davey Schwimmer's going to be walking by himself this year," she conceded.

"He and Amanda still bosom buddies?"

Jessie nodded.

"I wonder how long that's going to last."

Jessie didn't respond. Their eventual decision was already obvious to her; they would let Amanda walk by herself tomorrow. Wasn't that how they had chosen to raise her? Once a parent admitted the impossibility of shutting out the real world, it only made sense to prepare a child for its ever-increasing dangers, rather than futilely trying to protect against it. That was why Amanda had been going to public school ever since the first grade, a situation that Jessie's own mother found terrifying: it was as if they hoped that early, gradually increased exposure to the malignancies of urban living would immunize their daughter against its effects.

"She'll be okay, honey," Tod said softly.

Jessie smiled hopefully. "She always has been."

And so it was that the next morning, while Nick Van Lo discovered there was no mirror in his bathroom and cautiously shaved himself blind, Amanda learned she could begin a series of walks that would eventually alter the nature of her life. After slipping on her denim jacket in the foyer, she put her arms around her mother and then her father.

"Thanks a lot, guys. You don't want a turkey for a daughter anyway."

"Potato, you mean," Tod laughed.

The front door slammed shut, and Jessie put her arms around her husband. "Why can't there be a school for her in Presidio Heights?"

Tod kissed her softly on the mouth, and she decided he looked even better with the new gray at his temples.

"Do you want to follow her in the car?"

Jessie thought about it, then shook her head and sat down on the tiled floor. "I can't follow her every day, can I? We'll have to put our faith in human nature."

Tod knelt before her, cradling her fine-boned face in his hands. "Are you going to your studio today?"

Jessie moved her head back and forth slowly, savoring the touch of Tod's lips and tongue around her mouth. "Not until the afternoon. Ellen is finishing a piece this morning, and I promised I wouldn't disturb her." Ellen was the friend with whom Jessie shared her studio.

His hands moved down to the top button of her sweater. "Well, we can't have you sitting on the floor worrying about Amanda all day, can we?"

Jessie laughed in languid disbelief. "Tod, you're going to be late for work."

"Being a film critic isn't work," he reasoned, and unbuttoned the rest of her sweater.

The temperature of the tiles did not increase beneath their weight, and the unyielding floor did not fail to give them bruises before they rose. Jessie never really forgot about Amanda walking alone, just as Tod knew that even film critics have deadlines to keep. But as they picked up their scattered clothes and hurried, laughing and naked, to the shower upstairs, no one on earth could have convinced them that the magic spell of comfort and love surrounding their life would ever break.

Nick Van Lo spent the twenty minutes before he would meet Amanda Westerhays for the second time being lectured to by the principal of the John Swett School.

Calvin Shanker was a small, ugly man with a scalp disease that made his balding pate look like a slice of cooked ham covered with lint. At the moment, he was "frankly embittered" over the school system's assignment of Nick to teach "his" fifth-graders. "I don't know why you abandoned such an apparently promising academic career at Stanford, Mr. Van Lo, nor why those whom you abandoned would go to such lengths in recommending you for an elementary school teaching position. Nor do I see how eight years of Victorian scholarship prepares you to teach forty-four ten-year-olds this morning."

Nick stared back at him as neutrally as he could, thinking *you don't know how right you are*.

"Fortunately, for you," Shanker continued, "I don't have to understand very much in this job. When a very qualified young teacher elopes with a visiting Rumanian diplomat and flits off to the Carpathians without notice, and is replaced by a professional student who happens to have a certificate . . . it's easier to believe that it was meant to be, and just leave it at that, don't you think?"

Nick decided to swallow his pride and make an overture of sorts. "I understand your displeasure with these unusual circumstances, Mr. Shanker. I'd like to request your patience, and perhaps a little advice on how to handle fifth-graders."

Shanker was obviously mollified as he led Nick to the door. "Treat them like they were your own kids. Set the ground rules, stick to them, and they'll respect you for it. You've got my guarantee on it."

Almost every seat in Room 14 was filled when he entered it; even so, he noticed Amanda almost immediately. She was in the back row, ready to jump out of her seat with excitement when she recognized him. He flashed her a grin of recognition, then went over to the blackboard and wrote his name on it.

"Anyone who can't pronounce it gets left back."

No one laughed, so Nick picked up the attendance sheet and went through roll call. He made an effort to register every face with a name, but only succeeded twice. One was David Schwimmer, with the same given name as his son. David stood before him like a sweet-faced ghost from the freshly buried past. Nick had quickly continued on down the alphabet, until he reached Amanda Westerhays.

"Hi."

It was her: tall and thin with wheat-blonde hair, and fully aware of how cute she looked. He saw something coming, and decided to nip it in the bud.

"It's 'here,' Miss Westerhays, or 'present,' if you prefer. *Not* 'hi.'"

Even though Amanda sat down with the same foxy, knowing expression she had stood up with, Nick decided to lighten the moment. "Okay guys, July and August aren't that far gone—anybody want to tell us about his or her summer vacation?"

Several hands shot up in the air.

"Well I don't want to hear it." The others laughed, as expected. "What I want to know is, how many of you ran away from home this summer." The hands stayed down. "Seriously, who ran away from home this summer? Or anytime? Don't tell me none of you have ever run away from home. If that's true, I'm going to ask for a transfer."

There was a moment of indecision, and then one hand went up.

"David—I thought you looked like the type. So when was it?"

"Last Christmas."

"Last Christmas! Why'd you do it?"

"Because my sister got more presents than me."

"That's a good reason. How far'd you get?"

David blushed. "The PacMan machine at the candy store."

The entire class erupted with laughter, and David was hooted down. Then Amanda raised her hand.

"How about you, Amanda?"

She grinned playfully. "Tell us about *your* summer vacation, Mr. Van Lo."

The request spread across the class like a brush fire, and Nick had no idea how to contain it. My summer vacation? The three months still smoldered in his mind.

"My son Davey and I went camping in Yosemite." It was the summer before last, really, while his wife was at a seminar in Los Angeles. Nick had been inspired by a Prevent Forest Fires commercial; he hadn't gone camping since he was a teenager. They set up in a lean-to the first night, Davey falling asleep while Nick invented the origins of the winking constellations over their heads. "It rained the whole time. We had nothing better to do than eat Italian sandbags—that's what Davey calls ravioli—cold out of the can." Nick sipped Irish whiskey from a flask, giving the kid an occasional nip, and finally broke out a deck of cards, teaching Davey blackjack and Indian Guts, using raviolis as high-priced chips. "It got very cold that night, so we zipped our sleeping bags together like a giant cocoon, and pooled our body heat. When we woke up the next morning, we were covered with a film of snow." Davey couldn't believe it was possible to sleep with snow on one's face, and Nick agreed, speculating that they had frozen to death during the night, and were now nothing more than a father-and-son ghost team.

Driving back to Palo Alto, Nick had relaxed with the certainty that as long as there was a Davey, his marriage would survive...

A hand in the back of the class interrupted his thought. "Yes?"

"Does your son go to school here?"

This was what he had been afraid of. "No, he goes to school in another town."

"Why's that?"

"Because he's divorced," Amanda answered the persistent questioner. "Isn't that right, Mr. Van Lo?"

"That's right, Amanda"—and the morning recess bell rang in response to Nick's prayers. He stood by the door as the kids filed out. Finally, only Amanda and David Schwimmer were left.

The girl swung her braids at David. "Mr. Van Lo saved me and my mother from a crazy man on the street last Friday."

Nick winked at the boy. "Is it David, Dave, or Davey?"

An embarrassed grin: "It depends on the kind of trouble I'm in."

"He prefers 'Davey.' But *please* keep mine Amanda," the tall girl requested with mock supplication. "I can't stand 'Mandy.'"

Nick considered the crush Amanda was rapidly developing as he walked back to his Tenderloin room in the evening's fading light. Stopping at a pharmacy to buy some toiletries, he half-wished her mother's good looks hadn't convinced him to help out with the "crazy man" on the street. All thoughts about his flirtatious pupil disappeared, however, as he turned into La Casa de Dolores and heard the old woman's voice at the top of the stairway.

"Since I am not Lourdes Molina, Mr. Varney, I cannot fight your claim in a court of law. But rest assured that your eternal soul will be held accountable for your actions. Your soul, and the soul of the one you love."

Dolores's inflection was dry and final, as if she were reading from a book that had been kept locked in an airless box for centuries, a tome that dissolved into dust even as she spoke. Overheard out of context, her actual warning was ambiguous, but there was no mistaking the malevolence in her tone. Nick immediately felt sorry for whichever boarder she was addressing.

The Doctor met him at the top of the stairs, just as Nick looked to his right and spied the object of Dolores's wrath: a sleek middle-aged man in a dark, pinstriped suit.

"So how were the little monsters on your first day?"

Nick, visibly surprised by the incongruousness of the scene he had interrupted, failed to answer; but the Doctor, unperturbed, put his arm around him. "It's about time we were introduced properly. Will you do me the honor of stepping into my parlor, as they say in the insect world?"

The Doctor was clearly in his cups, and just as clearly eager to steer Nick away from the confrontation taking place a few feet away. Nick hesitated only a moment before grinning, and nodding his head.

His room was smaller than Nick's. Four paper bags, held together with masking tape, covered the lone window. The only chair in the room was laden with clothes; there was no bureau or dresser, and the rack in the doorless closet was broken. A little crate by the side of the bed held some loose papers, a notebook, and a couple of paperbacks. One was the *Autobiography of Bertrand Russell;* the other had its cover torn off.

Nick became aware that he was disappointed. Somehow he had expected more.

"Say, Doc. What was that all about out there?"

"Our devout and genteel landlady scaring off a prospective buyer," the Doctor answered, and emerged from the bathroom with two glasses in one hand and a bottle of MD 20-20 in the other. When Nick recognized the label, he could not suppress an embarrassed laugh.

"Is that why they call you the Doctor?" he asked, pointing at the bottle.

The old man poured each of them a glassful. "No—that's why they call *this* stuff the Doctor," raising his glass in a brief toast. "They named it after me."

"So then you *were* a doctor."

"That's right—I was a doctor. But when I said we should get acquainted, I meant with what we are today. I, for example, am a super of sorts."

Nick grinned. "And you know where I'm employed."

"Quite right." The Doctor was already refilling his glass. "It does no good to worry about what was; the past is best forgotten. And the sooner we accept our present lot, the less dissatisfied we will be."

Nick emptied his glass, thought about the taste, then blurted it out. "Have you always drunk this shit?"

"Scotch was my drink, but remember, we are speaking only of what is. Your fellow roomers, for example—they live in quarters once occupied by the slightly curdled cream of San Francisco society. But what does that matter to the man in the room next to mine? Charley the Tuna doesn't even drink much anymore. I think he's transcending this mortal plane; one day we will go into his room to find that he's left his skin and bones for us, and moved on. You can sense these things after a while. It is like being a medium, or a trolley conductor.

"Mr. Slater in the room next to yours can rarely walk after one in the afternoon, and I don't think he's taken a decent crap in years. Not a happy man, and do you know why? Because of that damn parrot of his."

"Yeah, I thought I heard a parrot a couple of times."

"You must have heard Mr. Slater. The parrot has been stuffed with sawdust for the last ten years."

"What a basket case," Nick muttered while filling his glass again.

"Yes," the Doctor agreed. "A true nut."

Another example of a man unwilling, or unable, to shake his past, the Doctor continued, and consequently going down with it. Leatherface, who slept across the hall from Nick, and was probably sleeping right then, had been a tank town co-ed wrestling dummy most of his sober life. One day, drunk, he married the woman who had pinned him in forty-five seconds the night before. She suffered a concussion practicing a trick fall soon after, and died in a hospital hours later. They had been married less than three weeks; Leatherface had met her that same month. But he retired from the ring, became a drifter, and ended up here.

"Knock on his door some time. You'll find him slumped on a stool in a corner, wearing that godawful Halloween mask he wore in the ring. Damn, damn. Have you noticed a little Japanese man, across the hall from Dolores's room?"

"You mean the one who says 'yo-yo-yo' over and over again?"

"That's the one. Yo-yo, we call him. I treat him occasionally for bedsores. His problem—"

"What about Dolores?" Nick was feeling his liquor; he knew what he wanted to know.

"Like the rest of the people in this place, she sleeps away most of the days, although she gets around plenty in that wheelchair at night. The half a mind she's got left is more than she needs to fend for herself around here, let me tell you; the other half went down with the Church, I think. Fresh towels are an acceptable vice, she'll say in all seriousness. But I've yet to see anyone pull the wool over her eyes."

"That cross she wears around her neck must weigh more than she does."

"I understand it's an heirloom," the Doctor answered vaguely, and then his eyes lit up. "I'll bet it's almost as old as she is!"

The old man guffawed, and dropped his glass to the floor. As the glass shattered, Nick thought he heard a faraway, crystalline laugh . . . and saw Dolores's cross nestled between two firm, young breasts.

Nick blinked. Where did *that* come from? He shook it off as the Doctor brushed away the broken glass and produced a second bottle of MD 20-20 from under the bed. For that round they just passed the bottle back and forth.

"John Swett's the name of your school, eh? Fine name. Got a reputation all over this city."

They both laughed, and Nick put his head down, realizing it was his turn to carry the ball. What could he talk about— his thesis on John Ruskin? Titled *Worms Beneath the Stones of Venice,* it was published proof that, not so long ago, everything had been going his way. The girl he had gotten pregnant, and subsequently married, was his advisor's daughter; the union had guaranteed him a future place in Stanford's literature faculty.

"My marriage was never right." His own words surprised him: why was he telling this to an old drunk he'd never spoken to before? Was he that smashed?

Yes, and that lonely. "Shirley was very young, and very infatuated with me. That's what I fell in love with—her infatuation. Married life quickly dispelled all our illusions, though, and nothing seemed capable of restoring them, not even the flings I had with my students. There were quite a few of those.

I remember, finally, Shirley asking me if I had been unfaithful to her. I asked her to define faith, and our marriage was over."

The pink liquid in the glass he held before him held no face below its surface, no message, no omen. "I used to tell my buddy Fred that our marriage no longer had a heart, but I was wrong. Our little boy was its heart—and Shirley drove a stake through it by making sure the courts gave her sole custody. He's all I love in this world, and now I've lost him."

Nick raised his head. The Doctor had fallen into a drunken sleep, hunched over on the edge of the bed. The second bottle had joined its companion on the floor, empty. Nick picked up the bag from the pharmacy, smiled down sadly at the sleeping man, and left.

He had barely noticed when Shirley's father revoked his scholarship and caused him to lose his teaching position. If Fred Olds hadn't set up this teaching job for him in San Francisco, he would probably have continued to float around Palo Alto, a ghost haunted by a little boy, a ghost no one wanted to see.

His mind still in that twilight zone of betrayals and regrets, Nick stumbled into his bathroom and deposited his purchases on top of the toilet tank. He set the last item in the bag—a small shaving mirror—on the tile ledge that ran over the sink. When he had tried to shave that morning and come up against a dark spot over the sink, a realization that had registered like a retinal negative in his memory, developing slowly in his subconscious, became clear: there were no mirrors in his room or, as far as he could tell, anywhere in La Casa de Dolores.

He looked down at his reflection. The light brown hair, thinning now, wasn't quite so wavy anymore. His narrow gray eyes, spaced far apart, eyes he could make intriguing or disturbing, were rather bloodshot.

Don't blow this chance, he told himself, recalling Fred's parting words at the Palo Alto bus depot. *It's high time you stopped punishing yourself, and started looking at this as a second chance*. That's what it was, even if he had to keep reminding himself of it, even if he was starting over in a Tenderloin flophouse.

Hidden Equations

THE TENDERLOIN, INCURABLE underbelly of the city built on the seven hills, was about to brush the surface of Jessie's life for the second time that fall. Its tendrils, borne on the ugly story her husband was carrying, would reach out and wind themselves around her heart.

She was far from the true source that morning, strolling with Tod and Amanda through the Japanese gardens in Golden Gate Park. As noon approached, the dew evaporated on the rolling lawns, and the three of them made their way to their traditional picnic site—the slope next to the Big Rec softball diamond. Once there, they joined other picnickers, resting roller skaters, and Frisbee tossers in watching the pick-up softball game.

Amanda spread out the 49ers blanket she had been carrying, and they plopped down in groaning, sighing unison.

"Mr. Van Lo's divorced," Amanda offered. "I know he's got at least one son. Davey."

"Just like your little buddy Schwimmer, huh?" Tod grinned. "I'll bet you know more about that man than his ex-wife does."

"That's enough, Tod," Jessie chided. Then, to Amanda: "I'll be meeting him next week at the parents-teachers get-together. That'll give me a chance to thank him properly for 'rescuing' us."

Tod's fingers snaked up the side of the picnic basket. "Steaks ready?"

Jessie gave him a mock-warning look. "Let's try to approach this properly, sir. If we eat right away, what are we going to do afterward?"

"Whatever we'd do now," he answered logically, "if we eat later."

Amanda grimaced. "You're not funny, dad."

"There's room for only one critic in this family, kiddo, and it's not you. Why don't you run off and play tag with one of those trees down there?"

Amanda knew when her father was kidding, and when he was also hinting that he wanted some privacy. This was one of those times. Maintaining her role, she gave him the finger and ran off.

Jessie could never get used to this sort of interaction. "What kind of relationship are you trying to build with that child?"

Tod lay back on the blanket and closed his eyes. "What does it matter? Freud says her fate was sealed before she entered nursery school."

"I know what Freud says." The truth was that Tod and Amanda had always gotten along well in a manner that never compromised his authority. It was a talent she felt she didn't share.

"So why did you send her off?"

"Something's sticking in my mind for some reason. I wasn't even going to mention it to you, but it won't go away." He rolled over on his side so he was facing her. "On my way home yesterday, I drove past the alley where they found Lisa Varney's body."

Jessie closed her eyes. Scarcely one week had passed since their lawyer's daughter had been murdered. Like most tragedies that are buried prematurely, what happened to Lisa would not lie still.

The Varneys had finished their supper at about seven one night. Rather than help her brother with the dishes afterward, Lisa volunteered to take the family dog for its evening walk. That "taking Buster for a walk" meant stopping by her boyfriend's house didn't escape her parents, but now that Lisa was fifteen, they had relaxed their rules a bit. Lisa and Buster left through the kitchen door at seven-twenty.

Two hours later, Vic Varney decided that his daughter had overstepped her bounds. He finished his drink and called the Martins' residence. the Martins had moved from Pittsburgh that summer, and he had met young John only twice. But when the boy told him that Lisa had left his house over an hour ago, Vic believed him. He paused only a moment after setting the receiver down before calling the police.

Buster wandered home just before midnight; he seemed a bit embarrassed by all of the activity at his master's house. By midnight, the police car had been parked in the Varneys' drive-way for over an hour. It had been that long since Lisa's body had been found in a Tenderloin alley.

The police had determined that her death had been caused by knife wounds on the throat. But Tod had learned from Vic that the conclusion was basically speculation. The rats in the alley had made sure of that.

"You never imagine these things happening to you or your friends," Tod continued. *"Homicide* . . . what does that word have to do with where we live? That's why I drove past where it happened. So I could see just how close it is."

He brushed his hair back from his forehead. "Jessie, it's so goddamn close, it's terrifying."

Jessie poured him a glass of beer, and asked the question her intuition told her he wanted to hear. "Is the alley near the property Vic Varney wanted you to buy?"

She noticed Tod tighten immediately. "You heard me on the phone that night? I didn't think you were in the room. Anyway, yeah, I guess that's part of what I'm feeling." He nodded. "A good part of it."

Jessie looked away. "Actually, I was just passing by the door to your office. What's it all about?"

"Vic was down at the Hall of Records doing some legal work for another client when he came across the deed to a nineteenth-century hotel owned by one Lourdes Molina. The place burned down in 1906, and he noticed something funny about the newer deeds.

"Well, you know Vic. He was down at the address that very day, offering the present owner—some old bat in a wheel-chair—twenty thousand dollars for the property."

"And she accepted the deal."

Tod noticed something unusual in Jessie's tone. "Yeah, she'd apparently been wanting to move to a nursing home for some time, so it all worked out well." He reached over and squeezed her hand. "We're not keeping the property, of course. Vic thinks he can turn it over in two weeks after it's in our hands."

"For how much?"

Tod laughed. "As Vic so crassly put it, for a lot of movie reviews."

Jessie winced at the words, and began to fuss with the picnic basket. She didn't want Tod to realize that she now understood what he was hiding.

3 lots/2 on record. And *$220K*.

The cryptic doodlings she had noticed on Tod's desk pad the night he spoke with Varney were now clear. The original hotel had sat on three lots; today, there were deeds for only two of them. The third lot had somehow evaded municipal records—and taxes—until Varney stumbled across it. The lawyer had no doubt explained the illegality of the situation to the owner when he offered twenty thousand dollars for the property—its real value was more like two hundred thousand.

A lot of movie reviews.

That phrase could have been the linchpin upon which their life turned. Vic Varney was a property lawyer, and the managing partner of a small real estate portfolio Tod's father had left him. Varney had parlayed the chronic housing shortage in San Francisco into a steady, hidden income that allowed them to live in Presidio Heights, ski in Aspen—and pretend it all came from reviewing films and restoring stained-glass windows.

"Did Vic mention the deal to the police?" Jessie asked. "I mean, there couldn't be any connection, could there?"

"Vic says the old lady can barely get around. And he's afraid that getting the police to ask questions around the property could screw up the purchase."

Jessie watched Amanda making her way back toward them from the far end of the field, and started setting up their lunch on the blanket. Tod was 42, eight years older than she; he had been keeping the real estate portfolio at arm's length long before they met. Because she understood her husband's embarrassment over this deal, it didn't bother her that he had bent the truth to keep the particulars secret. It was a form of protection, and she would have done the same for him.

Amanda was running up the slope to them, laughing. Jessie thought of the nagging, hidden equation between the property they were buying and the brutal murder of Lisa Varney. It was part of a world she didn't want to know, a world of hopelessness and death. She felt uneasy that they were involving themselves with it, even if it was through Vic, and only for a short time.

Offering Amanda her pick of the sandwiches, Jessie tried to put her troubling thoughts out of her mind. After all, it had been dark when Lisa left her house. Amanda walked to and from school in broad daylight.

The Root of the Matter

NICK TURNED RIGHT on Mason on his way home from school, swinging the imitation-leather attache case he had bought as the one concession to the respectability of his job. It swung easily, as empty as the day he got it.

The task of educating Room 14 was becoming easier as Nick neared the end of his first month at John Swett. He even had the opportunity to play the veteran teacher that day, when he encountered a nervous young woman cooling her heels outside the principal's office. When Nick discovered that she was just out of college and applying for her first teaching position, he offered her a detailed strategy on how to win over the unpleasant Mr. Shanker. He had no idea how her interview had gone, but the contact made him feel for once that his new life was finally taking root.

Walking up the flophouse stairs, he detected a whir of activity in the rooms, something unheard of in the house at four in the afternoon. He stopped by the first door and looked in.

Charley the Tuna was hunched over on the edge of his bed, the familiar sunglasses and beret not quite covering the quarter of his face that syphilis had eaten away. He was knocking down Dixie cups of red wine with someone who appeared to be a priest. Nick leaned against the doorframe; they didn't seem to be aware of his presence.

"No rush with the vino, Charley boy, it's on the executive priests." The priest downed his and poured another, still chortling. "Those execs don't touch the grapes, it's Scotch or nada for them. Why I'll bet if you looked in one of their chalices you'd find a Johnnie Walker label or two stuck to the bottom."

Charley failed to respond. "Not much getting through anymore, eh Charles? Well, don't sweat it. Not much being sent out these days anyway. Drink up."

Nick noticed a large black bag next to the priest, with the neck of a wine bottle bobbing out. He eased off the doorframe and was about to head on to his room when something the priest said caught his attention.

"Teeth giving you much trouble, Charley? That condition of yours must be hell on the jaw. Here, let me have a gander." The priest took the syphilitic's decaying face in two hairy hands, forcing open the mouth. "Yep, it's working its way through the enamel; meat inside isn't going to last long. It's a vile disease."

Apparently satisfied with his dreary diagnosis, the priest closed Charley's mouth and leaned back in his chair. Just then Charley looked up and noticed Nick. Nick looked away and strode quickly to his room.

The door was closed, his shoes lay scattered on the floor, and the attache case flattened his pillow as he splashed water from the bathroom faucet on his face. He looked for a reflection in the dark spot over the sink and saw the dentist's chair in his mother's office.

"Working through the enamel to the meat inside": not only was that problem eminently curable, the priest's terminology was all wrong. And those were just the details; the man had never even looked at Charley's jaw. Nick dried his face with the only towel he owned, then sat down on the bed, waiting for the priest to complete his rounds.

The knock came in less than twenty minutes.

"It's not locked. Come on in."

The priest entered, nodded, and looked for a place to sit. He was a swarthy, middle-aged man with body hair curling out from his cuffs and collar. Nick pointed to the chair by the dresser and the priest took it, tucking his legs in underneath.

"I'm Father Angustia. You're—"

"Nicholas Van Lo. My teeth are fine and I'll pass on the wine. Where'd you get your degree in dentistry, father?"

The priest absorbed Nick's rebuff and answered in the same jovial tone he had used with Charley the Tuna. "Not at Heidelberg, my friend. We urban missionaries are armed with a little medical knowledge, a lot of wine, and two lungs full of compassion. Believe me, we need it all."

"I fail to see any compassion in telling an alcoholic that the pulp in his teeth is done for when the syphilis has barely reached the jaw. Tooth decay is curable. The jaw is a different story— but then you never looked at his."

Angustia never took his eyes off Nick while reaching into his bag for a Dixie cup, which he then half filled with wine. The wine stayed in the cup while he spoke, giving him sustenance. "The basic reason for pain is decay. It is a vile disease. It is a disease of rottenness. And it is a hidden disease. It works in the dark, beneath the pink of our gums, within the secret places of our jawbone. If it is caught early, it can be removed in its entirety, destroyed. But if any of it is permitted to remain, it will spread until it reaches the heart and destroys the small fragment of life within."

"Reaches the pulp chamber, you mean—not the heart."

"I mean precisely what I said." And then the priest's intensity broke like a fever. "Did you mention where you got *your* degree in dentistry, my boy?"

"At my mother's knee. But it came without all the metaphysics." Nick crossed his legs. "Not that there's anything wrong with giving tooth decay a purpose and a face. It may be dealt with better that way."

The priest finally drank his wine. "Evil—and decay—have learned to hide their faces well in the twentieth century. The Church is like a boxer thrashing alone in the ring; it has been reduced to trading pieces of real estate and sponsoring bingo games. The modern theological crusader should not see himself as a warrior, but rather as a detective. Evil can no longer be identified by its sores; it must be tracked down, documented . . . and only then will the stake have an effect on its putrid heart."

Angustia's fervent words struck a chord inside Nick, a chord from the last century he couldn't quite pin. He knew he didn't want to think about it then, though. He also knew he wanted the crazy priest to leave.

"Well, father," he said, standing up, forcing Angustia to do the same. "I'm not a Catholic, and I have plenty of dental insurance. Maybe we can continue this talk some other time."

The priest picked up his satchel and took one step back. "Decay can spread beyond the mouth, young man. Look where you live. I hope you will have moved elsewhere when I visit next. For your own sake." He nodded a farewell, and left.

Nick dropped the attache case to the floor and lay down, eyes closed, on his bed. He had told himself that he couldn't move as long as he was making regular child support payments, but Shirley had already sent back his first check, uncashed.

It's high time you stopped punishing yourself, and started looking at this as a second chance.

Second chance, Fred? Nick smiled wearily: no, it hurt too much to call it that. This was his last chance to escape the traps he had been setting for himself for the past twenty years. And if he didn't know why he had chosen to make his stand in this room, he could at least recall the day it started, and the person with whom it all began.

A deep, earlier sadness welled up into his consciousness as he resigned himself to the four green walls. The bedsprings creaked beneath his weight like a door opening, a door that has been closed for a long time.

He was a boy, looking up at his mother, waiting for the secret signal that meant the visit to his father's grave was over. They only came once a year, on the anniversary of his death; the signposts of each visit were always the same, and gradually came to feel sacred by their very constancy.

There was the winding gravel drive inside the cemetery, lined with poplars, promising a wealth of stories in stone behind their branches. He would hold his mother's hand as they walked over to the gravestone and promptly let go when they found it. He always looked at the stone next to his father's first, and made sure the name was the same; the man must be his father's best friend by now, and they shouldn't be separated. Then there was the inscription under his father's name: *Korea. March 5, 1953*. That was the most savage word he knew, his war cry when he played commando. Korea.

His mother's gloved hand fingered the snap on her purse: the signal. The boy took her hand once more, and they walked back to the car in silence.

They never spoke on the long ride home. He knew the trip
back was like a waiting room for his mother, the time when
she left dad and came back to him. He felt sort of the same.
At the grave site, he thought of his father; going home, he
thought of what he would have told him if his dad were alive.
It was never stuff about school, or how he was doing on the
Little League team. Those things came and went so easily that
he didn't have to talk about them.

He would have spoken to him about the time two summers
ago when somebody broke all the eggs in the chicken coop
next door. The somebodies were he and Frankie Hayfield; when
they did it, nothing mattered more than each white-and-yellow
explosion, and the one right after. That evening, when his
mother said one of the servants next door had seen them smashing the eggs, he had burst into tears and blamed Frankie for
the whole thing. His mother had believed him.

He forgot about the eggs soon after; the Hayfields moved
away, and he almost forgot about Frankie. But he couldn't
accept the blind belief in his mother's face when he denied his
own involvement. The memory was an old sore that got picked
too often to heal; his tears of innocence were a betrayal that
could not be forgiven.

He and his mother stepped into the house, and still the
memory of his lie refused to leave. Even though it was not yet
dinner time, he changed into his pajamas and lay down on his
bed, face buried in the pillow, thinking of Snow White. It had
always been his favorite fairy tale, and his mother had told it
to him often. He was too old to ask her anymore, of course—
and on this particular night, too guilty. So he tried to take
himself back to that land of evil and enchantment, where the
evil queen had slowly taken on his mother's face, and he the
prince's, where he was still his mother's son, and Snow White
was his stepsister. But he didn't feel that way about his mother
that night, and the trick didn't work: he wasn't going to fall
asleep. Resigned, he went out into the living room.

His mother was curled up in a corner of the sofa, catching
up on her dental journals. She had also changed her clothes,
and was now barefoot, wearing only a loose housecoat. The
boy fit his body against the swell of her hips, saying nothing.
It was only a lie, and lies hardly ever bothered him later. But

how could he have cried for real? And why did she decide to believe him then, when so many other times she'd wrung the truth out of a lie?

She stopped reading when the first tear dropped on her exposed thigh. Her hand touched the spot where it landed, almost as if to determine what kind of tear it was; then, fingers in his hair, she asked him what was wrong.

Stifling his sobs, he told her.

He felt the hand on his head tense before withdrawing, heard the clashing of her thoughts, and sensed the passing of judgment. This was what he had wanted and, trusting, he waited for it.

She took him by the hand and led him into her darkened dentist's office, sitting him down in the chair. Still without speaking, she switched on the mirrored light just over his head, aiming it so he could see nothing in the room beyond the glare. Then she spoke. You were very bad, Nicky. How can I love you when you lie to me?

And she turned on the drill.

It's not easy raising a boy by yourself, she continued, as the motor's whine rose higher. I've tried being both mother and father to you—maybe it's too much to expect. Open your mouth, please. How can you keep such a lie for so long? Wider, please. I don't know whether to punish you or—

The drill was in her hand.

Or what. What do you think? Don't talk, don't move your mouth. I don't know, Nicky. I don't know. Then he heard her flick a switch, and the whining died. Go to bed, Nicky. You're alone tonight.

Nick turned over on his stomach, face buried in his pillow, unable to remember whether he had vengefully kissed Snow White that night. Twenty-one years had passed, and he could still smell the smoking drill.

He got up slowly and entered the bathroom. After plugging the bathtub's drain, he turned on the hot water and waited for the tub to fill.

That is where your problems started, Fred Olds had told him during one of their early talks. The root of the matter, if he'd pardon the pun. Because he was never able to differentiate between the paternal and maternal roles his mother had played all his life, his mind synthesized the image of the desirable female with that of the castrator. This was why he sought out sexual contact with younger, less threatening women...

Nick undressed and lowered himself into the bathtub, submerging his head, drowning the memory of those fatal affairs, and what they had cost him. Oxygen bubbles burst on the water's surface as he realized there was no choice but to confront the source of his pain. Otherwise, when he finally came up for air, it would only be to exchange one form of suffocation for another.

Unlikely Pairs

THE SELF-ABSORBED FACE in the vanity mirror barely noticed the transformation of her hair, and Jessie smiled to herself. The days when Amanda would allow her hair to be braided were numbered. Within a year there would be a request for a shag haircut, or worse.

"And what has Rapunzel been thinking about for the last twenty minutes?"

The corners of Amanda's mouth curved up self-consciously. "Mom, can I have a pet mouse? It's for a school project. Mr. Van Lo said he'd let me work on it at home."

"I'm starting to wonder about Mr. Van Lo's homework assignments. Maybe he can explain them to me at the open house tonight."

"Don't you dare! I'd die if he knew I talked about him at home."

Jessie was finished plaiting. "Okay, okay. We'll discuss the mouse with your father. Now turn around so I can look at you."

Amanda rolled her eyes before breaking down and smiling at her mother. The lustrous blonde braids framed her perfect face before coming to rest on the maroon of her corduroy bomber jacket. It was worth it, Jessie concluded as her fingers felt each thick swirl of hair: worth the time, the brushing, the arthritis she was probably developing in the service of her little, living doll.

"How long do we go back, partner?"

"Ten years, at least." Amanda played along with their game. "It seems like only yesterday."

They laughed together then, and hugged each other tight.

These were the moments Jessie would run through her fingers
when Amanda entered adolescence, when their bond would
initiate a painful, if temporary, rivalry. Her daughter had come
through many stages; some absolutely delightful, some definitely not so. Jessie knew they had many more to endure, and
many more to enjoy.

When Amanda finally pulled away, there was a mischievous
grin on her face. "Isn't it time to go, mom?"

Jessie grinned back in spite of herself, and glanced at her
watch. The John Swett School open house began in twenty
minutes, and she had to drop off Amanda at Davey Schwimmer's on the way. "I guess it is, sweetheart. Are you taking
any books with you?"

"Mr. Van Lo only wants us to watch the show tonight. We'll
do the report at school tomorrow."

"Just checking." It always embarrassed Jessie when a teacher
gave Amanda a TV homework assignment; she viewed it as
fodder for Amanda's complaints about being culturally deprived. ("The word is 'pop-culturally,'" Tod would correct.)

But Amanda's mind was elsewhere that night. Jessie thought
she learned where as they stepped into the cool night air and
walked toward the car, when she asked Amanda how she was
getting along with Davey.

"He's an ignorant child," Amanda answered tersely, and
slammed the car door shut. The Saab started immediately, and
Jessie backed down the driveway and into the street. Amanda
was growing up.

Her daughter had been friends with Davey since the first
grade. Their closeness had survived the traditional separation
of the sexes that goes on during those years, in what Jessie
guessed was a contemporary phenomenon. After all, Amanda
had never played with dolls, and Davey's parents never even
considered buying him war toys. Their friendship had always
been curiously asexual, in that neither assumed the gender roles
earlier generations sought out. Perhaps that was how Jessie
should interpret Amanda's derisive remark. As her daughter
approached puberty at a faster clip than her friend, she was
leaving him behind.

They paused at a traffic light, and Jessie was surprised by
the relief she felt learning that Amanda was drifting away from

Davey. It had been a long time since Amanda had read a fairy tale or a Nancy Drew mystery; for a while now, it had been either Judy Blume novels, or Jessie's own copies of *Vogue*. In the back of her mind, Jessie had always been worried about what would happen when they both turned twelve or thirteen, and sex became something more real than a Brooke Shields commercial.

The Saab came to a stop in front of the Schwimmers' Spanish-style house, and Jessie pulled up the parking brake.

"I'll be back for you by ten, dear. Say hello to your boyfriend for me."

"Mother, Davey Schwimmer means nothing."

Just checking—but the stridency in Amanda's tone still surprised her.

"Well, how do I look for my first meeting with your teacher?"

Amanda grinned. "Great, mom. Tonight, he's all yours." The grin flashed a light of unknown colors, and then she was running up the Schwimmers' driveway.

The banner stretched across one wall of the cafeteria read WELCOME, JOHN SWETT'S PARENTS. Nick read the message as he entered the hall, and immediately wondered, *Who is John Swett, and why are we welcoming his mother and father?* It was a feeble joke, but he resolved to try it on the first parent that approached him.

What else was he going to say? Even as he observed the milling couples all across the cafeteria making contact over cups of punch, he realized there was little he could offer to any parent wondering why Johnny consistently scored 140,000 points higher in PacMan than in arithmetic. Nick was learning quickly, and he felt most of his students respected him, but, as he had confided to a fellow teacher the other day, he was still driving by the seat of his pants.

He was on the verge of taking a stroll down one of the school's deserted corridors when a hand tapped lightly on his back. Turning around, he recognized the pretty, red-haired woman who had been waiting for an interview with Calvin Shanker the other day.

Nick smiled. "You wouldn't be here if you hadn't gotten the job, right?"

"That's right!" She impulsively took his hands in hers. "It went perfectly, thanks to you. I would have had no idea how to speak to that . . . horrid little man." She looked around nervously, giggling. "Shut up, huh? Anyway, I wanted to thank you properly, and introduce myself. My name's Eileen Morris."

"Nick Van Lo."

Eileen let go of his hands so she could squeeze him just over his left elbow. "It's only a substitute teacher's position," she confided. "But I just got my degree, so who's complaining? Shanker says the absenteeism is so high at this school that I should be in just about every day, anyway."

"I'm glad," Nick said honestly. "It'll be nice knowing one friendly face in the teachers' lounge."

The freckles on Eileen's country-girl cheeks disappeared beneath a furious, heartfelt blush, and Nick was suddenly struck by how long it had been since he'd had more than marginal contact with an adult outside of the guests at La Casa de Dolores.

Just then someone rang an old-fashioned playground bell, and the assemblage took their seats at the long lunch tables. Nick and Eileen sat down together while Calvin Shanker welcomed the parents and introduced the police officer who was the evening's keynote speaker.

The gray-haired man behind the microphone had come to talk about the threat of drugs at the elementary level. Readily conceding that little was being done to halt the flow of pills and marijuana into the playground, the speaker suggested that parents keep allowances below the rate of inflation, and their wallets and purses secure. Nick had heard it all before; he knew that if a kid with no money wanted drugs badly enough, he would turn to dealing.

His mind drifted to an encounter he had that afternoon while he stood outside the playground's chain link fence, watching some of his students playing kickball and jumping rope.

"You mind tellin' me why you been hangin' out in front of this playground the last half hour?"

Nick had turned toward the voice. It came from a beefy man of medium height wearing aviator sunglasses and an aquamarine leisure suit.

"Watching the kids play. Why?"

The man reached into his back pocket and whipped out his wallet, flicking it open with a practiced flourish to reveal a police badge.

"DeAngelo, Vice and Narcotics."

Nick felt his face flush as he responded. "I work here; I teach here at the school." He took out his wallet and showed the undercover man his union card.

DeAngelo glanced at the card, nodded, and handed it back. "Just a routine check. We been watching for child molesters ever since they found that Varney girl."

Then he leaned closer to Nick in a confidential manner. "Picked one of 'em up this morning. A grubby old coot, all stains and wrinkles, with the faraway eyes you see around here. The bum came this way from that direction," he pointed, "pullin' a little girl by the hand. Now the kid ain't resistin' or nothin', but the clothes she's got on tell you she's only in this neighborhood 'cuz of that goddamned bussin'.

"Now I know my Likely Types, *and* my Unlikely Pairs, so's I move in, ask the guy where he thinks he's goin'. Droppin' off his granddaughter at the school, he claims, innat offended tone these types always toss around. Par for the course, so's I check with the kid. A little blonde cutie name of Amanda, who just shrugs her shoulders. Ask her again, she shrugs again. Don't leave me with much, so I ask the coot for ID. I'm no dope, I knew he wouldn't have none. So's I send the kid off to school, and take the guy in. At the station he admits he's no grandpa, just thought he'd walk the little girl the rest of the way to school so's she wouldn't get in trouble. What're you gonna do? I left. Sergeant tells me later the guy was released. Fuckin' pervert, and they just let him go."

The undercover man grimaced and moved on. Nick had looked back at the playground one last time, and walked away in the opposite direction, the "little blonde cutie" on his mind...

A round of applause at the end of the speaker's cautionary sermon interrupted Nick's reverie, and he turned to Eileen for her reaction. She was already looking at him.

"Makes you want to swear off having kids," she whispered conspiratorially, and Nick reflexively put his arm around her as he laughed.

Eileen's own arm immediately slipped around his waist,

naturally and unobtrusively, and Nick finally faced what was happening. They were picking each other up. He liked her youth and directness, the way her light blue eyes twinkled; eyes men like him assumed could never feel hurt.

He didn't know if he was afraid of what she could do for him, or what he would do to her; either way, it was time for him to disengage. With his free arm, he pointed toward Jessie Westerhays, who waved immediately and moved toward them.

"That's the mother of one of my students," he explained to Eileen. "I promised to get together with her some time tonight."

Eileen shrugged wistfully. "That's okay, I understand. I probably wasn't being very professional, anyway. It was nice meeting you, Nick."

She hugged him briefly, and disappeared.

"I'm sorry, was I interrupting something?" Jessie asked, extending her hand.

Nick shook her hand and took in the pale silk blouse, the designer jeans, and heels. She was both older and better looking than he had remembered. "No, not at all. Just two teachers huddling together for support."

Jessie smiled politely. "Before we go any further, Mr. Van Lo, I wanted to thank you again for your support that afternoon, and to introduce myself properly. I like my friends to call me Jessie."

"In that case, make mine Nick. 'Mr. Van Lo' is for the likes of your daughter, although she seems to prefer 'Nick' also."

"I'm sure you're aware of how highly Amanda regards you. My husband and I are very grateful for the interest you've taken in her."

Nick briefly debated mentioning the vice cop's story to Jessie and decided against it. There was no point in frightening a mother with hearsay.

"Does that gratitude extend over to my television homework assignments?"

They both laughed.

"I see she tells you as much about us as she tells us about you. You'll have to forgive us. My husband is a film critic and—"

Nick touched her arm. "No apologies are necessary,

Mrs . . . Jessie. I often feel I'm taking the easy way out with those assignments."

A brief pause ensued, and Jessie glanced at her watch. "I've got to fly. I told the Schwimmers I'd be over for Amanda by ten, and it's a quarter of now."

"Davey's a wonderful boy," Nick offered. "I'm glad they're such good friends. And I'm glad we had an opportunity to talk."

Jessie shook his hand again, and left the cafeteria. As her heels clicked across the well-lit parking lot, she thought about how she almost didn't get a chance to meet him. That red-haired girl had been monopolizing him all night. Jessie could see why, though, and she could understand her own daughter's crush on the man. There was something mysterious behind his easy charm: an inward quality all those women bred on Gothics found irresistibly romantic.

Even a thirty-four-year-old wife and mother can see that, she kidded herself, and slipped the key into the lock on the driver's door.

Some Dreams Come True

NICK'S HANDS AND features are white, almost translucent. The cool, sickly smell of fungus overwhelms him as he sees the woman lying on an altar in the center of a vaulted room. Her body is slender, beautiful, sheathed in a shroudlike garment, the breasts still as death. Raven black hair frames her pale, sharply etched features. Two canines protrude from her mouth, pressing down on a full, bloodless lower lip.

This is why he has come: to make love to her. To make her breathe, bleed. To resurrect.

After kissing the cool forehead he raises the shroud, revealing her calves and her thighs, cold and smooth as marble. His lips touch her between the legs, searching for life, wetting her. Then his tongue makes the same discovery it has made every time it has been there. The delicate folds of her womb, those soft, cold lips, are covering parallel rows of fine white teeth.

He has been there before and, pausing only to bare the teeth, he reaches for the wooden stake strapped to his belt. But, just before he can bring the sharpened point down to clear the path, the ancient fear overwhelms him. His eyes close . . . he cannot do it. The stake drops to the floor.

Slowly he pulls the shroud back so that it covers her legs. Then he moves to the other end of the altar and tilts her head to one side, exposing her neck. The skin is dry, but soft. So are his lips. They come down, touch, and his canines puncture the skin. He draws in what little she has. It is not much, but it is the best he can do.

• • •

Nick rolled over on his bed and peered at the alarm clock on the nighttable: it was only an hour since he'd gone to sleep. But it had been different this time—disturbing, nearby. He realized he was wide awake.

Since childhood Nick had often dreamed of Snow White, lying within a glass coffin in a trancelike sleep, wakened by the kiss of a prince. As he entered puberty, of course, Prince Nicholas did much more than kiss the sleeping girl; he rattled the rafters with her, put her through enough contortions to wake a hibernating bear. Snow White would wake up, and they would live happily ever after.

He rose from the bed and slipped on his pants. Snow White failed to wake for the first time shortly after he married. She lay still and pliant as death while Nick tried everything he could think of to stir her, but she never woke again. Gradually, teeth grew to guard her womb, and Snow White became a pitiful ghoul starving for life. The dream of his youth was now the primal nightmare of his adult life.

He wedged his feet into a pair of tall, battered boots and put on a white dress shirt, then stepped out into the dimly lit hallway. He licked his lips, dismissed the idea of getting his coat, and plunged into the street.

The night was dark, and the wind was blowing, whipping his white shirt like a torn sail, pulling his hair back from his scalp. Bloodshot eyes glazed over, his head down against the currents, Nick moved up Mason, taking more space than a city sidewalk usually allows.

He saw an old woman wrapped in plastic bags, an empty bottle by her side, and a doll's arm cradled to her chest. She was wailing that she'd finally dried up—no more tears, or mother's milk. Her baby was going to die. The fingers gripping the rubber arm were hooked like a garden tool.

Nick sought shelter from the wind in a small, dark rock club. He ran his fingers through his hair and slid onto a stool at the bar. Behind him were several scattered tables and, on a makeshift platform, three boys dressed in black creating angry, jagged music on their instruments. Nick's head was aching, and he clamped it with his hands.

"Last call."

The bartender was standing before him. Nick said nothing

as his eyes bored into the bartender's, and flooded over at the lyrics he thought he was hearing. The words nibbled at the back of his memory, more real than his dreams: *ritual of blood*. The bartender heard nothing, but wanted no part of that look. He moved away to the other end of the bar, and Nick's stare, as if by instinct, fell on someone who had been waiting for it all her life.

She was a whirling vision in black on the dance floor, her slender figure at ease with every movement she made. Nick saw well-oiled passion in every hand gesture and leg kick—a passion that soothed as it cut. She was a vortex and a fireball, her force consuming her oblivious partner. Yes, the young man was almost invisible, because her darkly painted eyes were on Nick. She was dancing only for him. He felt strange new images crowd his consciousness, and knew he wanted her, had to have her, possess her.

She came to him after the song was over, wavy black hair framing her carmine lips, the dancing partner forgotten. Neither of them spoke as she put on a dark suede coat over her black shirt and pants.

They walked arm in arm, avoiding the white pools under the streetlights. Nick asked for her name.

"Judy Harper."

"Judith."

She laughed.

He hung her jacket in his closet and turned around. She was really quite young, and her lips were full. Then her eyes claimed him again, telling him to undress; as each garment fell to the floor, he understood more and more clearly that they were about to make his dreams come true.

Holding Nick's hands by his sides, Judith kept him inches away from the tips of her breasts as she brought her mouth over his. The kiss seemed to last forever, converting the oxygen in his lungs into a gas on the verge of combustion.

Finally, flushed and overheated, they came apart for air. She laughed first, exposing a canine made long and sharp by the gap on the other side of her mouth where the second one should have been. It was the perfect punctuation, he thought, licking his lip where the tooth had drawn blood.

Breathing hard, he shook off her grip on his wrists, and

wound himself around her body like a hissing, scalded snake. They stumbled over to his bed, but its shapeless boundaries couldn't contain them; their bodies spilled onto the floor, into the bathroom, against the walls. Nick felt her teeth and nails tearing his skin as he tried to suck out the liquid heat that was burning him like lava. Her fleshy lips molded themselves around his penis, threatening him with immolation, daring his fluid to explode. He buried his tongue in her mouth, in her vagina, as his fantasies ignited and his brain caught fire. Again and again he plunged into her, her legs wrapped around his waist, shaking her like a rag doll, never able to erase the doll's painted, devouring grin. No endearing words were uttered among the groans of lust and pain; no quarter was asked for, and none given. They came together, gushing streams of white, streams of flame, howling, hearts blistered in their pyre.

Some time passed before Nick had the strength to rise to his feet, to help Judith back to the bed. Neither of them spoke as they pulled the sheets over themselves, and gave in to their exhaustion.

Death, the unseen face on the back of love's head, had chosen to avert its gaze.

PART TWO

UNNATURAL LOVES

If I could be anything
in the world that flew
I would be a bat and
come swooping after you

—*Lou Reed*

A Mother Knows

IT HAD BEEN a quiet evening in Presidio Heights, with Halloween still three weeks away. Jessie, whose costume party was only in the early planning stage, had been reading *Second Heaven* while Tod worked on a piece he was submitting to *American Film*. Amanda, as had become her habit, had gone to her room immediately after dinner.

Shortly after eleven, Jessie and Tod turned off the lights in the living room, and climbed the stairs to their room. The click of the door's lock behind them signaled, for Jessie, an entry into the innermost sanctuary of their bond. This was the graveyard of downstairs disagreements, where the future was divined in whispers like tea leaves, where they talked about Amanda.

"I like the book I'm reading," she said, watching Tod pull his navy and green rugby shirt over his shoulders. "Our problems are nothing compared to those people's."

"I didn't think we had any problems," he joked.

"What do you think of Amanda's new pet?"

Tod tossed the rugby shirt onto a chair, and sat down on the side of the bed. "Well, I was a little surprised by its size. It looks more like a rat than a mouse to me."

Jessie unbuttoned the front of her shirt, and felt the air blow on the tips of her nipples. Her breasts were small, and she never wore a bra.

"She's acting strangely lately. She has very little to say, very little interest in doing what she's always done. I guess I'm saying she's not . . . being herself."

Tod, looking at her, almost forgot what she said. "You mean what *you* call 'herself.' She's growing, Jess. Changing by the minute, faster than you or I can acknowledge. I think she senses this . . . this insensitivity, and withdraws. Maybe she's a teenager already."

"But she's only ten!" Jessie pointed out. "I think it's more than that. She never sees Davey Schwimmer anymore, or any of her other friends. She just goes to her room. Every day, after school, after dinner. It worries me."

"Come here, mom."

Jessie stood before him, embarrassed by her fears, while he slowly pulled down the zipper of her jeans.

"Listen. For how long has she been going to her room—a week? Less than that? Maybe she's teaching her rat to do backflips."

Jessie shivered at the image as Tod's hands pulled down her panties along with her jeans, and he slipped to his knees before her. He kissed the inside of each thigh, slowly, letting his tongue join in little by little, so that by the time it reached her vagina and parted her lips she was bent forward at the waist, her fingers squeezing his skull as if this would end the trembling in her legs, as if she ever would have wanted the trembling to stop.

"Kiss me on the mouth," she asked, wanting to share her taste, wanting to feel the length of him flat against her. Naked now, his skin only slightly loosened by forty-two years, Tod entered her standing up, and their eyes drank from each other, a sip at a time, having forgotten how to be embarrassed by such intimacy, no longer considering that the source of this drink could ever dry. Her wetness inside, the sticky kisses their bellies gave each other, the saliva they shared, all this fluid, all this water, came from a bottomless lake needing no stone to ripple out: out, toward an unseen, mossy shore.

Later that night, the moonbeam aligned itself through the bedroom skylight as their architect had promised, illuminating Jessie's cheekbones and the short blonde strands that fell over her forehead. Her arm rested on Tod's bare back, which was rising and subsiding regularly with sleep.

She felt the air cool her skin and thought about what she had heard that afternoon: a tinny little voice on a cassette, a voice whose echoes were now keeping her awake.

Walking past Amanda's room on her way to prepare dinner,

Jessie had heard her daughter's voice behind the closed door. There was no one in there with her. Could Amanda have been talking to her rat?

Jessie had paused by the door.

She couldn't decipher the actual words being spoken, but it was obvious that the voice she heard wasn't talking to an animal. It was too animated, too fluid. Then Jessie figured it out. Amanda was telling a story.

Curious, Jessie knocked once and opened the door. Amanda whirled from her desk toward Jessie, but not before she depressed a key on her portable tape recorder.

Jessie knew immediately that she didn't belong there, and also knew that she had never felt this way before. Amanda confirmed her feeling in a coolly polite way.

"Mom, why did you knock if you were going to come in before I could answer? Would you like me to keep my door open from now on?"

Tod would say *good idea*, Jessie thought; she shrugged apologetically before leaving the room.

Walking to the kitchen, she recalled her belief that one taught respect by respecting others, and that the right to privacy ought to be respected in almost all cases. That this case might be an exception became clear to her when Tod came home from work and took Amanda with him on his weekly visit to the wine store, because that was when Jessie returned to Amanda's room, rewound the cassette that sat in the spools, and pressed the PLAY button.

"Once upon a time there was a little girl whose grandmother had given her a beautiful red riding hood..."

Jessie relaxed, and almost turned off the tape. She hadn't heard Amanda recite her favorite fairy tale in years; now, when those magical words in that priceless voice made her feel as if nothing would ever change, she remembered why she was hearing it in the first place. Her finger was hovering penitently over the power switch, ready to drop, when the familiar story began to change.

"Little Red Riding Hood was walking to school one morning when she met a wolf who offered to take her to visit her grandmother. Little Red Riding Hood said her grandmother lived in Pasadena, but the wolf said 'No, it's the one you never

met.' The wolf also said she'd get to school on time, so off
they went. When they reached grandmother's building, the wolf
let her in the door and left. But she didn't know what room
her grandmother was in, and that gave the wolf enough time
to go around the back, put on granny clothes, and sit in the
chair. When Little Red Riding Hood finally found the right
room, the wolf asked her to climb onto the chair with him.
After she did, Little Red Riding Hood looked at the wolf's
hands.

"'Gee, what hairy palms you have, grandmother.'

"And the wolf answered, 'The better to tickle you with, my
dear.'"

Jessie's hands had long since come together. There was no
longer any thought of turning off the machine.

"And then Little Red Riding Hood looked at the wolf's
teeth. 'Gee, what long, sharp teeth you have, grandmother.'

"'The better to rip out your throat with, my dear!' yelled
the wolf, and he dug his claws into Little Red Riding Hood's
neck and tore off her Adam's apple and drank her blood, and
sucked her guts out, and ate her up—"

The horrible tale came to an end with a sudden click, and
Jessie realized that must have been when she interrupted the
story. There was no time for her to even begin interpreting it,
however, because she heard the car doors slamming outside.

Suddenly, the whirring spools brought back Amanda's voice.
"A hunter passing by finally came in..." Amanda had obviously continued the story after Jessie had left. Her tone,
however, was quieter, more of a monotone. "The hunter cut
open the wolf with his knife and let out Little Red Riding
Hood. But by the time she got out of his stomach, she wasn't
a little girl anymore."

Jessie closed her eyes.

"She was a little wolf cub."

Jessie wasn't sure why she hadn't told Tod what she had heard.
Apart from the Freudian jokes he'd be sure to make, she knew
he would also make fun of her Pandora-like curiosity. But the
truth was that she didn't think he would understand, because
he wasn't a mother—and *that* she couldn't tell him.

Something was wrong with Amanda; something that had

entered her from the outside, and was now threatening to take her away. Her little girl seemed to have changed overnight. Jessie had even traced back the days until she had pinpointed when the change had occurred: the night she left Amanda at the Schwimmers' and met Nick Van Lo at that open house. It made no sense, but a mother knows when she is losing her daughter.

It was a horrible fear whose cause had to be isolated and eliminated. And that was when she truly became afraid. How does one bottle a vapor? For that was how she viewed Amanda's fading spirit—as a vapor being sucked away from her, disappearing from her hands.

The Worm in the Bud

NICK ADMIRED THE gushing fountain a while longer, then pressed the three books under his arm closer to his side and moved on. In minutes the pale grays of the library and the Civic Center faded into the glare of movie house marquees offering him honeysuckle, candy, maraschino cherries, and cheerleader she-devils in leather with ways of making you talk. Trudging home through the late rush hour crowds on Market Street, Nick reflected on Amanda Westerhays, who had come to dominate his daytime thoughts.

Ever since Nick decided that Amanda was the little blonde girl the undercover man had told him about—the one holding on to an old derelict's hand—he had viewed her differently, and become obsessed with the difference he, in turn, saw in her. Amanda wasn't so much changed, he felt, as *corrupted*. The cruelty with which she now treated Davey Schwimmer, for instance, went beyond simple rivalry for Nick's attention, or budding sexual jealousy. It had a malign undercurrent that alternately pricked, and repelled, his interest—

A shiver ran through him as he opened the front door of the rooming house and planted his right foot down on the rat by the base of the stairs. He turned it over gingerly with one foot, and cursed in amazement. The rat's carcass was curiously desiccated—just like the others he'd come across recently.

While climbing the stairs, he heard the rhythmic creaking of floorboards: Dolores was prowling around. They still hadn't had that chat about the children she had requested the night he moved into the house. Something about her always put him off. Her mind was sharp, her pronouncements amusingly eccentric, and he'd grown accustomed to her ruined mouth; it was always some little thing, something he couldn't rationally hold against her. The way the pale, translucent skin on her hands blended with the wheelchair's chrome, for example, or the obscene presence the cross on her chest emitted. Somehow he wasn't able to laugh about her the way the Doctor did.

She was slowly wheeling herself out of Mr. Slater's room—the one next to his—when he walked up.

"Good evening, Mr. Van Lo."

"Good evening, Dolores." He shot a glance over her head and into the room. Mr. Slater's stuffed parrot winked back at him. "Something wrong with Mr. Slater?"

He could never interpret her mouth's expression; perhaps that was what made him feel uneasy.

"No longer, thank the Lord, for He has taken Mr. Slater away from us. Although we treated him with every Christian kindness, I would never question the quality of his present lodgings."

"What did he die of? Never mind—stupid question, I guess."

"The Lord had need of him, and the Lord took him away. The Lord takes what he wants, Mr. Van Lo."

"Yes, I understand he took Old Man Pynchon a couple of weeks ago. He was kind enough to leave us the parrot."

She ignored the humor in Nick's remark. "Mr. Slater will have no need for that little creature. The dead are the dead." Then her fervent little eyes settled on the books under his arm. "What are those—educational books?"

Nick chuckled, holding them a bit tighter. "No, these are accounts of what's gone on in this city for the last couple of hundred years. A new interest of mine."

The expression on her mouth was still indecipherable, he thought, but it had changed. "Interested in the history of San Francisco!" she exclaimed. "My, what I could tell you about this city. I'm quite old, you know."

"That's right, I recall you telling me that the night I first arrived, when you showed me some old photographs. Could I see those again some time?"

"Yes, we really must plan on a long chat some night. We

seem to share so many . . . recollections." Her hands gripped the wheels. "And now, I must see the Doctor about letting this room. Good night, Mr. Van Lo."

She wheeled herself away, and Nick retired to his room, content to read his new books. They would keep Amanda and Slater from his thoughts until Judith came to deliver him.

And just as he was falling asleep, she came.

They could hear no sounds from the rest of the house; there were no lights burning save for the lone bulb in Nick's bathroom. The light filtered out to illuminate the lower half of the bed, where their feet were entwined in the loosened knots that follow lovemaking. The shadows took over again part way up Judith's thighs. Her head was cradled in one of his arms; his fingers idly tangled in her hair. They always felt comfortable with each other after sex. The silences that sometimes stretched for an hour after resulted because they were, quite simply, stunned.

It's like sticking my finger in a light socket, Nick said to himself. He had never made love like this, encounters that lifted his soul from his body by pounding it mercilessly into his marrow. He had never had a lover like Judith, with a knowledge that bordered on the encyclopedic, a youthfully perfect body, and a passion that made it all glow, that seared his senses on contact.

The more he saw of Judith, the more he realized she was as young as his Stanford undergraduates had been. He had seen her youthfulness shine through as the makeup wore off, a quality that helped him forget where he lived, and the fatal lack of marital passion that had brought him there. It was as if she had offered him the hope of future immortality every night they spent together. And yet this lovely, secret sweetness wasn't what was causing him to fall in love with her.

The love, he knew, came with the hint, the promise of the unknown. Now that she had her own set of keys, he'd come to expect her midnight arrivals, napped in preparation for them, and never asked why she left him each night just before dawn. You question a sorceress, he believed, only when you no longer believe in her magic.

"So how were the little monsters today," she asked lazily, tracing his earlobe with her finger.

"There's only one candidate for that title," Nick answered. "Amanda Westerhays, future star of *Dynasty* and *Dallas*." He smiled at a sudden image. "Make that *Dr. Jekyll and Sister Hyde*."

"Tell me about Amanda."

Nick paused for a moment, then rolled over to face Judith. "Would you consider me a pervert if I told you I was attracted to her?"

"You just told me, you pervert," Judith growled, and laughed.

"It's not like I want to defile her, for God's sake," Nick explained. "She's hiding something from me, and I want to know what it is. I like secrets."

His words hung in the air for a few moments, and then Judith spoke. "I have a secret to tell you."

Her hand brushed against his crotch while she shifted her body. Nick thought of the full, almost pendulous lower lip the dark concealed, and felt his penis swell. She felt it also, and sheathed it with her hand as her soft voice seeped into his consciousness.

"My mother left my father behind in Medina when I was born, and another guy in Chicago. We lived in Phoenix for a while, and by the time I finished high school we were in Los Angeles. I remember those places by the boyfriends I had."

The fingers had returned to her lap, and now it was his turn to massage her breasts. "I met my last real boyfriend at the start of senior year down in L.A. My mother didn't like him, but I was more in love with him than I've been with anyone before or since. Then one night, just as he was leaving our house, a police car picked him up. He was carrying a couple of lines of coke, and they sent him to a reformatory. Before he left, he told me that my mother had called the cops who arrested him.

"What my mother did to us left me ... shattered. Do you know what it is to lose all of the love in your life? It's such a cold, empty feeling ..."

She paused, sinking into the sensations his stroking hands induced. When she resumed the story, her words took on a dreamy, sensual tone, as if they and the story were one. "One night, almost like it was supposed to happen, little gray strands of smoke filtered into my room under the door. My mother worked late, so I was home alone. The smoke had no odor. I just saw it, growing like a spider's web in my room until it touched the ceiling, till it touched my throat, my lungs. I got up from my bed and opened the door. The rest of the house was the same, only smokier: all gray, wisping, the thinnest of tentacles. You could almost hear a hiss.

"I knew the hissing was inside me, the pain my mother had caused me starting to smoke, shudder, break me apart. And the house was going too, because it couldn't bear my hurt any longer. I sat down on the floor, watching, understanding it all. The gray gave way to yellow, orange, red. The flames announced themselves: we are fire. So alive, unquenchable. Sexual. It was life energy taking that house apart, taking me away to another world. The frame began to groan, because it couldn't weave and dance like the smoke and the flames. It was dead and had to collapse."

Nick's hands had frozen on her breasts, no longer feeling the erect buds that pressed into his palms. Eventually, they sensed his withdrawal and relaxed. "I was so happy, knowing I was going to die too, that I cried. I felt so warm, so free, even after the firemen arrived with their hoses and pulled me out of the house. They couldn't put everything out."

He felt her chest heave a bit, then subside; she was finished. Without a word he spread her thighs and entered her. Her stories went further, seemed truer, than his—and they frightened him sometimes. Her ravenous hunger, her unquenchable desire made their lovemaking seem like an eternal fall into a bottomless pit. It frightened him *because* it was what he loved about her.

She put her arms around his back, the lone flower in his barren life, and dug her nails into his shoulder blades. He pumped faster, shuddering at the terrible beauty of the image he saw each night, that of petals wrapped over the worm in the bud.

A Stranger in the House

THE SUPPER, SET on the Westerhayses' cane-and-glass dining room table, was roast beef and scalloped potatoes. This had been their traditional Thursday night meal since before Amanda was born. It had passed her stringent taste test for the last six years to become their unquestioned favorite. Jessie should have been surprised, therefore, that Amanda had only shifted her food about her plate with a loosely held fork. But she wasn't. Amanda rarely ate in their presence anymore.

My father would have shoved a forkful down my throat, Jessie thought wearily, but this evening, Tod was using a different method.

Tod pinned a medium-rare slice with his fork and suggestively slashed off a piece with his knife. Juice squirted from the knife's pressure and splattered the far side of the plate.

"Meat! Blood! Good!"

Amanda laughed delightedly, and Jessie settled for silence. Tod's clowning had never particularly amused her, but maybe it would encourage Amanda to eat the food on her own plate. Nothing else had worked.

Tod popped the oversized hunk of meat into his mouth and chewed it with all the delicacy of a Neanderthal. Swallowing was followed by a cluck of the tongue, and then back went the fork into the meat, a trident trapping a squid.

Jessie started to feel sick. "Tod, please."

Tod paused, loaded fork four inches from his mouth. "Whassa matter? A man caint enjoy his vittles after fourteen hours of tendin' his herd? Well, shee-ut."

Amanda burst out laughing again, and it was only after he

had finished taking his bows that Tod noticed the tears welling in Jessie's eyes.

"Can we go into the living room for a minute?" There was no mistaking the note of incipient hysteria in her voice.

"Why, sure, honey," rising from the table. "Excuse us, Amanda."

Amanda looked down at her plate, and her parents left the room.

"I'm sorry, Jess," Tod began, and moved over toward the bar in the far corner. "Would you like some brandy?"

"Armagnac," she answered lifelessly. "In the large sniffer."

Tod read the message, and brought her a generous amount. After they sat down on the couch, the soothing tone returned. "I shouldn't have acted like a clown. I know how you feel."

"It doesn't matter how I feel," she answered flatly, staring at the dark, cold fireplace. "She didn't eat her food. I haven't seen her eat in days."

"But that's the point," taking her hand. "She's obviously eating when we're not around. Didn't Dr. Seward say he couldn't find anything wrong with her? Isn't her weight perfectly normal for her height? I know how you feel," he said again. "But all this lack of appetite means is that she's investing her allowance in the Nestle company."

Jessie considered the hand holding hers, the way its adeptness at smoothing surfaces prevented it from sensing the abscesses beneath. "You only see her each night," she tried to explain. "At the table, and later for homework or games. When you're alone with her . . . when *I'm* alone with her . . . she looks through me. The way she says things . . . what she *doesn't* say . . . something is very wrong with her, Tod."

The hand rubbed her knuckles, insisting she was wrong. "I'd be a fool to doubt that Amanda isn't going through something difficult right now. But I think your perception of it is, well, colored by the pressures you put on yourself. The Halloween party next week's been taking up a lot of your time, and I'll bet you're already *worrying* about those two weeks in Mendocino that are coming up."

Jessie looked at him for the first time since they had sat down. "It wouldn't be fair to our friends for me to cancel the Halloween party now. But we can afford to lose the deposit I sent for the workshop in Mendocino. I'm not going anywhere until things get back to normal around here."

Tod looked at the brandy in her snifter: it was just about gone. He sighed, squeezed her hand once, and let go. "If we're going to be here a while, maybe you better go tell Amanda she can leave the table." Hastily he added, "Just so she knows you aren't angry with her."

Jessie nodded, and handed him her glass. That went right to my head, she thought as she stepped into the dining room.

Amanda's chair was empty, and her plate of roast beef and potatoes was untouched. She had moved over to Tod's seat, where she was licking the meat's juice off the empty plate. Jessie watched in horror as Amanda rubbed her mouth against the porcelain dish, lapping with her tongue. She had never seen anything so *unnatural:* it was as if Amanda were famished, ravenous.

Jessie gasped, and Amanda looked up from her plate. She locked her calm gray eyes on her mother's, and ran her tongue over her lips, licking off the pink juice in a slow, circular motion until Jessie screamed.

"Stop it!"

Amanda laughed and laughed.

"I would have said that she was probably just aping my own table manners tonight," Tod said quietly, "but that's not the picture you're painting. It sounds downright gruesome."

Jessie was seated across from him, slumped deep in the leather chair Tod's father had left him. Tod had wisely hustled Amanda up to her room as soon as he heard the uproar, but it had taken twenty minutes to get Jessie to tell him what had happened. Jessie, refusing his offers of drink and comfort, had wept silently all that time.

Finally, she felt ready to call him under the cloak of dread that had draped itself over her heart, the night she first felt she was losing Amanda. "I'm going to tell you everything I feel, and I'm not going to worry about how my words make me look. All I ask is that you listen to everything I have to say before you . . . explain it."

The light from the table lamp by his side confirmed his openness, and she began. There was more, of course, than the lack of appetite, the avoidance of former friends, the afternoons and evenings spent in solitude upstairs. There were the cold, alien stares, the formally distant tones that unexpectedly disintegrated into vitriol or rage. And there was Little Red Riding Hood.

"What was that?"

She told him of the perverted fairy tale she had heard on the cassette deck. Jessie's version was flatly stated, fatalistic; it presented the allegory as fact. And when she was finished, it was obvious that Tod had been affected by it in the same way.

"She's ten years old," he mentioned, as if in wonderment. "You never think a child can think those things, so you dismiss them. And she's left alone, God help her, to face her monsters as best she can." Tod gazed at Jessie with the groundswell of pain evident in his features. "I feel so sorry for her."

Jessie came over to him, put her arms around him, kissed the soft skin between his eye and ear. "What are we going to do?"

Tod rested the back of his head on her arm. "Talk to her more. Make sure she knows that we're available. That we care. Kids who go through what she's going through usually feel unloved, or unworthy of the love they receive."

"I can't imagine Amanda feeling either way."

Tod allowed himself to smile. "Certainly not unworthy of our love. Do you think we spend enough time with her?"

The pause before her response was more honest than tactful. "I've always felt you had a more balanced relationship with Amanda than I did. You've always been able to merge the role of father and buddy without tripping yourself up in the process. I really admire that," she smiled ruefully.

"But now Amanda's approaching an age where the sexual elements in your relationship are becoming more overt. I see her flirt with you—very innocently, of course—and I see that you don't respond. You don't respond, and I certainly can't do it for you. I'm the rival," she chuckled. "And yet she needs to be affirmed in this area, needs to not feel rejected. I think that's what's behind her giant crush on her teacher."

Tod nodded slowly. "But that's my problem, and I'll work on it. I'm going to really work on it, in fact, while you learn all those esoteric stained-glass techniques in Mendocino."

Jessie started to protest, but he raised a hand. "I insist on making the most of this golden opportunity, Mrs. Westerhays. Frankly, you'd just be in our way."

She looked up at him. "It's not going to be that easy, Tod. And I'm afraid her problems go . . . deeper than prepubescent rejection. I'll tell you what. I'll make an appointment with Mr. Van Lo next week, and see if he's noticed any change in Amanda's behavior recently. If her problems extend to school, then I'm staying."

"And if they don't, you're out of our hair for two weeks. Deal?"

She rose and kissed him deeply, for a long time. She was glad she had told him everything. "Deal."

"Somebody better go up and tell her a truce's been declared," Tod suggested.

"Let me do it." A thought occurred to her, and she laughed. "I can't trust the two of you alone anymore."

Jessie crossed the living room and started to climb the stairs. The hallway above her was dark; Amanda had gone up without turning on any of the lights. Suddenly Tod seemed very far away.

When she reached the landing, she stopped and looked down the hall. The door to Amanda's room was closed; in the darkness, it was marked only by the sliver of light emanating from the doorsill. She's living as if she were a stranger in this house, Jessie thought, and recalled Tod's words: *I feel so sorry for her*.

Jessie walked down the hall and knocked softly on the door. When Amanda failed to answer, she opened it a crack. Amanda was lying on her bed, crying.

The tears immediately came to Jessie's eyes, and she sat down next to Amanda, passing a hand down the little girl's face. "What's wrong, baby?"

Amanda looked up at her. "Mommy, I'm scared."

"I know, baby, I know," and hugged her fiercely, having absolutely no idea what could be wrong. "Do you want to talk about it?"

Amanda sucked up the fluid in her nostrils and cleared her throat. "Mommy, am I adopted?"

The question released a floodgate in Jessie's heart. *Adopted? How could you possibly think that?* These thoughts broke in a tidal wave of relief as her little girl's heartache became something she could understand, something she had felt herself, something all children feel. It was natural. It was normal. She was holding her daughter again.

"No, honey, you're mine and your daddy's daughter, our baby . . ."

Jessie reminded Amanda of all her baby pictures, of the photo showing her in Jessie's tired arms at the hospital. She recalled the trip to the Great Salt Lake when Amanda had been only two, an event Amanda couldn't possibly remember, but part of her history all the same—

"But mom. What if at the Salt Lake, say, someone switched babies on you? 'Cause all babies look the same at that age, and you might not have noticed, right?"

Jessie laughed at the question, at the sober, insistent tone in her daughter's voice. "Believe me, Amanda, by the time you were two years old, I knew every square inch of your scrawny little body. Nobody could—"

"How about at the hospital? You wouldn't have known me then, right?"

Jessie did not respond so easily this time. The question would have seemed innocent, childish, even silly, to anyone else—but a mother knows. Jessie had always *known,* somewhere inside, hours after Amanda had emerged from within her. When those blind little lips had wrapped around her nipple, and her milk had miraculously come forth, she had admitted and accepted it. Now she was forced to accept, to admit, what her child's tone and manner signified, what her insistence veiled . . .

Amanda did not want reassurance. She did not want the truth. She wanted to be told that she was adopted. That this was not her true family. That she was a stranger to this house.

That she came from, and belonged, somewhere else.

Love and Death
In the Tenderloin

Nick was tucking in his shirt before one of the dark spots on the wall when he first heard the sounds.

He had just finished bathing in preparation for a not-so-casual visit to the Doctor's room. Other than the rat situation—which was a legitimate health hazard, flophouse or not—his purpose in paying a call on the old man was rather hazy. He liked the old guy, and for more than the aura of depth and mystery he emitted. There was something paternal about him, albeit in the sad, failed way Nick had viewed father-figures since his real father had let him down by never returning from Korea. He hoped the bottle of Scotch he was presenting to the old man would warm his heart as well as loosen his lips. Because there *were* questions—

He heard the sounds again. They were a soft patter, steps creaking lightly on the floorboards, small objects being shifted. Sounds that would never draw any attention, except that they were coming from what had been Mr. Slater's room.

Had the room been let already? He didn't think so; there would have been other sounds, more noticeable ones than what he was hearing now. The more closely he listened, the more it seemed that whoever was in there didn't want to be heard.

Quietly Nick stepped out into the hall and put his ear to Slater's door. Hearing nothing, he felt the doorknob to see if the room was locked. It wasn't, and he decided to open the door.

The room was dark, but he couldn't find a light switch. From what the hallway lights allowed him to see, the room looked the same as it had the other night when he had encountered Dolores leaving it: a neatly made bed in contrast to the broken dresser with soiled garments hanging from it; empty wine bottles in every corner; unopened boxes of Ritz crackers and a moldering hunk of cheese half-wrapped in newspaper on a chair; the parrot perched on its stand with the help of wire, green breast stuffed with sawdust, its glassy eyes reflecting Nick's gaze. It was as if Dolores had no intention of renting the room—as if Slater were still living there.

Nick sensed a presence in the room; not Slater the constipated drunk, but a malignant, watching... something. It pervaded the space, overpowering even the stench Slater had left behind. It made Nick glance over his shoulder to make sure the hall door was still open, and hesitate before trying the door to the bathroom.

But there was nothing in there either, except a pathetic little turd floating in the brown water of the toilet bowl and specks of dried blood in the sink. Nick shook his head. The poor bastard, he was thinking, when he heard a noise out in the room.

He darted out of the bathroom just in time to see the hall door closing. He reached it in two seconds, gripped the knob and pulled. The door stayed shut. He yanked harder, again and again, and still it would not open. The presence he had sensed moments earlier was no longer in the room; it was in his head. In that moment the sweat spreading from his armpits turned into cold, insidious fingers, his breath into a rancid gas. The fear was blind, mindless; its tendrils pulled and tugged at his psyche with no pattern or logic until his fingers, momentarily freed from the lockjaw of his brain, remembered to twist the knob, and the door opened.

He stumbled into the hall, and saw a form disappearing into the shadows at the far end. But he was still too shaken to pursue it. And what would he be able to prove?

He stepped back into the room and forced himself to confront his fears. A quick glance confirmed his suspicions; the only possible hiding place was under the bed. It seemed that everything could be dismissed as easily as the form he had seen ducking into darkness: odd noises in an old building, a sudden air current shutting the door, a wino going back to his room after urinating. Forget the whole thing, he told himself, and turned around to leave.

That was when he saw the closet door.

It was on the left of the hall door; he couldn't have seen it coming in, and hadn't noticed it when he ran out in pursuit of that sound. Someone could very easily have hidden in the closet after hearing him fumble with the doorknob, and escaped while he was in the bathroom. Just to make sure, he opened it.

It was empty except for a coat hanging from a hook, and one gray rat, sucked dry.

"Hey!" The Doctor's eyes were glued on the bottle of J & B cradled in Nick's arm. "Who's that you brought along with you?"

"An old flame," Nick answered, handing over the bottle. "Risen from the dead."

"She's welcome back anytime—you only live once, right? The hell with my plumbing!"

Nick sat down on the bed while the Doctor fetched two glasses, babbling all the while. Finally he sat down next to Nick and poured three inches into each glass. A delicious shudder ran through him with the first taste.

"So what do I owe the pleasure to, my boy?"

Nick took a sip from his glass and told the Doctor about the curiously desiccated rats he had been finding lately. He deleted, for the moment, any mention of what had gone on in Slater's room.

The Doctor brought his feet together before responding. "Rats are a part of San Francisco, son. Right around the time of the Great Fire, the rats of Chinatown brought the plague to this city. Imagine—the Black Death in twentieth-century America. Where there's men, there's scum, and disease, and death. And if you've got those items, you're going to have rats. They'll always be around, and plenty of *them* get sick and die. I'm not a veterinarian, so I won't pretend to know what makes them dry up like that."

"You mean you've seen them?"

"Of course I've seen them! Do you think you're the only person living here? An ugly sight they are, too. The exterminator's been notified but, between you, me, and this J & B, it won't help. There'll always be rats."

They were silent for a while, working on the Scotch. The bottle was half gone when the Doctor put his hand on Nick's knee. "There's more on your mind than a couple of rats, am I right, son?"

"A dead rat in the hall . . . on the stairs . . . okay. But—" Nick told him about the one he had found in the closet, the noises he had heard, his certainty that someone had been in there. "How does a sick rat get into a closet that's been shut for at least a week?"

The gleam in the old man's eyes came from more than whiskey. "The rat I can't explain. Never had too much interest in their behavior, why some want to die on a staircase, another in my shoes. That's right. As far as what you heard—that could've been any of the fellows living here, scavenging for any liquids Mr. Slater may have left behind."

The Doctor grinned. "A sharp boy like you is probably also wondering why that room hasn't been cleaned out and rented, like it would've been anywhere else. The answer is that this flophouse is run by a woman for whom the word 'history' has no meaning. She is old; her life is history—to you—and so now is Mr. Slater's. But, confined as she is to a wheelchair, her memories *are* her life. For her, they still live. Mr. Slater is alive; the parrot still caws. And this place is a grand hotel, with 'Lourdes' on everyone's lips, instead of 'death.'"

Lourdes: the name reminded Nick of a dream . . . and those photographs Dolores had shown him. "Who was she?"

"A beautiful Spanish woman who appeared in San Francisco over one hundred years ago. She converted a bordello located on this very spot into a grand hotel. Lourdes was shrewd, but her real strength was in her beauty. It was said no man could resist her, and her lovers were the most powerful men in the city."

The Doctor paused for a moment, and Nick had a fleeting image of an orgy: *they were already ripping off their clothes, sinking to the floor.* "Don't let Dolores hear this, but one of them was supposed to've been the archbishop. The place went down with the catastrophes of 1906, and Lourdes was never heard of again. Some, though, said it was the scandals, the corruption she seemed to breed—and not the fire—that brought about her downfall."

"And Dolores?"

"Dolores owns this place. It bears her name. But sometimes she thinks that Lourdes is going to return, and claim the house as rightfully hers."

Nick drank slowly, his eyes on the paper bags that covered the window, keeping the world from an old man who could no longer handle any part of it. Now Nick knew why he had come bearing the J & B: to raise the blinds for one night, to let him witness how a man like the Doctor could be wise, and good, and fail.

"Quart's almost gone, Doctor—how'd it feel? Bring back the old days?" He saw the broken-veined eyelids blink. "Tell me what happened."

The Doctor gave him a queer look, as if Nick didn't really know what he was asking; then he nodded. "It was in Korea, thirty years ago. I was a surgeon in a mobile army hospital, drafted like most of the other medical people. I was fresh out of school, and soon learned that the rules were different out there in the mud and the snow. You cut fast, sewed faster, kept the bodies moving. No four-hour operations. Decide who had a chance, who didn't—and decide quick. Some chose according to color, some depending on what side of the bed they'd gotten up from that day. And one man would live, another would die. I tried to stay above it, be impartial . . . what a joke. No one can stay above death. I was as bad as the rest; the only difference was that I couldn't take it. It was making me sick. At the end I was willing to do *anything* to get out of there, away from the choices no one has a right to make.

"And my chance . . . my choice . . . came. The son of a U.S. senator arrived in my ward, guts all torn to hell. He was going to die without intensive care, but we didn't have enough plasma to sustain him through an operation—he had a very rare blood-type. Then I was informed that if I saved the boy's life, I could go home with him.

"Well, I saved it, and I went home. I saved it by stealing the blood of another wounded man who had the same type. There wasn't enough plasma to save both, I told myself before starting. So I used what plasma there was, and then I hooked up that other boy and sucked the blood out of his body. I condemned him to death to spare myself the pain of condemning others. So I came back to the States, received an award from the kid's old man. And here I am now."

The Doctor looked up at Nick, expecting rejection, but found him lost in thought. He waited, and finally Nick stood up.

"Thanks, Doctor. And good night."

But the old man was agitated, wrestling with something inside. "Nick, boy . . . you deserve a chance. What a man's done . . . it comes back to him. I've given you all I can for now. Just remember—it all comes back, looking no different than it did the first time. And then . . . it's all up to you."

Nick nodded, but his thoughts were in Korea. He paused by the door. "Remember what their blood-type was, Doctor?"

The old man told him.

"Funny," said Nick, feeling the sadness swell. "That's mine too."

He walked slowly down the hall, the rats forgotten, unaware that the Doctor's parting advice and mention of Lourdes would cost the old man his natural life. The talk had brought back images of his father's grave, images of life gone askew from the very start, as if that were its very purpose. They were images he had long since grown tired of, feelings he knew could only hamstring the modest new life he was trying to create here.

Instead of continuing toward his room, he turned down the stairs and headed out into the street. He hadn't gone more than twenty feet before he saw Judith.

"Hey."

She was wearing a loose-fitting striped seaman's jersey over white pants and thonged sandals, and she looked wonderful.

"Leaving without me?" The overripe lips parted like curtains before her pearly teeth, before that perversely long tongue that excited him more than he could account for.

"I felt like taking a walk," he began. "I wasn't going anywhere in particular."

She read his mind, then stretched out her hand and said, "Trust me." He gripped it, and she took him away.

Once they were settled in the back of a streetcar, he told her about the boarders dying off one by one, and the curiously empty rooms littered with rat carcasses. Judith let him tell his story to its completion, then fixed him with a knowing look.

"All you have to do is move."

Nick felt his cheeks blush, and stammered that he hadn't saved enough to move; Judith just smiled. "You don't have to explain anything to me," she soothed. "I don't mind if you want to pretend you've wandered into the plot of a horror movie. You live there because you need to—that's no big confession. And I have a confession to make, too. I need you just the way you are."

By the time they got off the streetcar it was almost one, and they could smell the nearby night surf from where they stood. She took his hand again and led him across the highway to the water. They made their way through the rows of parked cars—teen-agers hanging out—that divided the Great Highway. Once Nick had realized where they were going, he had suggested splitting a hot buttered rum at the Cliff House, but Judith had shaken her head. Now, as they descended the stone steps that led to the beach, he looked to his right and the aptly named restaurant perched on jagged cliffs three hundred yards away. With the waves crashing against the rocks below, the moonless sky above, and its own lights winking, the Cliff House reminded him of a mad scientist's laboratory.

Judith had already taken off her sandals, and waited for him to remove his shoes and socks before moving south, away from the cliffs. The sand felt cool and moist beneath his feet, pleasantly contrasting with Judith's warm, dry hand.

"I went home with a waitress," he sang jauntily, "like I always do . . . How was I to know-oh . . . she was with the Russians too."

She pinched his butt. "I'm no waitress!"

"Are you with the Russians, then?"

She bit his earlobe in response, and slipped her arm around his waist. Judith felt good, the sand felt good, and he responded with a curious blend of hurt feelings and surprise when his heel came down on half-buried driftwood, and a sliver embedded itself under his skin.

"Shit! Aw, shit!" he barked, and sat cross-legged in the sand to examine his throbbing heel. Judith plopped down in the sand next to him.

"Let's see your foot."

Feeling like a child, Nick lifted his foot, holding his thumbs on either side of the spot from where the pain was emanating. "It's a splinter," he explained.

Judith took the foot in both hands like a corncob, and licked the area around the splinter. The touch felt tingly, tickling him.

"This is only going to hurt for a second."

Her lips shaped around his heel like a plunger, and Nick felt her teeth prick the skin. She began to suck, and it seemed like his very blood was being drawn from his pores by the vacuum effect she was creating. His head lolled back, his shoulders sagged, and he felt the delicious, tidal pull of surrender. When the splinter left his skin he gasped, but she was right, it had only hurt for a moment. He felt like a new man as her lips and tongue, their task completed, unabashedly sculpted his heel.

Finally she looked up, lips parted, tongue poised like a cobra, that lone canine flashing . . .

"Judith, how did you lose that tooth?"

"Which tooth?" The response was quick, girlish.

"The upper right canine, Miss Harper."

Judith ran her tongue through the appropriate gap, and Nick found himself getting hard. Raising one knee to his chest, he nodded and asked her again.

"My mother and I were in Phoenix then," she began. "She was still suing her second husband for alimony and child-support payments, and we were living in a trailer park.

"A lot of families in the park were Christians, the born-again kind that go to churches with neon signs. By the middle of the summer I was going out with one of the Christian boys. Being fourteen and poor, that mainly meant hiking and necking in the hills behind the park.

"One afternoon I was waiting for him at our favorite spot, but his pious geek of a brother came instead. He didn't mince any words—called me a heathen, a slut, and welfare trash, and warned me to keep my corrupting hands off his little brother if I knew what was good for me.

"That was when I noticed why he'd jammed his hands into his trouser pockets. He was trying to hide an erection. It made me want to laugh, but instead I just smiled at him, as sexy as a fourteen-year-old can be. And he started to stammer, and paw at the ground with his feet like a bull, all the time licking his upper lip.

"I licked my lip too, as slowly as I could. I think my tongue was still out when he hit me."

She shrugged at Nick. "His fist split my lip, and the bastard ran away. My tooth was just about knocked clear of my mouth. My mother took me to a dentist who just glanced at it and pulled it out. After that we went to the police, but the family had pitched camp and left."

The explanation of the missing tooth was a nasty story, Nick thought, even though he had felt like laughing when Judith had described that repressed boy's frustration, and over the way she said *Christian*—almost as if it were a pagan cult.

He gave her a playful poke on the jaw and followed through by grabbing her hair in his fist. He brought her back to his mouth; they kissed for a long time before undressing. Making love in the sand with the black waves lapping at their feet, Nick felt the swooning pull of the void, drowned in the tidal nature of Judith's love. He was possessed by the blackness he saw, drawn headlong toward it, as blind and helpless as a newborn kitten. Time stopped, other worlds became visible, his lover transcended the moment, and he whispered *Lourdes*.

They spoke very little on the streetcar ride back, and Judith transferred after only a few stops. Nick didn't want her to leave, and thought of following her, but decided against it. Maybe it was better this way; maybe there could be no other way. In a relationship like theirs, each moment was all-important, all-consuming; choice was hardly ever involved.

Soft gray light greeted him as he got off the streetcar on Market Street and walked back to his room. All around him the Tenderloin prepared for bed: the strip joints were being mopped, the projectors in the hard-core houses cooled in their brief daily respites, the whores and masseuses lay down in their own beds, all alone. The winos and bag ladies began to snore on benches and in doorways, strewn on garbage piles, under makeshift cardboard roofs. The jungle night, with its young

and hungry marauders, had passed for them, and they knew
that when a policeman lifted the newspaper from their faces,
he would find them alive.

Walking past an alley, Nick noticed two denizens of the area
who hadn't yet decided on sleep. One of them reminded him
of Old Man Pynchon, a wino at the other end of the hall who
had recently died. The old man was propositioning a woman.

She was about fifty, a good twenty years younger than he.
She was wearing black rubber calf-length boots with metal clips
on the front, the sort Nick's mother had made him wear when
the snow turned to slush on the streets. Her dress was a faded
violet, made of some thin material that could never keep her
warm in the night. Around her shoulders was a transparent
stole made of disposable plastic trash bags. One of her hands
held a supermarket bag bursting with rags; the other one was
trapped like a chubby pigeon between the old man's fingers.

Nick thought of the way the old and decrepit had always
reminded him of vampires, always sucking up to the young,
the warm, the living. He watched with a fascination that bordered on horror as the old man draped his brittle claw on the
woman's tit and flashed a curdling saw-toothed grin. Nick
moved closer as the couple stumbled deeper into the alley. The
woman had let go of her bag by now. Her hands hung limply
while the old man cooed to her, kissed her purple lips, tangled
his twiglike fingers under her watch cap.

The old man yanked at his zipper and Nick took a step into
the alley, realizing they were far too gone to notice him. Now
the old man had her hand inside his pants; Nick could hear the
pitch of his cackle lower. The old man's chancred lips sucked
at her eyes, her cauliflowered ear, sucked at every pore for
life, and Nick began to feel the terrible beauty of the moment,
saw her wrist jerking by his fly, his hungry mouth on her neck
now as an affirmation, an espousal of life. Even though she
couldn't have been penetrated, the French term for orgasm—
la petite morte, the little death—went through his head as she
sagged, too heavy for the old man, and slumped against the
alley wall.

Nick left then. There was something in that alley he didn't
understand, but felt very close to all the same. He thought of

being inside Judith, and the horrible hollowness the Doctor must feel; how, like the two sides of a coin, you couldn't have love without death. He flipped the coin in his mind, and watched mesmerized as the two images blurred together into the face of the future he felt himself surrendering to.

Inside the Lunch Box

IT WAS QUARTER-PAST two, and Nick's students were filing past his desk to get their coats and lunch boxes before going home. Nick was tidying his papers, still thinking about his conference with Jessie Westerhays two hours earlier, when Amanda came up to him.

"How was your date with my mother?"

"Very informative. She told me about that pet rat I gave you for a science project. Somehow that had slipped my mind."

She dismissed his comments with a contemptuous smirk. "Is that what she said? Well, she doesn't know *anything*."

Nick drank in her Cheshire-cat smile, then jerked his head toward the back of the classroom. "Get moving, Westerhays. It's time to go home."

He had finished straightening out his desk and was about to erase the blackboard when Amanda's eerie words—spoken in that grotesque tone kids affect when they try to sound harsh—charged the room's atmosphere.

"If you take my lunch box, Schwimmer, I will cut out your tongue with the art scissors. And fill the hole with glue after all the blood comes back to me."

He should have thought more about the tone, about the curious meaning of her threat. Instead, he reacted against her inflated ego, and the humiliatingly preferential treatment he had been giving it for too long. A grin settled like a death mask on his face as he slowly walked to the back of the room.

Amanda had the lunch box pressed to her chest with both arms. She shifted them so that Nick could make out the four faces of the rock group Kiss.

"Miss Westerhays, there is nothing so special about you, or your Kiss lunch box, that excuses your threatening a classmate. You'll be eating whatever's inside it in the principal's office for the next two weeks."

"But I don't want David Schwimmer looking inside my lunch box," she whined. "It's mine."

A thought raced through his head. "Let me have it, Amanda."

Nick held out his hands, waiting for her to give it to him. At first she shook her head and clutched it tighter, but when she saw that he was not going to be put off, her grip loosened. A smile that did not belong on a child's face spread over hers. She handed it to him.

Nick gazed at her expression, not quite able to accept it, before opening the lunch box.

He looked in, then snapped it shut.

The knock on his classroom door had come a few minutes after the children had left for lunch. Nick had tossed the chocolate milk carton he had just emptied into a waste basket and licked his lips before answering the door.

"It's good to see you again, Jessie," he greeted brightly, and took her hand. Her clothes were much more appealing to him today: baggy black pants, short boots, and a soft leather jacket over a white blouse. But the smile she offered him was so fragile that he immediately knew he would need all the tact he could muster for their conversation.

He pulled out a chair for her from his supply closet, then sat down behind his desk. "I'm afraid the message you left for me wasn't clear. Did you want to go over Amanda's academic performance?"

"No. Why? Is she doing poorly? The first marking period isn't even over yet."

Nick shook his head. "No, her grades are fine. I was only wondering . . ."

"Why I'm bothering you so early in the school year?" Jessie kept her purse in her lap as she began to explain why she had come. "Frankly, Mister—Nick," she smiled briefly, "my husband and I have been very perplexed and upset by Amanda's behavior at home recently. To put it simply, she hasn't been herself."

"And you'd like to know if she's exhibiting any of the same behavior here at school. Could you give me some examples?"

Jessie catalogued her observations for him: Amanda's lack of appetite, her adoption fantasy, the twisted fairy tales...

"Well, I don't think I've noticed any wish to be rid of her parents. And as far as her appetite goes," he grinned, "I'm afraid I don't watch what Amanda puts in her mouth *that* carefully."

Jessie shook her head, missing his humor. "It's so hard to explain, you have to see it for yourself. Her attachment to the rat you gave her, for instance..."

Nick uncrossed his legs beneath the desk.

"It got sick almost as soon as she brought it home, but she would spend hours talking and playing with it. I noticed it was gone yesterday. I guess she brought it back."

Nick got up and walked around to the front of his desk, so that he was closer to Jessie. "Amanda used to be pretty close with Davey Schwimmer, right?"

Jessie nodded.

"Well, she's certainly having some difficulty relating to *him*. Amanda's obviously a very bright, precocious little girl, and I can understand how some of the other children might bore, or even annoy her. There's not much I can do for her in this area, though—it *is* a classroom. The efforts I have made haven't been too successful."

"I'm surprised her feelings toward you don't influence her more." She grinned. "My daughter's got quite a crush on you."

"I'm flattered," Nick responded in his most charming tone, "and the feeling is mutual."

They both laughed.

"Seriously," he resumed, "I'm quite fond of Amanda. She's a very special child. And that, finally, is the impression she leaves me with. If she tells me one day that her father's John Glenn and her mother's Sally Ride, I promise to call you right away. In the meantime, I wish I had forty other students just like her."

Jessie rose and took his hand firmly. The relief in her face was evident. "Thank you so much, Nick. I feel so much better knowing that"—a pause, and a smile that melted him—"that

Tod and I have a friend who really cares for our daughter."

"My pleasure." He led her to the door. "Say hello to your husband for me."

"Of course," she answered, then had a second thought. "Better yet, why don't you say it yourself? We're having a Halloween party this Friday, and I'd be delighted if you came."

Nick was caught off-guard by the impulsive invitation; to him, it was like a ticket to another world.

"Well..."

"Bring someone, if you'd like. It's a costume party, but don't feel like you've got to spend a lot of time dreaming one up. I'm sure there'll be plenty of other party poopers," she teased.

"Okay, okay," he nodded wearily, and smiled. "A definite maybe. And now, I've got a chemical warfare demonstration to set up for Earth Science class."

"See you on Friday," she laughed, and left the classroom.

But that was three hours before, Nick thought: three hours before the lunch box's contents forced him into the corner he found himself in now, finally having to choose.

He stared at the rows of empty seats before him. Why hadn't he been open with Jessie from the start? He couldn't tell himself that it was in order to prevent needless worry; the strength beneath the porcelain was precisely what made Jessie attractive to him. Anything he could dish out, she would take—including his certainty as to what little girl that vice cop had saved.

Did he really have a crush on her? The way she'd gazed at him in class that morning, for instance; a look more acquired than provocative, like lipstick on her mouth or a wiggle in her walk. He had surprised himself by winking at her then, as if that were the appropriate response.

But this was different. It had happened, and he had seen it. The fact that he was actually debating whether or not to tell Amanda's parents about what he had found foretold his eventual conclusion: it was his secret. He was staking off the mystery of Amanda's behavior for his own private investigation. She had finally bewitched him, after weeks of hopelessly prepubescent flirting, bewitched him by acting as if she herself were bewitched. The spell that enveloped him hid the enormity of the responsibility he had assumed. It never even crossed his mind that he could get burned. All he could see was the fire's red glow, illuminating the severed head of a white rat he had found in her lunch box.

Halloween

THE NIGHT OF the Halloween party was foggy, cool, and moonless. Once the floodlights in the Westerhayses' backyard were turned off, what was yet to happen that night would do so in darkness; what was to be found, would be stumbled across by the blind.

Tod Westerhays turned on those floodlights at seven o'clock, just before the first guests arrived. They revealed a long table laden with cold cuts, three garbage pails full of ice and beer, and scores of black and orange streamers fluttering from the trees that marked the property's perimeter. Two tall loudspeakers sat on one side of the patio, which had been cleared for dancing.

In the foyer of the house a red-haired woman was arranging bowls of candy on a plastic folding tray. She was wearing a long-sleeved black dress that descended to her feet, and buttoned on the front all the way up to the cameo brooch at her throat. As she moved, her red hair swung lifelessly between her shoulder blades.

"Amanda, would you please come down here?"

A little blonde witch in flowing black robes and peaked hat eventually descended the stairs in response to the call, and Jessie immediately noticed her sulking expression. She determined not to let her daughter ruin her mood.

"You're much prettier than the Wicked Witch of the West *I* saw in the movies," Jessie complimented. She breathed an inward sigh of relief that Amanda had not dressed up as Little Red Riding Hood.

Amanda kept her eyes on the floor. "That wig you're wearing looks like a floor mop."

"May I ask why we're in such a good mood tonight? Or should I guess?"

Amanda's mauve-streaked cheeks flashed. "You know perfectly well that I detest Davey Schwimmer. But you invited him to this party, *and* to spend the night. Is that a good enough reason?"

"Amanda, I've already told you that the Schwimmers are going to another party in Marin, and are going to be back very late. We've asked them to let you spend the night there on other occasions, so we couldn't very well turn them down this time. I'm sorry, but all I can suggest is that you swallow your differences for one night."

Amanda popped a Hershey's Kiss in her mouth, and chewed it dejectedly. "I can't believe I'm baby-sitting on Halloween."

"It's not my fault that you turned down two invitations of your own, my dear, after deciding that you were too old to go trick-or-treating. You've been drafted to greet our guests at the door, and hand out candy to any children who ring. If that's not good for you either, then you can take off that costume and go to your room."

Jessie did not wait for an answer before striding away, nervously adjusting her wig.

An hour later, the patio was full of people drinking and dancing to the Beatles' songs blaring from the speakers. Jessie, sipping on a beer herself, noticed that most of the costumes fell into the historical category—Romans and cavepeople, mostly—or Universal Studios horror: Frankenstein couples, phantoms of various operas, and a bevy of ghouls. Her early favorite for Most Ridiculous, however, was a man in a three-piece suit with an E.T. mask over his head. This corporate E.T. was drinking beer from a straw through each of his outsized nostrils.

After a while she noticed that Amanda was no longer by the front door. She and a pint-sized Count Dracula—Davey Schwimmer, no doubt—were haranguing Nick Van Lo by the food table. Nick was dressed in a fair approximation of a jacketless nineteenth-century hero: Lord Byron in shirtsleeves, she mused, and thought about the coincidence of their costume choices.

Finally, after sampling a series of finger sandwiches that the children concocted, he glanced her way. She started to wave, then held her hand breast-high. In her role, a look should be enough.

It was. He stuffed a couple of finger sandwiches into the children's mouths, and walked toward her, puffy white shirt glowing in the artificial light.

"Lord Byron?" she asked, curtsying.

"I'd thought Heathcliff myself, but what the hell," kissing her hand. "To whom do I have the pleasure of speaking?"

"Sarah Woodruff."

He cocked an eyebrow. "The French Lieutenant's . . . ?"

"Woman," she finished for him, and they both laughed.

"We must share another interest besides the Wicked Witch of the West."

Jessie finished her beer. "I'd thank you again for all your help in that department, but I'm afraid you'd think me maudlin. I'd also introduce you to my husband now, but I have no idea where he is. His costume is a big, dark secret."

"I'm sure I'll meet him sooner or later." He looked about at the dancing couples. "This is quite a bash. Do you have one every year?"

"Not quite what you expected from the parents of one of your students, eh? Actually, this is our second. Last year's was much livelier. It wasn't quite so cool." Jessie paused, watching swaths of fog passing before the floodlights. "Are you new to the city, Nick?"

"I arrived twenty minutes before I came across you and Amanda." Jessie looked away, and Nick, embarrassed, hurried on. "From Palo Alto. That's where I lived the last nine years."

"Yes, that's what Amanda told me. You have a son there?"

Nick nodded. "But I'm here, and there's no going back. Snow fell on my tracks a long time ago."

Their conversation, she realized, was drifting away from the party, and into the fog. She smiled, and changed the subject. "Did you have a hard time finding an apartment? I'd throw my hands up if I were moving into the city now."

"Remember where we first met?" His grin was open, challenging. "I found a room right across the street." He gave her the address.

"Why would you want to live there?" she blurted, and instantly gripped his wrist. "I can't believe I said that. Please pardon me."

"Strange place for your daughter's teacher to be living, huh? I don't mind your question, but I don't think I can answer it."

"Then don't." She looked up at him questioningly, searching for an exit. "Why don't we waltz instead?"

Nick placed his hand on her shoulder, and she felt the moment poise for a leap into a different century. Moving briskly in the modest circle they cleared for themselves amidst the other dancers, Nick and Jessie laughed delightedly at the image they were striking. Looking into his eyes, Jessie realized that she was only intensifying the intimacy of their contact, rather than dispelling it.

"How about switching to a jitterbug?" she asked as lightly as she could.

Nick smiled, and came to a halt. "Actually, I should be going. I have to meet someone very soon."

Jessie let go of his hands, and gestured at the costumed couples surrounding them. "This engagement still has a ways to go. Feel free to bring your friend back later, if you'd like."

"I very well might." His hands stayed by his sides. "It's been a pleasure, Miss Woodruff. Say good-bye to your husband for me."

Jessie nodded, and watched him walk over to where Amanda and Davey were sitting. Davey's mouth, stained brown with chocolate, blended with his blackened eyes to give him a fixed, surprised look. Nick rubbed his mouth playfully with a napkin, pulled Amanda's hat down over her face, and disappeared into the fog seeping back from around the side of the house.

"Lady, can I use your phone to call home?"

Jessie whirled around, and was swept up in the arms of an energetic E.T.

"Tod, that better be you."

"Who else wears three-piece suits to Halloween parties?"

Jessie pushed him away. "You should have come by earlier.

Nick Van Lo just left without meeting you."

"Oh." The giant turtle head looked as friendly as ever. "What's he like off-duty?"

Jessie looked back toward the side of the house. "He's living in a rented room in the Tenderloin. Isn't that strange?"

"He just got divorced, right? Sounds like he's punishing himself," Tod shrugged. "Happens all the time. Listen, I'll see you later. My nostrils are getting dry."

Jessie watched the walking pumpkin weave through the crowd of dancers, and walked over to one of the garbage pails for a beer.

I felt a tremor somewhere, Jessie admitted; before the ground closed and she could deny all, she wanted to think about what had happened with Nick. She hadn't felt the powerful gravity of flirtation—the way it weighs down each word with other, pulsing meanings, how it hurtles the next moment at you with the silent force of an underground river—so strongly since she had married Tod. She couldn't help but be curious about a man who was so different from her, who needs to hide, who likes to run—

"I guess you're drunk, huh?"

Jessie's eyes snapped away from the lip of her beer bottle and over to Amanda, who stood next to her, hands on hips. Something was wrong, she realized immediately, noticing the angry red blotches on Amanda's face.

"What's wrong, hon?"

"What's wrong, hon," Amanda mimicked, curdling her lips. "Did you call him *hon* too? You made an ass out of yourself flirting with my—teacher!"

Jessie looked about for a place to set her beer. It was important that she get Amanda inside before others heard her.

"Don't bother looking for him, *Mrs. Westerhays,*" Amanda sneered, misreading Jessie's glances. "He's gone, and he's not coming back. What would he want with you? *He belongs to somebody else.*"

Jessie would have slapped her daughter hard enough to draw blood, had she not felt the looming presence by her side. She turned to her right and smelled the moldering odor of a huge man in a crudely stitched leather half-mask. It's one of Tod's drunken professor friends, she thought, but only for a moment. The air of decay whispered *wrong* to her; the cold, drowned eyes behind the mask's slits shook their heads.

"Hello," Amanda greeted sweetly. Jessie saw the corner of the monster's mouth twitch in response.

"What's the problem, mister?"

The man barely acknowledged Tod's arrival. Jessie, to her horror and disgust, saw Amanda reach out to take the giant's hand. But before she could respond, Tod stepped between them and grabbed the man by the lapels.

"Listen to me, bud—"

It was as if the huge man weren't really there; no sooner had Tod seized him than the lapels tore wetly, like some fungus, from the jacket. Jessie felt that if Tod were to place his hand on the masked man's chest, it would have sagged like cardboard in a rainstorm. Conversely, the masked man looked at the E.T. mask as if Tod were something *he* could crumple, someone he'd just as soon chew and spit out.

She stepped back, pulling a resistant Amanda with her. The guests, she noticed, had grown quiet. At first she assumed that they had noticed the confrontation between Tod and the silent man. But then she saw that they weren't looking in her direction—they were looking all about.

There were more of them.

They may even have been there all along, drifting in and out of the little groups that had set up like points of the compass along the party's periphery. You had to focus so as to see them, had to concentrate to learn they were together: the tall, gaunt, loose-skinned ones, others etiolated, with the formless features of gas-filled cadavers. Silent and vacant, moving slowly like the fingers of the fog, they were all in costumes that weren't *really* costumes.

Who are they, Jessie wondered, and remembered that bleeding derelict's face . . . that man who spoke gibberish at her and Amanda from a torn, lipless mouth.

(Something chewed off his lips.)

She didn't really know what would have happened next; but suddenly the tension centered around the hulk in the leather mask broke. The man grinned a good-bye that was little more than a baring of his teeth, and lumbered away toward the street; his friends silently followed him into the mist. Before he disappeared, however, the man in the mask paused, and waved.

Amanda waved back.

"Nick. Why were you calling me 'Lourdes' before?"

He propped his head on one bent arm and admired the curve of Judith's belly where it disappeared into maroon panties.

"Just playing. That was one hundred years ago—*se acuerda, mi dama?*"

She didn't respond, but Nick could tell by the way she jerked on her boots that his offhanded answer hadn't satisfied her. Had there been any indication of how she was feeling . . . before? He touched the scratches on his chest and shoulders, felt more on his back. She had been a wonderful Lourdes—ruthless, but incredibly adept. Without explaining why, he had described the costume he wanted her to wear that night: a white gown that exposed her back and the swell of her breasts, silver clasps on her wrists, the throat left bare. *(The rippling black hair, the gaunt, ravenous cheekbones, lips so ripe they conjured the odor of slightly rotting fruit.)* That was how she came to him that night, and with the secret christening of a new name and personality, his fantasies had crystallized into a session that left his legs feeling like mauled tubes of jelly.

The truth was that he was feeling too good to worry about her right then. "You called me all sorts of names, right?"

She whirled around, eyes flashing. "Don't you ever want to . . . want to just fuck?"

Angered by her anger, he countered her thrust. "Do you want me for anything other than fucking? Come here in the middle of the night and never stay past five . . . do you realize I've never once seen you in the daylight? Ask me to make love to you," he sneered. "Where are you going now? Why won't you tell me? I'm starting to think you're a goddamn vampire."

She said nothing while she gathered her things, then came over to the bed. Nick felt somewhat self-righteous, but the abused tingling in his groin was still there. He put his hands on her shoulders and brought her face down to his, and kissed her. They kissed until he gasped in pain and pushed her away.

Her mouth was smeared with the blood she had drawn with her teeth. "Good night, Nicholas," she whispered, and closed the door soundlessly behind her.

Nick stumbled into the bathroom on rubbery legs and splashed water on his swelling lower lip. The throbbing itself was an indicator of how fantastic their lovemaking had become. Fantastic, he had to admit, in every sense of the word; they hadn't made love straight in a long time. That was why he couldn't understand her sudden anger at being called Lourdes; it wasn't the first night she had assumed the role.

After toweling the stubborn bubble of blood dry, he returned to his bed. Still feeling a little self-righteous about their fight, he asked himself why she kept coming back. The sex was better than any he'd ever experienced, but he had the feeling that wasn't what kept her in his bed night after night. Sometimes, at the height of their lovemaking, he would see a light in her eyes, a light that grew into heat, then flames, threatening to consume while it licked, drawing him closer, as if he were a moth.

But she was gone now, the alarm clock on the dresser read not quite eleven, and Nick did not want to lie awake in the arms of his unanswered thoughts. On any other night, he would have walked out of this neighborhood and down to the Embarcadero piers, where the vast emptiness of the night would inevitably dispel his thoughts. This night, though, was different; for once, there was a lamp signaling to him in the darkness. All the elements were there at the Westerhays house, waiting, cryptic, poised.

He slid his boots on after his pants. In the next hour, the shards of his life would lock into focus.

The door to Amanda's room opened, and Jessie peeked in. Davey and Amanda looked up like startled raccoons from a board game they were playing on the floor.

"Don't you kids ever get tired?"

"We were drinking Coke all night, mom," Amanda answered. "I think the caffeine affected us."

"Okay, well, don't stay up too late," she smiled, and quietly shut the door.

The party had sputtered to a close shortly after the derelicts left. Jessie didn't reproach her guests for feeling that the festive mood of the evening had unalterably soured; the truth was that she also had wished the party to end. There was too much she had to consider.

Amanda's jealous outburst over Nick Van Lo, troubling as it was, meant much less to Jessie than the cold lick a phantom tongue had given her heart, when Amanda said hello to that giant in the leather mask. Because there was no way she could rid herself of the suspicion, absurd as it was, that Amanda had met him before.

After turning off all the downstairs lights, she paused by the banister. Her long-tressed wig was perched jauntily on its base.

Jessie picked it up, and thought of the fear she had felt that evening, the reawakening of her intuitions about Amanda's condition. An exchange of waves was all it took to make her certain there was something else, something outside Tod's vision, and hers. It was the same feeling she got from Nick Van Lo, she realized as she climbed the stairs: the tickling brush of danger. He could never mean something to someone like her, because he wasn't real. He was only a fantasy, a Gothic character oozing a nectar of vulnerability and danger, managing to make her feel both intimate and uncomfortable.

Entering her bedroom, she saw the E.T. mask sitting on a chair, and Tod passed out on the bed. Slowly she unbuttoned the long black dress she was still wearing, and let it fall to the floor. Her body was tingling unpleasantly, as if she had drunk a pot of coffee. But after another glance at Tod's sodden form, she decided to settle for a hot shower.

The steam shrouded all the sharp chrome edges of the bathroom as Jessie reached languidly for the soap. One more adjustment of the knob and the needles jabbing the wings of her back would become painful; at the present level they were as soothing as a massage. She sometimes stood in the shower for twenty minutes before soaping herself; the knob, starting somewhere near the lukewarm notch, invariably ended just shy of scalding. Breathing in the vapor, she could barely move. Her legs had felt this weak only after giving birth to Amanda. It was as if her muscles had atrophied into jelly.

And with the deterioration of her natural tautness had gone

her senses. The vapor prevented her from making out the grooves on the bath spigot, and the hissing steam drowned Tod's drunken snoring outside the door. Touch was all she really had left: a fusion of the molecules on the soles of her feet to the bathtub Formica and on out to the tile. Without peeking from behind the shower curtain, she could see a film of steam coating the floor, walls, and ceiling, even droplets coagulating on the mirror. Perhaps some steam was escaping beneath the bathroom door and into the bedroom cold. She could sense it was cold out there, just as she could sense Nick's first hesitant footsteps.

Closing her eyes, Jessie imagined dismissing her suspicion, picturing the room behind the door. Everything was dark; she had turned off all the lights before entering the shower. If someone unfamiliar were to enter her bedroom, he would probably bump into the bed, but Tod would never awaken. The tips of his boots would then snag the black dress on the floor, and the orange wig tossed next to it.

Jessie took a step back in the bathtub, trying to feel any further insinuations of movement in the bedroom as the jets of water reddened her rounded belly. There was no way she could know if he had picked up the dress, if he was now feeling the fabric's texture between his calluses, if he had raised it to his nose, inhaling her essence, re-creating her, finding her. There was no way to know if, out in her bedroom, he had breathed life into the folds of her dress and lovingly taken her into his arms, because Nick had opened the bathroom door.

The droplets on her nipples, warm as the sweat of lovemaking, turned clammy with cold as a billow of steam escaped into the bedroom. Jessie shivered with fear, even after the bathroom door had closed, insulating her once more, making the temporary change in temperature seem like a malfunction of the plumbing. With the influx of adrenaline her vision improved so she could almost see his form behind the curtain, playing with her pale lipstick, drawing an ancient symbol on the clouded mirror, his movements as silent as his footsteps, the padded muscular silence of a great cat. The drone of the water turned into a roar, the chrome shone and reflected warped images of her shoulders and collarbone.

She stepped back as quietly as she could, reaching down for the razor, the stream of water now caressing her mound.

The water and heat had anaesthetized her sensations enough
so that a neat slitting of her wrists would go unnoticed on the
other side of the curtain. She could visualize her flowing pink
deliverance, not a sound uttered, bravely standing on drained
legs, her life oozing out of her skin, joining the clear water
and disappearing through the drain, leaving only a grinning
white husk for the unsuspecting intruder on the other side.

Then her stomach betrayed her, emitting a low moan of
hunger or pleasure. Jessie froze, anticipating a lunge through
the curtain. But there was no sound, no movement, and she
relaxed her arms enough so that the razor slipped from her
grasp and clinked against the side of the tub. Again she stiff-
ened, one hand pressed instinctively to her vagina . . . and again
there was no sound. The feeling that it was all a dream seeped
in with the steam, opening her lips, lowering her lashes just
as the curtain tore open.

Jessie could not scream through the vapor. She leaned back
silently against the tile, one hand clutching her neck, the other
still massaging her vagina. Then he was in the shower also,
softly removing her hands as she sliced her heel painlessly on
the fallen razor. Like water, like steam, he filled and drained
her at once, her mouth, her throat, her breasts, all the way up
to her intestines, all the way down to where no sound is heard.
Her head craned up, mouth open and eyes shut, she sensed the
heat and the steam and the sweetly acrid wafts melding with
her terrified panting. And sated, spent, she slid down to the
bathtub floor, the fingers on her crotch relaxed, a dull smile
allowing trickles of water to salve her parched mouth.

The grass by the sidewalks of Scott Street were already winking
with dew as Nick drew near to the Westerhayses' home. The
long walk past the revelers of the Polk Gulch area was achieving
his desired effect.

The questions of the last hour had steadily given way to a
bittersweet acknowledgment of the depth of his involvement
with Judith. He wasn't so much in love as possessed by her;
he wasn't so much fascinated by her life-force as addicted to
it. It was as if her blood were so rich he could live off it too.
And that was how he felt: as if she were nurturing him back
to a strange new life.

"That college life wasn't for you," she had told him one night. "And I don't think you lost it—I think you threw it away, as far as you possibly could." She was right, of course, as she always was in matters of the soul. That world seemed very distant this night.

He reached the house then, and took in its darkened windows. The party he had come for was over. Was he hesitating because of Amanda, and the secret they kept sealed in her lunch box? Or was it her mother that he sought: Jessie, confession, and deliverance? Nick thought the latter, and crept toward the house.

There was a soft light visible from the side; it came from a window just above a row of bushes. He moved below it, and there, crumpled like a failed poem at the bottom of a wastebasket, he found Davey. Wrapped in his Dracula cape, his little mouth still stained with chocolate, he lay with his eyes open, dreamlike. It was as if he were gazing at something so rapturous, so hypnotic, that he never felt the tiny savage bites that had ripped open his throat.

PART THREE

THE VAMPIRE KILLERS

To escape from horror bury yourself in it.

—*Jean Genet*

The Shadow of His Doubts

THE MORNING WAS an embarrassment of brightness, like every other day that week. Slashing rays of sunlight reflected on the casket as it went in headfirst, filling the hole that had been cut into the gently swelling side of the hill. The enormity of the shock had left no room for grief in the ceremony. Now that Davey's plundered veins were restocked with embalming fluid, he was being returned to the earth.

Nick was standing beside the Schwimmers as the gathering began to break up. He avoided speaking to them, just as he had avoided Tod and Jessie Westerhays. Dressed in sober, striking black, they had stood to one side of the congregation, and left as soon as the ceremony was over. Nick noticed that Jessie had kept her eyes averted from him throughout.

It was all too intimate to be comfortable, he reflected.

He had kicked at their door late that night; when Jessie finally opened it, she found him holding Davey's body in his arms. They stood motionless for a moment then, and Nick took in her still-damp hair, the kimono she had thrown on, and that look of dread: a look, he felt in his bones, directed at *him*.

Tod joined them in the kitchen minutes later, knocked sober but still groggy. It was he who finally called the police, while Jessie raced upstairs to check on Amanda, and Nick sat down next to the butcher-block table that bore Davey's weight. After a while the Westerhayses returned to the kitchen, where they all waited in silence until the police arrived. As the sound of a siren drew close, Nick remembered exchanging one last, naked look with Jessie.

The inspector in charge of the case made Nick explain why

he had returned to the Westerhayses' home—and why he had
wandered into the side yard—several times before dismissing
him. Nick left as Tod prepared to go over to the Schwimmers,
and Jessie told the inspector that Amanda had been retching
for the last hour, and would be unable to answer any questions.

There were only two mourners left now, two men in ap-
propriately somber suits. One of them motioned to Nick as he
turned to leave. He could tell what they were from their approach.

"Mr. Van Lo? I'm Sergeant Blake. This is Detective Steinmuller." He flashed a badge. "Inspector Vicente wanted to
know if you saw anyone. Suspicious or otherwise. On your
way to the Westerhays house."

"Or earlier in the evening," Steinmuller added.

Nick thought about how the plainclothesmen disliked com-
mas, and shook his head.

"The Westerhayses described four to eight intruders in their
backyard last night. Derelict types. Other guests have confirmed this."

"They must have arrived after I left, then. Either that, or I
took their appearance to be costumes. It was Halloween night,
you know."

"That doesn't leave us much to go on. David Schwimmer
died from loss of blood due to a severing of the jugular vein.
The fatal wound appears to have been caused by indiscriminate
bites on his neck and throat. What you might expect an animal
to do. But the expression on his face was not the sort you find
on victims of animal attacks. So. Do you have any ideas?"

"Yes, I do." Nick paused, allowing himself a smile that
made his pain a little more bearable. "I think he was killed by
a vampire."

The detectives looked at one another, nodded curtly, and
strode away. Nick turned once more toward the grave site, then
made his way down the slope.

The possibility that it may have been a psychopath or some
rabid animal had never crossed his mind. What else would he
have thought after studying fantasies like *Carmilla* and *She*
over the last ten years? He had even written a paper once on
its sexual overtones. And then there were the words of the first
cop on the scene: *another one.*

Another what?

Throat attack. Like that Varney girl they found in an alley last month. A couple of Tenderloin derelicts have registered complaints lately, too, though they weren't all that clear as to what happened.

He wondered what he would have said if the detectives had asked him if he had any particular suspects in mind. Is one decapitated rat and precociously seductive behavior sufficient evidence to accuse a little girl of vampirism? No, he would keep his accusations to himself until they grew hard enough to drive a stake through the heart of his doubts . . . and that of a ten-year-old vampire.

Riding a bus back into the city, his thoughts went back to the overlapping emotions he had felt when he found Davey. The first had been horror, sweetened with sadness only to be curdled by guilt. Should he have known? Slowly the guilt abdicated its hold to a cold, vindictive anger aimed from its very inception at Amanda. Pointing the finger in her direction answered too many of his own questions.

He wearily got up from his seat at the same Greyhound station where he had first arrived in early September, and crossed Market on his way to the flophouse.

As far as he was concerned, his struggle with Amanda had been in the open since yesterday afternoon, when he had read the children a very vague explanation by the principal concerning Davey's death. Nick had decided to deliver a eulogy that would allow Davey's classmates to say good-bye to him, even if they didn't know why. Gathering them together just before school let out, he had spoken of the meaning of the word *spirit*, how it wasn't an individual thing but something they all shared. That their spirit had existed before they were born, and would continue to exist long after they died. And that when Davey had died, a little bit of their spirit—the part that had been in him—returned to them, put Davey inside all of them, brought them all that much closer together.

Amanda had come up to him afterward, wide eyes almost liquid, and placed a hand on his arm. "You know, Mr. Van Lo, I just wanted to tell you," pausing, sincere as only a child can be, "that I'm really glad Davey's dead."

Yes, he hated her, and blamed her. His certainty about it

had grown as her chillingly beautiful face became all he could see, as that preternatural calm threatened to best him. That silent, reptilian confidence was what first formed the word *vampire* on his lips. There was no longer anything childlike about Amanda: the shadow of his doubts had sprouted wings. He now found her rare sugar-and-spice poses almost lewd. Previously, he had dismissed his preoccupation (infatuation?) as a residue from the nether side of his Victorian studies. At least it was comforting to know, as he stepped back inside La Casa de Dolores, that he had succumbed to the spell of a vampire, rather than to the cult of the little girl.

Alone

IT WAS VERY cold outside that night, cold enough that plain thermal warmth wouldn't do. In the Tenderloin the street people stamped their feet and hugged their triceps under the figurative heat of sex-show marquees, all feeling a tacit union because tonight's isolation was brought on by the weather, brought down equally upon all.

Nick, out on the street again, passed through them like a lost icebreaker cutting through floes, fists jammed into the pockets of his suede jacket. He was moving aimlessly, treading the same sidewalks every night, avoiding his only possible destination.

Suddenly, he stopped.

The cadaverous face grinned knowingly and moved on. Nick looked back at the receding figure. Could it have been Uncle Bill? They'd said Bill had died five days ago; he had watched the Doctor airing out his room. The man he had just seen was more gaunt, chalkier . . . Nick walked away. On the street now, he was seeing them everywhere.

That afternoon he had come home from John Swett to find six dried-up rats arranged neatly in front of his door. Furious, he'd stormed into the Doctor's room without bothering to knock. The old man was sprawled in a corner, stone drunk and—Nick thought later—scared to death. He had nothing to say about the rats.

"Tell me what's going on, you old fucker." Nick leaned over him threateningly. "Forget the rats. What is happening to all of you winos? You're dying like flies."

"Flies die in the winter," the old man croaked. "But they're always back by spring."

Nick paused while he deciphered the old man's cryptic words. "Doc, you're scared shitless. You're so scared even that pink stuff won't wash it away. I know something's going on, I've seen some of the dead ones, moving around. And the rats. The rats are part of it. Are they all vampires?" He kicked the old man's thigh. "Or are you one of them too?"

"It's all the same," the Doctor announced in a lifeless voice. "We're all half dead, all addicted to liquids." He coughed out a hideous laugh, then muttered. "Get out. Go on, son. Leave me."

That had been three hours before. Now he was back in front of La Casa de Dolores and, one week after Davey's funeral, no closer than ever to its secret. None of the vacated rooms had been let, and he had *seen* them. But the only connection between Amanda and these undead derelicts was the cautionary tale of a vice cop.

He entered the flophouse and trotted up the stairs to the second floor landing. The Doctor's door was open, and he could see a light inside. It couldn't hurt, he decided, to pump the old man one more time.

"Good evening, Mr. Van Lo."

Dolores and her wheelchair were parked in the middle of the Doctor's room, chicken-claw hands folded in her lap. It was as if she'd been expecting him.

"Good evening to you, Dolores. Is the good Doctor in?" Even as he smiled, though, Nick could already sense the worst.

"The Doctor is no longer with us," she recited the now-familiar litany, fingering the cross on her chest. "The good Lord took him away just a while ago. We must pray—"

"Another death, Dolores?" The news raked up anger and a sense of loss in him, rather than grief. "How many is that in the past two months? *How many are left?*"

"Must we reduce ourselves and the dear departed to numbers? Please lower your voice, Mr. Van Lo. I have sensitive hearing."

There was no calming Nick, however. They had cut into him one time too many. "Of what did he die?"

"Of what do all these afflicted souls die? Alcohol? Drugs?

Malnutrition? Brain damage, cirrhosis of the liver, degenerates' disease? I do not conduct autopsies, Mr. Van Lo."

"Well, somebody will. I'm not going to let go of this one. Where was his body taken?"

Her ruined mouth shifted again, expressing—what? "I have no idea. His relatives took him away just an hour ago."

"He had no relatives!"

She actually laughed then. "*Somebody* came for his mortal remains. They introduced themselves as his relatives."

"Who sent for them?"

"I thought you did."

He felt like overturning her wheelchair. "I'll be moving out as soon as I can, Dolores. Consider my room empty by the end of the week."

"It's yours until the end of the month, Mr. Van Lo, and we'll all be moving out by then. I can't maintain this place from my wheelchair. No, the Doctor's passing signals the passing of La Casa de Dolores into younger hands. It's the Lord's will. I only hope the rest of the lodgers have as easy a time relocating as you seem to think you will."

Nick turned away without a word, and stumbled down the stairs and out of the house. The old man's death, he was sure, wasn't the sadistic crime of bloodlust that Davey's had been. It had been preordained ever since that drunken night when the Doctor spoke of his own and the house's history, and warned him against . . . Himself, Nick had then thought; now he knew that the Doctor had meant vampires. He realized with alarming clarity that, right then, he needed to talk with someone who knew him well, knew him . . . before. There was only one person he could think of. Stepping into the phone booth on the corner, he dug in his pockets for some quarters, and dialed the number with fumbling fingers.

"Hello!" Fred Olds' voice sounded as cocksure as ever.

"Fred—it's me, Nick. Nicholas Van Lo."

"Nick!" The tone was one of surprise, but Fred adjusted quickly. "Where in hell have you been keeping yourself? We'd given you up for dead."

"I need to see you—I need your help. Tonight."

Fred's voice never lost its professional smoothness. "Could you tell me what happened?"

Nick didn't want to risk losing him before he even started. "When you get here, not before. You'll understand after I explain."

A long pause. "I think you'd better give me an idea of the problem, Nick, or I can't come."

Here we go, thought Nick. "A lot of the roomers in the hotel I'm living in have disappeared in the last couple of weeks. The landlady says they passed away in the night and were taken away, yet she never seems to know *where*. But the thing is, I've seen some of them walking around afterward. And... they're different."

"So they couldn't pay their bill, and the lady tossed them out," Fred answered matter-of-factly. "But the landlady doesn't want to admit it. And when you see them, they're embarrassed to say hello."

"There's more," Nick said softly. "One of my students had his throat ripped out on Halloween night."

"Why, that's awful! I can see why you're upset."

"I think a ten-year-old girl killed that little boy."

Nick could hear the catch of breath on the other end. He hesitated for a moment, and plunged in. "Her name is Amanda. I've always felt... drawn to her, as if she had a deep, unexplained hold on me. As if she were a vampire. I know it sounds like an excuse, and that's what I thought it was for a while. But now, it's what I really think. That's what I'm afraid of."

"That's what you're *afraid* of." Fred's tone was low, threatening. "Now you listen to me. I encouraged you to mow through these weeds in your mind. When you told me you were banging your students, I winced, but I didn't say stop, because it seemed to be the only way. It brought down your marriage, your career, but it gave you a fifty-fifty shot at saving your own life. But this... *a ten-year-old*..."

Fred let his words sink in. When he felt they had hit bottom, he continued. "They say some problems can be resolved by simply perceiving them as what they are. But you know what your problem is, boy—and you're tracking it down, wrestling it to the ground, and rolling in the dirt with it. 'But she's a vampire,'" he mocked. "'She killed one of my students.' You disgust me, Van Lo. You're sick."

The line went dead.

Nick slumped against the booth, feeling the awful solitude
envelop him once more. Now that he'd blown it, he realized
he never should have mentioned the word *vampire* to Fred, not
after the psychiatrist had analyzed Nick's recurring dream of
the woman sleeping on the altar.

Vampires are the embodiment of your neuroses, Fred had
once told him. *In dreams they often refer to an underlying wish
for incestuous relations, usually resulting from repressed sexual desire. When you can plunge that stake right through those
teeth, you'll be free of it. As free as the rest of us, anyway.*

He would have to tell Fred one day that there were worse
things in life than harboring dubious sexual fantasies . . . things
like having one's blood sucked by a vampire.

Tomorrow, with the coming of light, he would be brave
again. He really had no choice; there was nothing else left in
his life. Davey was dead, half the roomers had disappeared,
and now the Doctor was gone. All he could do was pursue the
shadows that crept closer each day.

But tonight he was scared: scared of whatever was brushing
the blood strokes around him. He didn't want to be alone
tonight. And as the awareness of his own solitude threatened
to boil over into despair, he fished into his pocket and pulled
out another quarter. The operator gave him Eileen Morris's
phone number, and he dialed it immediately, before he could
change his mind.

"Hi, this is Eileen. I'm not home right now, but . . ."

Nick rested his forehead against the telephone box, and
waited for the recording to end. He couldn't think of where
else he could turn.

The recording beeped, and he spoke wearily into the receiver. "Hi, Eileen. This is Nick Van Lo. I was calling to see
if—"

"Hello, Nick?"

"Eileen?"

"I always leave the machine on, even if I'm home. That
way I can screen my calls. Listen, I've already changed into
a sweatsuit for the night. Do you want to come over?"

Nick smiled. "If you're sure it's all right."

"No, it's not all right. I asked you over because I like making
life hard for myself. Do you know my address, you bozo?"

The smile grew wider. This was what he needed. "Yeah. I'll be there before you hang up. Thanks, Eileen."

Twenty minutes later, she opened her door and took him into her arms.

"It's good to see you, Eileen," Nick said huskily as they disengaged.

"It's always good to see someone," she answered, and winked. "Can I get you something to drink? I've got nothing that costs over three dollars."

"How about a beer?"

"I think there's a six in the refrigerator. Go over and sit down on the couch while I bring back a couple."

Nick sat down and took in the tiny studio apartment. Like half the addresses on Upper Polk, it had a view of the Golden Gate Bridge that made the utter lack of space bearable. The exposed brick walls met a polished hardwood floor that had room only for the couch Nick was sitting on, the coffee table before it, and a rocker in one corner.

Eileen came back with a glass of beer for each of them, and curled up on the other end of the couch. "So what's up, teacher? Having trouble with one of your students?"

Nick blinked with surprise. "As a matter of fact, I am, but . . ." He knew already that vampirism wouldn't ever make sense in her life. He was glad for that, and decided to let it rest. "I just didn't feel like going home."

"Oh." She took a sip of beer, and turned back to him. "Anything wrong with where you live?"

Nick nodded. "Yeah. People keep dying." He briefly told her about the dwindling wino population. "Living in such a flea-pit, I guess I shouldn't be surprised."

Eileen wrinkled her nose. "So why do you live there?"

"People always seem to ask me that," he said, more to himself than to her. "Not that I mind—I just don't know what to say."

"Then don't say anything. You're supposed to let a guy talk if he wants to," she grinned, "but I'm certainly not going to *force* you."

"Let's try it the other way around," Nick said lightheartedly. "What's going on in your life?"

"Well." Eileen stretched her legs and took a deep breath. "As long as you asked . . . there's this guy I'm seeing."

Nick reached over and squeezed her thigh. "That's more like it. I'm all ears."

"His name's Matt Hemphill. He's a cab driver—that's how I met him—and I could really fall for him. He's cute and sweet and all that, but . . ." She paused, searching for the right words. "Hanging around with him is an adventure, like he's one of the Hardy Boys or something. Every date has its own special mystery, its own excitement. Do you know what I mean?"

"It sounds wonderful," Nick answered honestly, and held one arm out to her. "Where's the cloud?"

Eileen slid over to Nick's side of the couch and rested her back against his chest. "The cloud is that he's nineteen years old. He's a very resourceful boy—I mean, don't ask me how he got his hack license—but he's still a boy. I'm worried that going out with an older woman will screw him up."

They both laughed at the absurdity of her sentiment, and Nick pulled her closer for a moment. "True love overcomes everything except old age and death, my dear. It positively *buries* an age difference of four years."

"I don't know about true love, true lust is probably more like it. I feel like a teacher seducing one of her students."

They sipped their beers in silence after that, and Nick felt Eileen relaxing against him. This was all he had been looking for, he thought: to deny, for one night, the tomorrow there was no escaping.

The minutes passed, they set their empty glasses on the coffee table, and still neither of them spoke. Some time after Nick had closed his eyes, he felt Eileen shifting to face him. He looked into her light-blue eyes, felt the calming effect of the surf on a faraway shore, and kissed the air between them.

"Let's go to bed," she suggested softly.

"What about your friend? Matt?"

Eileen wrinkled her nose again, so that she looked like a slightly incredulous kitten. "Do you want me to call him to make sure it's okay?"

"I want you to do what's right for you."

Eileen looked down for a moment, then back at Nick. "Do

you know why there's such little morality in dreams? Because no one really gets hurt. As long as no one's hurt, there's nothing wrong. And no one's getting hurt tonight."

Nick ran a hand down the side of her face, and asked her where the bed was.

"You're sitting on it."

Laughing, she yanked him to his feet, then pulled out the mattress from the convertible couch. She let him take off her sweatsuit, and helped him undress. As they lay down on the bed, the glow of a streetlight lit pinpricks of light in her hair.

Nick pressed his lips softly against hers, and reminded himself that he should go no further. He had no right to entangle an innocent person in the web being spun about him; he had no right to even offer the choice to another. And if he couldn't involve her, he couldn't let this night get any closer to his heart, and the fear that dwelled inside.

Tipping her chin up to him, he whispered that they should just go to sleep.

Eileen hesitated only a moment. "We're good friends, aren't we, Nick? We're friends because we care enough to never hurt each other."

There was no way he would have refuted her words that night; no way he could have foreseen the serpentine paths betrayal will take to reach its destination, the realm of pain. He could only look into the brightness of her eyes and ask, why can't I fall for you? Is it because I'll never get lost inside?

Eileen, flattered, turned away from the intensity of his gaze. Nick took advantage of the break in the moment to whisper good night, his isolation unbroken.

Angustia's Return

DUSK WAS SETTLING earlier, just as it had the rest of that week, and its lengthening shadows caught up with Nick as he reached the door of La Casa de Dolores.

Four days had passed since he had sought refuge at Eileen's apartment. In the classroom, Amanda sat silently by the window, watching him, as if she were biding her time. Little by little, he was admitting to himself that he didn't know what to do next. There had been nothing to spur him into action, nothing to prevent him from dreaming each night of the sound of Judith's key slipping into his lock. It seemed like the creaking wheels of his own destiny had also come to a stop since she dropped out of his life.

After ascending the staircase two steps at a time, he was a little short-winded as he turned left toward his room. With the raspy noise his own breathing was making, there was no way he would have heard the sounds of a struggle in the Siphon's room. But the door to the room had been left carelessly open, and what was going on inside stopped Nick in his tracks.

Someone had the Siphon pinned against the wall with one inflexible arm. Nick watched as the derelict's neck muscles distended in a futile effort to break the other man's grip. A muffled laugh came from the attacker as he bore down on the Siphon, almost flattening him against the wall. Then, grunting obscenely, he buried his face in his victim's neck. Nick stood by the door, transfixed, as the Siphon's head snapped back, as his terrified bloodshot eyes fixed themselves on Nick's. Their gazes remained locked over the slurping sounds, the sounds of the Siphon's life being drained away . . .

Gradually the tension relaxed, and the Siphon fell limp, his arms draped loosely over his killer's shoulders. Nick still could not move—not until the shoulders shifted and he recognized, just above the dripping fangs, Leatherface's gray mask. The black eyes behind the slits were on him, and Nick was not about to find out what they wanted. He ran: back through the hallway and down the stairs, out the front door and into the street.

He didn't know where he was going, or what he was looking for, but the question was answered for him before he reached the end of the block. Two cops walking their beat took one look at him and blocked his path.

Nick knew what he looked like, and spoke first. "There's been a murder," he began, and caught his breath. "At La Casa de Dolores, down the street. I think he's still there."

The policemen glanced at each other, and then one of them spoke into the walkie-talkie strapped to his shoulder. "Probable 187, Turk and Mason. La Casa de Dolores. Request 1025."

"Let's go," said the other one, and they ran back to the flophouse as sirens drew near. Two police cruisers squealed up to the curb and four more cops hurried out.

"Where?"

"Second floor," Nick stammered. "On the right."

The police kicked open the front door—Nick remembered he'd left it open—and charged up the stairs. Nick followed them, taking no notice of the crowd that was already forming, or of the hulking priest in the back carrying a black satchel. As he climbed up the staircase, he had a sickening premonition of what they would find: nothing.

Why would the vampires leave evidence of their existence behind? Davey was different, he had been killed by a child. But the roomers had disappeared without a trace; the Siphon, regardless of what Nick had seen, would be no exception.

He was preparing excuses for this possibility as the cops burst into the Siphon's room, revolvers drawn. But much to Nick's surprise, the Siphon was still there, face down on the floor, his spilled blood creating a halo around his head.

A plainclothes detective Nick hadn't noticed before crouched over the body and lifted the head by the hair. The Siphon's neck had been slashed from ear to ear. The detective reached under the dead man's neck, picked something up in a handkerchief, and let go of the head.

He stood up slowly. "He did leave us something." And Nick saw a long, rusted kitchen knife.

The room gradually grew more crowded over the next two hours as a police photographer, a fingerprint expert, and two or three reporters jostled around Nick and the cops performing their various duties. He was still in shock from what the knife had prevented him from telling the police: the truth. They may as well have hidden the corpse, he thought bitterly. No one's going to believe what I saw.

That was when he saw the priest.

It was Father Angustia, the one who had been at the house—when was it, anyway?—examining teeth. *Examining teeth,* he repeated to himself, and watched with increased interest as Angustia insinuated himself effortlessly into the flow of events.

"I'm here to give this man his last rites," he whispered to the lieutenant in charge, and proceeded to perform the sacrament of Extreme Unction on the Siphon. The rites took only a few minutes, and were marked only by Angustia's glances, Nick realized, in *his* direction.

When the lieutenant finally told him that he could leave, he wasn't surprised that the priest unobtrusively left the room and followed him out into the hall. Nick turned to face him, girding himself for the inevitable confirmation of his suspicions.

"I haven't noticed you examining teeth lately, Father."

Angustia picked up the challenge. "It certainly seems as if I should have been, don't you think?"

Nick hesitated for a moment, refusing to return the priest's smile. "Maybe you'd like to check out mine."

"With pleasure."

They repaired to Nick's room, where Angustia promptly straddled the lone chair. "May I offer you some wine?" The tone was familiar, ironic, a comment on the manner he had employed when they first met. Then he added more seriously, "I think you're going to need it, Nicholas."

Nick nodded, and Angustia poured three fingers into two Dixie cups. Nick took his and sat down on the edge of the bed.

Angustia wasted no more time. "Could you tell me what happened in that room?"

Nick told him in detail, omitting nothing. Leatherface's bloody visage was still clear in his mind.

"So the knife was planted near the body after you'd run off to get help."

Nick shrugged. "I didn't see him use a knife."

"Well of course not," Angustia snapped. "You saw him use his teeth."

Nick flinched at the words; they were ten times more horrid when spoken aloud, rather than in his own head. Angustia noted his response, and patiently altered his approach.

"I am the Senior Researcher at the Archives of the Roman Catholic Archdiocese." A pause, and a smile. "When I'm not examining teeth, that is. Some years ago, while writing a monograph on Ambrose, one of San Francisco's archbishops in the last century, I came across certain secret ecclesiastical documents of the period. These documents altered the direction of my life, they *gave* me direction, you might say. They led me to this house, and to the conclusion that what you saw this evening really began over one hundred years ago."

Angustia leaned forward imperceptibly. "The papers told of Ambrose's infatuation with Lourdes Molina, a young woman who owned one of the city's grand hotels. The gravity of the situation, however, came to official light only after the deaths of Ambrose himself and his brother, a monk named Emilio. The repentant tones of Ambrose's will, a testament written one day after Emilio's death, left little doubt as to how deep Ambrose's involvement had been.

"My curiosity was first pricked by the fact that, despite all these ominous allusions to Ambrose's will, no record remained of the will itself. The Church, my boy, saves everything. So I set about searching for the mysterious will. I finally found a copy of it in the journal of a 'spiritual undertaker' who was sent here to investigate Ambrose's death. And I found something much better."

The priest paused. "Ambrose's diary. It told a story that whetted my appetite to such an extent that nothing since has ever been able to slake my hunger."

Ambrose first met Lourdes at a charity ball held at one of the posh Tenderloin hotels. Her reputation had preceded her, of course. Her dalliances with some of the most powerful men in the city were well-known in the highest circles, and combined with a hard, cold shrewdness to make her hotel a stylish and prosperous enterprise. He was to learn more later, as he joined the roll of men who helped smooth over the periodic scandals and "disappearances" that permeated her establishment.

The archbishop fell under her spell that very night; she had that combination of youth, beauty, wit, and barely suppressed danger that older men find so enchanting. They became lovers, and Ambrose wrote poems to her breasts, her lips, her hair, her teeth.

Hopelessly entangled, he anguished over, yet inevitably tolerated, not only shadowy crimes, but black masses held in the sacristy of his cathedral, blasphemous orgies lubricated with consecrated wine. Lourdes enjoyed humiliating him, and grew bolder as the strength of her chains became clear. She received guests at one of her balls wearing a gown that would have failed to contain her breasts were it not for an ornate clasp— the archbishop's titular cross.

Ambrose's inability to extricate himself from this fatal involvement threatened to spill the messy affair before the general public's eye; it eventually came to the attention of his half-mad, solitary brother. Emilio was aware of his brother's uncanny dependence on Lourdes, and had come to suspect the supernatural, even the demonic. After making one final plea to his brother to see reason, Emilio decided to pay a visit to Lourdes at her hotel.

He was never seen again. When Ambrose discovered his brother's disappearance, he confronted Lourdes. All his diary says about the meeting is that some of her teeth had been knocked out. But afterward, Ambrose finally broke away from her. His valet found him hanging from a beam in his bedroom. His will confessed the exact nature of his relationship with Lourdes, accused her of vampirism and other crimes, and pleaded for forgiveness in the next world. It also asked that his remains be burned immediately. "It is both significant and ominous," Angustia pointed out, "that his request was carried out, in direct defiance of ecclesiastical law, by the very priests who read the will."

Nick thought of the similarity between how Lourdes and Judith lost their teeth, and how Judith had disappeared on the night that Davey died. Even as his breath grew short, he decided to bide his time. "What happened to Lourdes?"

"Apparently more people had known of the extent of Ambrose's involvement than he had supposed, because unofficial protection for Lourdes's hotel came to an end shortly after his death. Her fortunes declined steadily after that, and the 1906 fire put an end to her reign in that hotel."

"You mean she died in the fire?"

"No. I simply mean that she was never seen again. There is no record of her death in this city, just as there is no record of her birth. But her hotel is still here . . . and you are living in it."

Nick looked at him steadily. "I know."

"Ah. So you know."

They sat in silence then, eyes locked together in a death grip. More than just a passing on of information had taken place; it was as if their words had bonded them. Nick knew this, knew what Angustia was thinking, knew that this strangely fortuitous meeting was really no accident at all, that it was just as fated as his residency at La Casa de Dolores. So he waited for the half-dreaded, half-longed for words to come from the priest's mouth, the question that could only be answered with an oath.

At last they came, in a rare, quiet tone. "My boy, can you believe in vampires?"

They struck Nick like a trance-breaking slap, a confirmation and a liberation. Then he looked at the priest's face again. It was the face of a man who knew the truth, and feared and respected it. Nick checked his feelings in deference to it, and simply nodded his head.

Angustia took in the nod and proceeded as if there had never been any question as to what his response would be. "Lourdes is in this city now—I know it. Her spirit pervades this flophouse you call home. I sense it growing stronger, more blatant every time I visit."

He reached for the wine bottle and refilled their cups. "I also sense that tonight's . . . episode is not your first brush with her work. When did you first suspect the truth?"

Nick held back Judith's name, and described his suspicions

about Amanda; from her increasingly aberrant behavior to his own interpretation of Davey's gory death.

"A little girl," the priest mused. "Clever. Now tell me what you have seen in this house, and how you first heard of Lourdes."

Nick went over the litany of not-quite-dead roomers and desiccated rats, of strange noises in the night and his fateful conversation about Lourdes with the Doctor. "I think he was actually trying to warn me."

"A sliver of remorse," Angustia cut in harshly. "That man runs the building. He must be connected with Lourdes."

"I don't know about that. He's dead too."

"Dead!" Angustia half-rose from his chair. "You saw his corpse?"

"No. Dolores told me the same night she told me she's selling the building." And, even though they no longer seemed important, Nick mentioned the old photographs she had shown him.

"Yes, Dolores." Angustia rolled her name slowly off his lips. "That's Ambrose's cross she wears about her neck, you know."

"Then—"

"Then she is part of the conspiracy, no doubt. She's old enough to have been one of Lourdes's servants. At least that one is harmless, pinned as she is in that wheelchair. But the Doctor's death and the sale of the building—things are coming to a head. I don't suppose she told you who the buyer might be?"

Nick swallowed. The time had come to confront his greatest fear. "No, but I have a pretty good idea."

"Who?"

"My girlfriend."

He recounted the devouring nature of her sexuality, her unexplained disappearance every night before dawn, and her curious anger at being called Lourdes during sex. He wondered why he hadn't suspected her before. "I think she's running Dolores off this property by killing everyone who lives here."

"She isn't just killing them, though, is she?" Angustia chuckled evilly. "Tell me, what does she look like?"

Like a panther in human form, Nick thought, and described

her lustrous black hair, her mountain-pool eyes, and her tooth. "One of her canines really stands out, because the matching one on the other side is missing. She told me the brother of one of her boyfriends knocked it out."

"When did you see her last?" Angustia asked quietly.

"Just before I found Davey Schwimmer's body."

They looked at each other for a moment, absorbing their tacit conclusion. It was Angustia who finally spoke. "So the enchantress is back, still young, and still enchanting. She has latched onto you, my boy, counting on your loneliness to regain her hotel. That explains why she hasn't satisfied her thirst with your blood yet. We are told in vampire lore that the bloodsucker must be invited into a home by an untouched being of its own free will—it cannot enter otherwise."

"What about Amanda?"

"The little girl may be a child vampire, or simply an accomplice, afflicted but still human. And she may also be Lourdes herself. Folklore also warns of the infernal leech's ability to alter its physical appearance."

"Hmmm," from Nick. "I never heard of that."

The priest smiled. "No reason why you should have, my boy. Vampires are usually the concern of arcane scholars."

Nick grinned for the first time that night. "I majored in Victorian literature. Does that qualify me as an arcane scholar?"

"It most certainly does. The Victorians were quite scrupulous in their cataloguing the powers of, and antidotes against, vampires. Which is fortunate for us, because it's basically all we have to go on. You have, for example, noted the lack of mirrors in this house?"

Nick nodded, unwilling to reveal his obtuseness, and the priest continued. "We also have the weapons of the Church." And he removed a small crucifix from the satchel.

"You aren't a believer, eh Nick?" He had noticed the shadow passing over Nick's face. "Don't you see . . . what else can we go on except the passing courage this wine has given us, and the knowledge we've acquired?"

"Our knowledge tells us that Lourdes wore Ambrose's goddamn crucifix at a ball. I think I'll pass on the cross and go heavy on the garlic."

Angustia thought hard before responding. "Yes, only superstition claims that this will ward off the vampire. But where do we know anything of creatures that suck the blood of the living and move only at night, except in superstition?" He pressed the crucifix into Nick's palm. "If we accept what the dark side of the coin tells us, we may as well accept the light."

Nick examined the priest's gaze, and saw a luminous mixture of obsession, alcohol, and fanatical zeal. He couldn't think of a more inappropriate place to find logic. But Angustia wasn't going to take no for an answer.

He closed his fingers about the crucifix, and made a mental note to obtain a real weapon. "All right. Now where do we go from here?"

"We go to the city morgue—tonight." Angustia reached into the bottom of his satchel and withdrew a wooden stake with a wickedly sharp point. "The Siphon is still awaiting his true last rites."

Pretender to a Home

WHILE NICHOLAS VAN LO allied himself with Father Angustia, and discovered the comfort of purpose in his Tenderloin room, Jessie Westerhays hiked among the redwoods and sequoias of Mendocino, and admitted that she was lost.

She had arrived at the Northern California Autumn Arts and Crafts Workshop the week before, three days after Davey Schwimmer's funeral. After that tragedy, Tod had to convince her not to cancel her reservation at the workshop, but Jessie knew how little "convincing" had really been needed. No matter how she or Tod rationalized her attending the two-week seminar, it felt like she had run away.

It had all come crashing down on her that night, when Nick Van Lo had stood before her with a dead child in his arms. For a single devastating moment, the little black-cloaked body had been Amanda's, and the man bearing it, her daughter's fated murderer. Had his hands been wrapped around Amanda's neck while Jessie trembled with the fantasy of her own breath being claimed by him? Even her belated recognition of Davey, and Nick's account of how he came across him, could not dispel the complicity Jessie knew she shared in that moment, and for that crime, with Nick.

After that, there had been no way she could continue to pursue the virulence infecting her daughter; the virus's dizzying reconfigurations had rendered her helpless. Lisa Varney had been murdered, and now Davey. How could she allay her increasing pessimism at warding off the danger circling over Amanda? The problem lurked in an unseen corner of the world

they lived in, and its greatest strength was that it never went
away. Jessie had finally conceded that she couldn't confront it
alone, but there was no support network to cover for her when
her back was turned, or catch her when she fell. The workshop,
which would keep her 150 miles north of her problems until
Thanksgiving, arrived like a reprieve. It offered two weeks in
which to recover.

The noonday sun streaming in through the windows of her
cabin illuminated the large stained-glass panels Jessie had been
working on since her arrival. Destined to go in the French
doors she foresaw in the bedroom, the windows were coming
along surprisingly well. Jessie appraised them one last time,
then put down her soldering iron. She was scheduled to meet
with her advisor for lunch at the dining hall. Before slipping
on her down vest, however, she picked up the telephone and
asked the compound operator to dial San Francisco for her.

Tod answered the phone on the third ring. "Hey, babe!
How're all the artists getting along up in the woods?"

Jessie smiled. "Quietly. The ones who expected an orgy
have gone home already, gravely disappointed. How are you
two doing?"

"One week after you left us? Well, we're still alive." Tod
laughed. "Just kidding. Everything's fine. I've been eating very
rare steaks with garlic *every* goddamned night, and it's heaven."

"How does Amanda feel about that?"

There was a slight pause. "Frankly, she has yet to join me
in one of these feasts."

"Oh, Tod. How can you be so irresponsible?"

"By shelling out five bucks of lunch money every morning,"
he answered, unperturbed. "She gets the dough if her weight
remains constant at my new daily weigh-ins. As of today, she's
up a half-pound, so whatever she's eating is okay in my book."

Jessie sagged against the oak wall, and apologized. There
wasn't much else she could do.

"Forget it, kid. I know how you felt when you left, and I
can imagine how thinking about it all alone up there wouldn't
make it any easier. I help her with her homework each night,
and put her to bed by ten. I've mentioned Davey's death a bit,
just to see if she's hiding any of her feelings, but I swear she's

digested the whole mess. *We* should only have her stability."

Jessie nodded. She wanted to get off. "Well, that's encouraging. Anything else up before I go?"

"Yeah. Vic's gone back to work again, and with a vengeance. He called to say that the building is now ours, and should be somebody else's before Christmas. That means a vacation in Pago Pago, if you like. Other than that, just forget us and try to have a good time. I may not understand women," he concluded with a devilish laugh, "but I sure understand little girls."

"Okay, you sicko. I'll see you in nine days."

Jessie slowly lowered the receiver to its cradle. She didn't want to spend Christmas in Pago Pago; she wanted to spend it with a family that was healed. But that possibility was out of her hands for the moment, since she had run off up here and abdicated control.

"I'm a pretender to a home," she punned, trying to jab herself out of her lethargy. But all she felt was a curiously liberating shame.

The Siphon's Last Rites

THE DARKNESS SETTLING over the city took on a special meaning for Nick as he put down a fourth shot of Old Crow: it augured a time when those he feared stretched and flapped their wings.

It was just past six-thirty, and the other drinkers around him pressed closer to the bar for the last thirty minutes of happy hour. But for Nick, a pale ghost among the crowded, flushed faces, it was still eleven o'clock of the previous night, and the location was the city morgue.

He and Angustia had taken a cab over to the morgue, where the priest once again impressed him with his ability to bluff his way into normally restricted areas.

"I'm Father Keneally from the St. Francis Home for Men," he told the receptionist at the information desk. "I understand one of our charges was brought in here about an hour ago—a homicide at La Casa de Dolores." He gave the address. "I would like to see the body for identification purposes."

The receptionist leafed through a pile of papers before him. "This should be it. John Doe, advanced age, throat lacerations. He's on tray Thirty, in the basement. Take that elevator over there. An orderly will pull the slab for you."

They rode the elevator down in silence. Their plan was brutally simple. Once they found the Siphon, Nick would feign illness to get the orderly out of the room. Then Angustia would lift the sheet covering the Siphon, plunge the stake into his heart, and saw the stake off at skin level. By the time Nick and the orderly returned, Angustia would have the sheet over the corpse once more, and no one would be the wiser.

The morgue's basement was the opposite of its bustling, dirty lobby: white, cool, narrow, and antiseptic, as if its echoing corridors were bathed in subliminal blue light. Nick stayed close to Angustia as they followed a series of blue arrows to the morgue room. When they encountered a police orderly outside the door, Angustia repeated his story and gave the man the tray number. The orderly stretched, opened the door, and led them to number Thirty.

Standing as he was behind Angustia, Nick couldn't see the tray's contents as it was pulled out of the wall. He did, however, hear the priest whisper *my God* softly to himself, and he closed his eyes, unwilling to face the glazed eyes and bared fangs. It was only after he realized that Angustia and the orderly weren't moving that he stepped around the priest and looked down at the tray.

It was empty.

"Happens all the time with John Does," the receptionist informed them minutes later. "Thirty's in Twenty, Twenty's in Sixteen, and Sixteen got lumped in with Seventeen because nobody could separate what was left of them into two baggies. Know what I mean? Try again tomorrow morning. Regular staff will be in then. Maybe they'll know where he walked off to, heh heh."

Once they were in the back seat of a taxi, Nick had told Angustia that he didn't want to go back to the flophouse. "Not tonight. Not after everything that's happened."

The priest placed a hairy hand on Nick's knee. "Spend the night at the rectory. There's a spare room that's always prepared." He paused. "But if we want to stay abreast of what Lourdes is doing, you are going to have to return there. I'm afraid it's a chance we must take."

Nick had agreed, and retired to the rectory's cheerily simple guest bedroom. He lay awake all through that night, thinking not of Siphon, but of Judith.

Angustia had viewed his involvement with her as a master vampire taking advantage of a lonely man, and dismissed it. But the priest hadn't slept with her, didn't know that even as she drank Nick's semen, he had eaten her as if she were a rare, intoxicating mushroom, whose poison induced a delirium he could never resist. If he was a victim, he was a very willing one.

Perhaps she had already attacked him. How else could it all have seemed so natural? The incendiary sex, the dreams, the perverse fantasies and desires all sprouted together, so organically, like a fungus. He had been drugged, paralyzed like a small woodlands animal before the blinding light of a vampire.

Yet, for some reason, she had been unwilling or unable to take his life. It was the only card he had to play. He admitted the possibility that he was still under her spell, and pledged to extract vengeance.

Eileen Morris had substituted for Nick the next morning while he answered questions in police headquarters. Inspector Vicente wanted to know how he had gotten into the habit of discovering murder victims, and what he knew about the murder of Lisa Varney. The police learned nothing new from him, but he now had another name to add to his list of vampire victims.

Nick spent the entire afternoon at the library reading Transylvanian superstitions, trying to match them up with what little he and Angustia knew about the vampires they were pursuing. Most of what he read struck him as rather ineffective, such as the adage about painting a set of eyes on a large black dog's forehead to ward off a vampire. Perhaps it was all a matter of taste, he mused, sipping another tumbler of bourbon—what struck your fancy worked, and what didn't, didn't. For him it was the classics, the ones his Victorian romancers employed: safety in the sunlight, or from the blaze of a fire; death by impalement or decapitation.

Impalement or decapitation. But first they had to find one, and to have any hope of that he would have to get back to La Casa de Dolores. The clock over the bar read seven-forty; he was now on his sixth tumbler of Old Crow, and the sky outside wasn't getting any lighter. "Don't forget that they also know what you saw," Angustia had reminded him. "She will come back for you soon. If God is with us, we will be ready for her. But in the meantime, keep your door locked, and don't leave your room after dark, no matter what you hear. Our time is the light."

The light was gone now, but that couldn't be helped. It had taken six ounces of bourbon to build the courage to go back there. Angustia didn't want him in the hallway after dark. But when else were they going to encounter the vampires?

His question was answered less than two blocks away from where he had formed it, as the bar's din became a memory replaced by the twin rhythms of his heartbeat and footsteps. His, and the ones behind him.

He stopped dead and swiveled. The street was empty except for one old wino standing on the corner he had just passed. Nick moved on, thinking he had been scaring himself, and tried to regain the rhythm he had lost by stopping. But it was no use. His stride could only counterpoint the footsteps that were following him. He glanced over his shoulder without slowing down: it was the same bum who had been standing on the corner. This time the bum didn't stop.

Nick cursed himself for having drunk too much, and tried to will himself sober, but there was no way. He was drunk, and he was scared, and his legs refused to do what he was ordering them to—*run*.

Turning the corner to his own block, he caught a glimpse of the man. His face had been shrouded in darkness, but it reminded him of the Siphon, and it was smiling. Nick knew the smile from countless boyhood films: it was the smile of slow, inexorable death. Having seen it, he could barely accept it. *Me? It's my turn to die?* The very thought was so unbelievable and yet so sure, in a dream-logic way, that when he tripped over his own feet on a curb and fell down, he could not get up.

Instead, he lay there on his hands and knees, breath coming slowly to him, the approaching footsteps filling his mind, an underground grotto with a trickling, seeping stream of images—the images of his own death. Only a few more steps now, and its cold hand would grip his neck, its lips breathe the stink of mouldering bacteria in his face. The touch . . . The stench . . .

A hand settled on the nape of his neck. It felt cold, like a dead fish.

Nick screamed and rose up like a woozy sprinter coming out of his starting blocks, staggering toward La Casa de Dolores. He would get there ahead of his pursuer, he knew; death never runs. It was simply a matter of whether he could get past the locked door in time.

When he reached it, the shadowy figure was still half a block away. Nick pulled out his key chain and almost panicked when he remembered that the flophouse keys were on the same ring as the six that went to the John Swett School. His fingers stuttered over the keys, clumsy with fear and alcohol, and the Siphon—for that was who it was—stood ten feet away when he finally found it. The nauseating odor poured over him as he slammed the key into the lock.

The door flew open with the force of his movement, and Nick rushed in, whirled, and put his shoulder to the door. The familiar image of that grinning face dissolved into pinpricks as Nick heard the lock click into place.

He knew the Siphon was still out there, but there was no way he could get through the door. Nick leaned his back against it, fingered his room key, and looked up the tranquil staircase. After he caught his breath, he was going to his room, lock *that* door, and draw himself a bath. The water would be scalding, and he would finally allow his mind to melt—

A key was being slipped into the lock.

He could hear it turning as he spun and backed away (he lives here, he's got a key), felt the blond hairs on the back of his neck prickle as the door swung open with a triumphant creak, and stared at the creature he had known as the Siphon. He could still see a semblance of the wino, but the coarse, matted hair under the coonskin cap and the sores on his ears and nose were now only accessories. The being before him had become a gaunt-cheeked, reeking ghoul with a ravenous grin that bared the three fangs inside its gaping maw.

Nick moved backward one step at a time, eyes locked on those of the creature before him, mistaking his inability to scream for asphyxiation. When his back foot bumped against the first step of the staircase, he turned and scrambled up the stairs on all fours like a pathetic, frightened sand crab suddenly exposed to sunlight. His feet seemed to slip on every third step, but mercifully made enough noise to prevent him from hearing just how close the creature was. One backward glance was all he needed; the Siphon, staggering from side to side like a drunken pioneer, was making his way up the stairs one step at a time.

Once he reached the top, Nick never looked back. His room key was still clutched in his right hand, and he covered the distance to the door in twenty running strides. He was behind his locked door before the Siphon had even gained the top of the stairs.

Nick knew there was no way the creature could possess a key to his room, but he wasn't taking any chances. He unscrewed the chinning bar he had set up in the bathroom doorframe, and gripped it in one hand, belatedly realizing it was more like a baton than a billy club. Seconds after he turned off the room light, he heard the shambling footsteps just outside. Nick leaned against the wall, ready to come down and across with the chinning bar the moment the door opened.

His heart skipped a beat as the knob slowly turned to the right. But then it reversed direction, jangled up and down, and was still. The footsteps shuffled away, and Nick sank to the floor, eyes closed, the chinning bar across his lap. He sat there for the next forty-five minutes, as the presence outside his door returned twice, fumbled with the doorknob, and went away. Finally he rose from the floor and lay down on the bed, fully dressed, and allowed his muzzled thoughts to stretch.

There would be no sleep for him tonight, but he would get even. Starting the next day, there would no longer be any sleep for the vampires.

The following night a pair of unlikely vigilantes patrolled the Tenderloin streets.

Father Angustia, wearing a black poplin jacket over his black shirt and Roman collar, strode slowly down one sidewalk, intently scanning the faces of the night people who walked toward him, and those leaning against lampposts and doorways. His ramrod-straight posture was only partly due to the stake he had taped vertically to his back. Angustia periodically darted a glance across the street to the opposite sidewalk, where Nick was moving in the same direction.

Nick had found Angustia at the Archives in the early afternoon, after sleeping away the morning. The Senior Researcher's office was sparsely furnished: one large desk and two straight-backed chairs. Two of the walls were lined with books; on the other two hung a painting of the Temptation and a crucifix. Like Angustia, the room was all business. Nick had sat down in one of the chairs and told him of his near-fatal encounter with the Siphon the night before.

The priest deliberated over Nick's story before responding. "Lourdes has been saving you for some purpose of her own," he began. "But it seems we can't count on her stooges to do the same. You'd better move into another hotel as soon as possible."

Nick nervously fingered the brown paper bag he had brought with him. "What about the vampires? We can't just have them prowling the streets at night."

"You yourself said their rooms are empty. Where do you suggest we start looking for them?"

Nick's response was prompt. "Where the Siphon found me—in our neighborhood. The Tenderloin."

Angustia smiled. "Then it's time, isn't it? Tonight we go looking for them." He paused. "Tell me, son, do you know how to carve a stake?"

"I'll do my carving with this." And he reached into the bag on his lap, removing a mahogany-handled hunting knife with a seven-inch blade.

Now he could feel the knife's reassuring heft bumping against his ribs with every other stride he took. Earlier he had cut a hole in the lining of his suede jacket's inside pocket, so that he could carry the knife without it being noticed. The shiver he had felt moments before when a patrolman crossed his path—a guilty reflex over the concealed weapon he was carrying—had reminded him of how unbelievable, how *criminally insane*, their mission would seem to anyone else.

The mission was swiftly building to a climax, he knew, and not just because a vampire had stalked him the night before. Angustia had told him that afternoon that, thanks to the Church's connections at City Hall, he should be hearing from the Hall of Records the next day as to who was buying La Casa de Dolores. Lourdes's time as the unseen, untrackable specter of their lives was drawing to a close.

Nick's thoughts were sharply interrupted as he crossed the mouth of an alley by one long, dying yelp from its depths.

After alertly pressing himself against the side of the building in front of him, he craned his head around and looked into the darkness. With effort he made out the silhouette of a man crouched over a small, limp form. The man's back was to him, he couldn't *see* what he was doing back there, but the sounds told him more than he needed to know. Below the frenzied wrestling and staccato groans he heard unmistakable tearing sounds, chewing sounds, the licks of a rasping tongue. Nick knew what was happening in there, what the little unre-sisting thing was: another Davey, dying.

He looked away from the nightmare in the back of the alley and across the street, but Angustia was nowhere to be seen. Why did he have to find one on his side of the street? His left hand, knowing there was no other choice, slid over his shirt toward the knife handle protruding from the inside pocket. His fingers had just closed around the carved, polished wood when the Siphon emerged from the alley.

Nick would always be thankful that the eyes in that blood-smeared face didn't settle on him, that the staggering, somehow *drunken* creature under the coonskin cap chose to head away from where Nick was standing, breath trapped halfway up his windpipe. He could still see that long tongue lapping the skin about it for food, for sustenance, when steely fingers closed around his left wrist.

It was Angustia, and Nick closed his eyes, releasing the air from his lungs in one cracking sigh.

"What happened?" Angustia muttered under his breath.

Nick pointed into the alley. "In there."

They rushed in and found what the Siphon had left behind next to an overturned garbage can. It was a scrawny black-and-tan mutt with part of an ear long since missing and mange covering half its ribs. The little dog's stomach had been torn out. What was left of its organs lay between its legs, providing a luminous bridge for the roaches scuttling into its belly.

Nick turned away from the gruesome sight and retched against one of the brick walls. When he finished, Angustia placed a hand on his shoulder. "It could have been worse. It could have been a human being."

Nick looked back into his eyes with cold fury. "It was the Siphon. And he headed back the way we came."

He was less than two blocks away when they saw him, listing to one side, occasionally supporting himself on a parking meter. Nick and Angustia, walking side-by-side now, stayed almost a block behind him, hoping he would lead them to Lourdes. (Judith, Nick thought. Judith Harper. That is her name now. She is the one I am hunting.)

Their path, however, soon took a familiar appearance to Nick and, after the Siphon made a final turn, his destination became clear to both men: he was going back to La Casa de Dolores. With their quarry only thirty yards from the flop-house's door, Angustia snapped his fingers, and the two pursuers broke into a run. They dashed around the Siphon to the doorstep, and turned to face his approach.

A look of confusion clouded the Siphon's ravaged features like a passing shadow before he snarled menacingly, fangs bared. He took two steps toward them, then stopped. Nick's flashing blade was only six inches from his chest. If the vampire had any doubt as to what he should do then, Angustia resolved it for him by fishing in a pocket for his cross. The Siphon never saw it. He spat like a cat, and moved off into the night.

Nick looked questioningly at Angustia.

"He'll have to find some sort of shelter before sunrise," the priest said, slipping the cross back into his pocket. "All we have to do is stay close to him. If we're lucky he'll take us to a more interesting location than his old room."

So the two men set off again, easily keeping up with the figure ten yards in front of them. Occasionally, the Siphon glanced over his shoulder, and always found their eyes boring into his. Nick remembered these moments later, remembered the raw animal fear in the Siphon's eyes as the point when his own doubts hardened into a driven, vengeful purpose. These creatures could be cornered and killed—and they knew it.

Then, quite suddenly, the Siphon was gone. He had made a right turn, and when they followed seconds later, it seemed as if he were momentarily obscured by the milling traffic. Half a block further, however, they knew. The vampire had lost them.

"He's got to be somewhere on this block," Angustia insisted angrily. "We checked the alleys and doorways, and there's no way he can flat outrun us. He must have ducked into one of these joints." He pointed at the tangle of red-yellow-and-white signs that effortlessly lit the street behind him. "A bar, a strip joint, or that porno theater."

Nick peered at the different blinking messages. "There are no bars on this block, just strip joints, and I doubt any bouncer would let a ghoul like the Siphon into his place." He looked at Angustia, grinning. "Looks like we're going to the movies."

The priest shook his head, pointing at his collar. "Not me." He continued, but failed to stifle a blush. "I'll wait out here. If you find him, keep an eye on him, but don't let him see you. He can't stay in there forever, and we'll get him when he comes out."

Nick nodded, then went over to the box-office window of the all-night theater and paid the bored Oriental man behind the glass five dollars for a ticket. After one last look at Angustia, he entered the theater.

The theater's small, dank lobby was empty save for one ripped plastic couch and a coffee machine. A sign on the wall read NO SOLICITING. Nick smiled in recognition of what it really meant and, parting a black curtain, entered the auditorium.

After focusing on the screen's bondage action until his eyes adjusted to the dark, he surveyed the sloping, low-ceilinged room. Only about a quarter of the hundred-or-so seats were filled, and he quickly spotted the Siphon. Nick quietly took a seat in the last row, an area cast in even deeper shadows by the overhanging projection booth.

The ensuing hours passed as if in a vacuum. No one budged in his seat—not the Siphon, not some drowsy customer with an aching bladder. The only movement was the passage of cigarette smoke through the beam of light bringing the images of pleasure and pain to the screen. Nick watched three features twice without falling asleep or getting excited, and came to realize that some men preferred their sex thrown up on a wall, where only the flick of a light switch was required to end their subjugation.

Then the overhead lights came on, and the theater manager stuck his head through the curtain. "Okay, everybody," he announced wearily. "Show's over. Wake up. Time to go."

Nick watched from the darkness underneath the overhang as the theater's patrons slowly rose, stretched, and filed out.

The Siphon, joining the tail end of the procession, slouched past Nick without noticing him.

He thinks he's safe now, Nick realized. But I wonder where he's going? It must be daylight by now.

It didn't take long to find out. Once in the lobby, the Siphon took advantage of a small disruption by the theater doors to slip into the men's room. Only Nick saw him go in. After debating what to do, he approached the manager, a stout, middle-aged man with a cyst over one eyebrow.

"There's some crazy old geezer hiding out in the john."

"What else is new," the manager shrugged. "I'll send someone in for him. Thanks."

Nick thought about what the vampire had done to the dog in the alley, and decided to be as honest as he could be about the potential danger of the situation. "Maybe you'd better call the police. He pulled a knife on me in there."

The manager shook his head. "Thanks for the tip about the blade. But we take care of our own problems here." He turned toward the ticket window. "Johnny!"

The Oriental man appeared.

"A little trouble in the john. Some old fuck with a knife."

The two men moved toward the rest room, and Nick stayed close behind them, his left hand hidden inside his jacket. Then the manager opened the door.

"The sun's coming up, mister. Why don't you..." His words faded away in the emptiness that greeted him. Panicking, Nick looked about the room. On one side there were three stand-up urinals under a long, cracked mirror, which in turn reflected three stalls. No feet were visible under the doors, but only one door was shut. The manager stepped in front of it, looked at his assistant, and kicked it open.

The Siphon exploded on him from his crouch on the toilet seat, knocking him backward onto the tiled floor. Nick saw the terrified, frozen expression on the man's face, the vampire's hands slipping around his throat, the baring of the oversized canines. He pulled out his knife and moved forward. Just then a shadow flashed past him, and the Oriental crashed the side of his shoe into the Siphon's temple, sending him sprawling across the floor.

The manager, quickly regaining his composure, jumped to

his feet and grabbed one of the Siphon's arms while his assistant secured the other. Together they cautiously raised the thrashing, snarling vampire to his feet.

"Careful, John," the manager warned through clenched teeth. "This guy's rabid."

Nick quickly put his knife away and held the rest room door open for them as they dragged the vampire into the lobby. The weak rays of early morning light were visible through the ticket window. That was when the Siphon began to scream.

"No! Please! The sun! Let me stay! Please! Not the—" The words became garbled, incomprehensible *(unbearable,* Nick remembered later) as Nick opened the outside door and the other two struggled to get the shrieking vampire through them. Then the Siphon, beyond desperation, planted one foot against a doorframe; the two men couldn't pry it loose without releasing one of the arms.

They looked up at Nick.

Nick, grim faced, kicked the wedged leg on the side of the knee. The Siphon's shrieks melded into a howl of pain, the leg came free of the doorframe, and the other two men heaved him onto the sidewalk, six feet from where Father Angustia stood.

The Siphon landed in the fetal position, his hands balled into fists and drawn in against his stomach. The convulsions lasted less than a minute; to Nick he looked like an autumn leaf cracking and writhing under a low flame. When it was over, the vampire's flaky, parchmentlike skin was sucked in like a prune.

"John, call a fucking ambulance."

Nick and Angustia looked over at the manager. He couldn't believe what had just happened in his theater. "The lunatic must have had a coronary," he muttered, and turned to Angustia.

"Father, isn't there anything you can do? Last rites or something?"

Angustia smiled at Nick.

The Trap

OVER A GREASY-SPOON breakfast less than an hour later, Angustia had tried to discourage Nick from going to John Swett that morning and proving, once and for all, that Amanda Westerhays was a vampire.

"You haven't had any sleep," the priest had pointed out. "Not to mention what we've both been through. Call in sick and spend the day in bed at the rectory. Don't forget that I'll be finding out who's buying the flophouse today. We're going to have another busy night."

"We've only seen them at night," Nick responded, his eyes reflected in the fresh cup of coffee before him. "The sunlight killed the Siphon. I have to know why she's different."

"But she's just a little girl!" Angustia exploded. "She's not important now!"

"She is to me," Nick said softly. "If she's not one of them . . ." He didn't want to say what it would mean, to him.

Angustia slapped the Formica counter with his spoon. "And just how do you expect to *prove* anything in a classroom full of children?"

"I'll think of something," Nick answered softly, and slid off his stool without saying another word. And later that morning, over a school lunch he could barely taste, the plan took shape in his head.

It was more than a clever idea, he decided. It was a goddamn bear-trap . . .

"The years from six to twelve," Roberta Allen announced to the students in Room 14, "are perhaps the most important in our lives—the years in which we go from babyhood to the very threshold of maturity."

Miss Allen, a young dental hygienist from the dentistry program at the university, was visiting Nick's class that afternoon. She had brought several charts and displays, and a prepared speech containing nothing he hadn't already taught the children. After fifteen droning minutes, she reached the point of her presentation that Nick had been waiting for.

"Now that I've pointed out the changes you all can expect *your* mouths to undergo," Miss Allen continued, "let's have a closer look at a set of teeth that have already had these transformations." She looked mischievously over at Nick. "Mr. Van Lo, could we use you as our example of a well-developed mouth?"

They always need a volunteer, Nick said to himself as the class burst out laughing with unfocused anticipation. He walked over and stood comically erect by her side, hands locked behind his back.

"Please open your mouth wide, Mr. Van Lo."

Nick opened it as widely as he could, hoping his eighteen hours of coffee breath wouldn't knock her out. It was important that this demonstration be carried out to its conclusion.

Miss Allen reached into her carrying bag and withdrew a small metal prober with a sharp, hooked point. "As long as you don't jerk around, Mr. Van Lo, you won't get hurt." She winked at the class.

"Now these," lightly touching his mouth with the prober, "are the front teeth and lateral incisors. Most of you already have these teeth in, just like your teacher."

Nick planted his left foot firmly on the floor, and rested the right one on his heel.

"Some of you have also lost your baby molars, and replaced them with"—tapping the appropriate teeth—"the bicuspids."

Nick shut his eyes tightly.

"Now in two or three years—when you're all teenagers— you'll lose your baby eyeteeth and replace them with"—moving the prober one tooth over—*"canines."*

Nick's right heel slid forward as if on a banana peel, throwing his weight—and his head—back. There was no way the prober's hooked point could *not* have caught on the inside of his lower lip.

"Oh, no!" Miss Allen gasped. The blood welled between Nick's lip and gums, and slowly seeped into view.

"Here, let me help you." She was clearly horrified. "You ... You ... This has never happened to me before." And she daubed the cut with ointment from her carrying bag.

The bleeding was quickly quenched. "Thank you," Nick said graciously. "I'm afraid I slipped. It's much better now."

"Well, good ... good ... I guess we can't use your mouth ..." The woman was still agitated. "Maybe I should wrap this up, get going."

Nick smiled without disagreeing, and Miss Allen quickly packed her props and said good-bye to the children. After ushering her out the door, he turned to face the class. They were all still somewhat stunned—all except Amanda, who was staring at him with unabashed curiosity.

Nick had an image of an impoverished prospector striking a vein after a lifetime of drought, and felt his heart beat with anticipation. "Take out your decimals workbook. Start working on page forty-four, and keep on going until you finish the section."

It was time to get his proof.

He stood up and slowly paced around to the back of the classroom. Pausing there, he bit down on his injured lip until the blood flowed again, and he had to dampen the wound with his tongue to keep the sluggish stream from trickling down his chin. Then he resumed his pacing, and finally came to a halt next to Amanda. Under the pretext of examining her work he bent over her, hands clasping the sides of her desk, bringing his head down to her level, tongue still over the lip.

Amanda angled her head slowly, trying to gauge his intent. When Nick had her undivided attention, he lifted his tongue to the roof of his mouth, allowing the blood to seep out. Now he could only wait to see if she would give herself away.

Amanda's tongue lolled, and the pencil in her hand slipped from her grip and fell off the desk. The word in her look was desire, a desire that translates as hunger, while the little stream of blood ran down Nick's chin. The eyes jerked away twice only, when the first two drops of blood fell from his chin and spread in twin stains on her worksheet. From then on they were riveted on the source of the blood, the jagged incision on his lip. Her mouth began to lift, imperceptibly at first, then a bit faster, and Nick felt a desire to have her bite the bait welling within him.

Amanda's mouth opened like the drawing of Cupid's bow, and beads of sweat trickled down from Nick's hairline; the blood was coming freer now, as if it were attracted to her lips. He couldn't bear it any longer; he closed his eyes and waited those last few seconds until Amanda's mouth closed on his lip.

The second they were in contact was an eternity; the feel of her lips, teeth, and tongue was an ancient scripture. The blood couldn't have been gushing, but that's what it felt like: a sweet river of life rushing to its mouth. He thought of that term again. The little death.

Then the principal's voice slammed into him, each word a nail sealing his coffin. "Mr. Van Lo, step out into the hall. This instant."

He felt like dying right then.

Dead Flowers

NICK JAMMED THE quarter into the slot and dialed the number again. It was growing dark.

He had been trying to reach Angustia all afternoon long, but the priest had never returned to his office after lunch. Nick had spent the last three hours darting between a little diner where he'd sipped countless cups of coffee, and the phone booth on the corner. The catastrophic events at the school that morning had shaken him worse than he had anticipated. A tic had developed on his lower lip after fifty-five hours with almost no sleep; it was centered, he felt, on the fateful cut.

Then, finally, a male voice answered on the other end of the line. "Archives. Angustia here."

"It's me, Father. Nick."

"I suppose you've been calling to find out who the mysterious buyer of La Casa de Dolores is. This is much bigger than we thought."

"I'm calling about Amanda." Nick told him about the inspiration to tempt her with his own blood, the unexpectedly dangerous reaction it induced, and finally, the principal's untimely intrusion. "I was fired on the spot. He mentioned the possibility of criminal charges depending on how much Amanda chose to remember."

"That's the least of our worries. Amanda is not going to be in any shape to testify against anybody after we're through with her. I *am* worried about the blood she took from you—it was a fool thing to do. We don't know what effect it may have." Angustia shifted forward in his chair. "Now listen to this. The

Hall of Records called me this morning with the name of the buyer. His name is Tod Westerhays."

"My God," Nick gasped. "That's her father."

"That's what I assumed. *Everyone* around you is involved in this thing, and after the bite you received, I don't think we can afford to wait any longer."

Nick remembered the fear in Jessie's face when she opened the door and saw Davey in his arms. "Where do we start?"

"At La Casa de Dolores," came the prompt reply. "It's the object of all her machinations. We'll start in the basement and work our way up. Even if we don't find anything, we can make it uninhabitable for her. From there we'll go and pay a call on the Westerhays family."

The All-American vampires, Nick thought, and then Angustia continued. "I'll meet you in your room between seven-thirty and eight—there are some provisions I have to pick up first. Once you get there, lock your door and don't open it for anyone else. But before you go back there, make yourself a stake. That hunting knife isn't going to be enough tonight."

The empty feeling in Nick's stomach told him that the priest was right. But . . . "Where do you buy a stake?"

Angustia laughed richly in the shade-drawn darkness of his office. "You *buy* a stake at a plant store. They're called rose-bushes. When you're back in your room, use that knife of yours to whittle it into shape."

"Okay." Nick felt drained, exhausted. "If you can get there sooner . . ."

Angustia slowly brought down the receiver. His free hand slowly ran over the pile of sharpened stakes next to the phone. He was worried about Nick, who leaned back against the glass sides of the telephone booth, eyes closed.

Nick was worried, too. What had he done to himself in allowing her to bite him? He hadn't meant for things to go that far . . . and that long, horribly seductive moment came back to him. He now thought he knew how succumbing to a vampire would feel, and knew he didn't want to be tempted again.

He finally stepped out into the cool night air, felt the breeze on his tainted lip, and allowed his mind to clear. He had to find a plant store. The nearest ones he could think of that would still be open were on Polk Street.

But the next hour passed in a fruitless search to find an open store. I'm not going to find one tonight, he said to himself, still standing in front of the last one he had tried. *And it's getting darker.* He took a long look up and down the street; there was no one within a block of him. Breathing deeply, he stepped back and kicked the doorknob as hard as he could.

The door, splintered free from the jamb, flew open.

Nick couldn't believe it. He hesitated, looking around again, sure that someone was watching him. But the street was deserted for a block and a half, almost as a favor to him. He grimaced and went in, closing the door behind him.

The store was dark and crowded with greenery; Nick knew instantly that he was going to need a flashlight. He made his way over to the cash register. Fumbling around underneath, he finally came up with a heavy watchman's-style light.

Keeping the beam down low, he began to prowl around, making his way over to the far side. There, lining one short length of wall, were several stout potted rosebushes. Nick picked one up. It was much too heavy to haul all the way home; he was going to have to dig it out of the pot.

It was harder going than he had expected, and he found himself thinking enviously of dogs ripping holes in the earth. But his fingers burrowed patiently into the moist, compacted earth, scattering the dirt on the floor, and finally the dirt's hold on the rosebush began to loosen.

That was when the door opened behind him. Nick froze, and switched off the flashlight. The door closed, and he heard cautious footsteps pad past him. Peering through a part in the rosebush he saw a slender young man with a small-caliber pistol in one hand. He must have been in a back room the entire time, Nick realized.

The man was at the cash register now, checking to see if it had been opened. Satisfied that it hadn't, he reached under the counter for something. The flashlight, Nick thought: he's looking for the flashlight. The man fumbled under the counter for a few more seconds, then jerked up, looking about nervously. Without hesitating, he moved toward the far wall. He's going for the light switch, Nick thought. Or to call the police. Either way, I'm dead.

Nick leaped from behind the rosebush, brandishing the

flashlight; the proprietor turned around in time to see Nick lunge and bring the flashlight down on his neck. A groan stifled the man's scream, the pistol fell to the floor, and he put his hand on his already-swelling neck. Nick looked into the man's eyes: he was petrified. Moaning, Nick struck him across the side of the head. The man staggered, but remained standing. You're supposed to fall, Nick thought with rising panic, and hit him again in the same place, slicing open the man's cheek. Blood spurted out, and the man fell.

Nick stood over him, panting. Don't think about it, he repeated to himself. Tearing his eyes away from the unconscious body, he dropped the flashlight and went back to the rosebush. He brought it down hard on the floor, smashing the clay pot into pieces.

As soon as he was out of the store Nick started running. He got halfway to the flophouse before he thought his lungs would burst; the rest of the way became a gasping, stumbling nightmare, ducking into alleys and doorways with every passing car, before every approaching form. The adrenaline rush that had come with his assault on the man with the gun had been supercharged with a mushrooming hysteria that prevented him from thinking about anything, including what he had just done. By the time he reached La Casa de Dolores and staggered up the stairs, small pinpricks of black were dotting his vision. Moving swiftly down the hallway, he could only think of collapsing on his creaky old bed.

But when Nick opened the door to his room, the rosebush clutched to his chest, Judith was there waiting for him.

"Roses! An entire bush—for me? How romantic!"

She was lying on her side across the bed, naked. Looking down at her, seeing the flicker in her eyes, at the tip of her tooth, he wondered for a moment if he were hallucinating. He shut his eyes and opened them again, but she was still there.

So this was it. "They're for you, all right. Vampire."

"That's right, Nicholas. I'm a vampire." And she started to rise from the bed. His grip on the rosebush tightened in time with the spread of her smile, the ends of her mouth lifting maliciously, the tongue rising like a waking, hungry snake. Then her eyes caught fire and her lips flared back, exposing her beautiful teeth. Nick forced his fingers to loosen. She was close enough now for him to smell her scent, feel her heat.

His fist caught her flush on the cheek, and sent her sprawling back on the bed.

"You bastard!"

She was rubbing her jaw now, and Nick could see the frustration seething in her eyes. He could hurt her; actually knock her down. This awareness gave him the confidence to start what he had to do. Reaching into his pocket, he took out the hunting knife.

"What are you going to do with that?"

The fear in her tone pleased him. He glanced over to her, smiled, and whispered, "Whittle."

"What?"

He leaned back against the dresser and began to break off the branches. Rose petals scattered on the floor. "Whittle. A stake. A rosebush stake. Understand?"

The blood drained from her face. "Nick—Nick, you're crazy. Don't—"

She made a dash for the door. He reached her just before she touched the handle, and threw her back on the bed.

"This is your last night on earth, Lourdes."

She hesitated as if she were confused, before speaking. "That's what you called me those last few times . . . right?"

"Yes—the time you bit my lip. Don't you like being called by your true name? Or has it been so long that you've forgotten it?"

"Nick." Her voice quivered, and she covered herself with a bedsheet. "I am not . . . Lourdes. Please. If you'll just tell me what's going—"

"Shut up!" Her body had begun to shake, and it was affecting him. He didn't want that. He forced himself to think of Davey. "Shut the fuck up." A pause, building the venom. "Vampire."

She looked up at him then, as if only just understanding what he meant. "You really think I'm a vampire?"

He didn't answer, busying himself with the rosebush instead. His feet were in a pool of pink petals; the knife hand had started to shave the trunk.

"Nick. Nick, listen. Aren't vampires strong? Can't they turn into bats? If I'm a vampire, *how come I can't get out of here?*"

He knew she was crying now; he knew it was a trick, and refused to look.

"Why didn't I . . . drink your blood, whatever, any of those nights we spent together?"

"Because you needed me alive." Angustia's explanation proved itself. "To invite you in."

A small silence, a feeling that *she* was silenced, until she broke it. "Nick . . . how did I get in tonight?"

He looked down at her face; it was open, a child's face. Amanda's face. A vampire's face. "I don't care how you got in. I just know that you've never spent the night." He saw her flinch, and pressed his advantage. "A romantic couple like us never managed to stay together long enough to see the sun rise."

"I had to get to work, Nick. I'm a nurse's aide trainee. You can call and find out."

He smiled cruelly. "Why didn't you tell me before?"

"Because . . ." Her voice dropped to a whisper. "The job is part of my probation. They were sure I set fire to my mother's house. I didn't want you to know yet, because . . . I love you. I didn't want to lose you."

The words cut deeply, bringing up the red in his cheeks. "It's too late for that now. I know everything—the Westerhayses, Ambrose, this hotel—everything. You've destroyed too much already, Jud—" He caught himself. "We killed the Siphon last night. Tonight it's your turn." He stopped, then repeated himself without quite knowing why. "It's too late."

"Are you sure?" The tears were streaming now. "Don't you know you're all I have? I could never hurt you. I've missed you so, Nick. I can't live without you."

"Liar—you're all around me." The words came without prior thought. He looked down again at the ugly thing his hands were forming, and allowed the blade to nick his finger. The blood came up, not to tempt her as he had Amanda, but to punish himself for what he was going to do.

"I have to go to the bathroom."

He let her pass, waiting until the door closed behind her, and starting hacking at the end of the trunk. (Judith looked quickly toward the sink, then all about the bathroom. When she spied Nick's toiletries on top of the toilet's water tank, she moved swiftly toward them.) He knew he was losing his resolve, his certainty of her guilt; and knew that a vampire's greatest weapon was guile. (There was a double-edged razor next to a can of shaving cream. She picked up the razor, opened it, and removed the blade.) Someone was going to take this stake tonight, but he no longer knew who. Then the door to the bathroom opened.

"You won't be needing that, Nick."

He turned and saw that the true meaning of love is sacrifice, something a vampire cannot do. Vampires keep their blood; Judith was spilling hers over the petals on the floor, from four cuts on the insides of her wrists.

PART FOUR

CHARNEL HOUSE

Toutes les femmes sont fatales.

—*Maurice Chevalier*

Idyll Under a Shroud

IN THE DREAM, Jessie could watch unseen as the seven dwarfs fussed about the sleeping form of Snow White. From the concern in their wrinkled faces, and the gloom that hovered in the air, she could tell that the dwarfs were despairing of Snow White ever waking.

Jessie turned over in her sleep then and, in one of those shifts of perception whose rules operate everywhere except in our filtered waking lives, she suddenly recognized Snow White as none other than her own daughter, Amanda. And no sooner had Jessie realized this than the dwarfs hovering over Amanda stepped away from the bier, and stood revealed as the strange, ruined men who had appeared at the Halloween party.

None of this surprised Jessie; part of her had known Amanda was under a spell ever since that night, and before. That same part also knew it was not up to her to save her daughter. It would be another.

The dwarfs whispered among themselves as he entered the room, dressed as he had been on Halloween night. Nick put something down by Amanda's side, then looked down on her with an expression of longing Jessie recognized, but couldn't place. The longing was for love, and for death; Jessie finally remembered the feelings as her own, alone that night in the shower. Nick bent low and kissed Amanda softly on the lips.

When Amanda awoke, Jessie knew she was no longer her daughter, but that was all right, so long as she was alive again. Jessie cried in her sleep, and started to wake, as the dwarfs laughed for joy, as Amanda rose slowly and rubbed her eyes.

She was different: older, simpler, and more beautiful than ever. Nick was waiting for her by the foot of the bier, and Amanda came to him. The dwarfs hugged each other, Amanda opened her arms, and Jessie woke shrieking as Nick picked up the stake he had brought, and turned it in his hands.

As she slipped on her nightgown and searched for her slippers under the bed, Jessie attempted to defuse her dream by interpreting it. There was no doubt that Amanda was going through a phase, and the appearance of those men at her party had never been explained. And if Amanda was Snow White, then wasn't Jessie the wicked stepmother? That was how she felt in her Mendocino cabin, responsible for whatever would happen to her daughter during her absence. Even the stake was laughably clear; Jessie obviously feared Amanda's eventual deflowering, and coming of age.

If it was all so clear, however, why was she dialing her home phone number in the early morning light? And why was she going to tell a startled Tod that she would be on the first bus to San Francisco the next morning?

Because of *him,* she admitted to herself. The rest of her dream was neurosis, but Nick Van Lo was for real. He had tapped on the window of their life when he became Amanda's teacher; she had let him in on Halloween night. Now, sprung full-blown from the forehead of her repressed desires, he was loose inside their surprisingly fragile world.

The phone rang four times before she heard Tod's distant greeting.

"Tod, is Amanda all right?"

She could imagine him poised to hang up on her; instead, he cautiously asked her what she meant.

It's already happened. "Did Nick Van Lo . . . do anything to her?"

"Jesus, how'd you know that? I mean no, she's fine, he didn't really hurt her . . ."

Tod explained how the principal had called him two days before, and told him of what he had witnessed in Room 14. "The only real damage was the bloody lip Amanda gave him. Shanker threw Van Lo out of the school, and is only waiting for word from us to press charges. But Amanda seems fine, and I feel like we shouldn't put her through a messy trial. So what happened, did Shanker call you up there?"

"I dreamt it. Just now."

"Holy shit," he said quietly. "That's impressive. I wish I could say it was only a dream, but . . ."

Jessie smiled as the sun peeked over her windowsill. "But it's all over now, and she's all right. We all are. Listen—go back to sleep. I'll be on the first bus out of Mendocino today. Check the schedule, and meet me at the terminal. Both of you."

She hung up, and slept for another hour.

Twenty-four hours before Jessie's subconscious tried to warn her that Amanda was in mortal danger, Nick Van Lo had slipped another quarter into the coffee machine in the waiting room of San Francisco General. His shaky fingers pressed the BLACK button—not the way he often drank his coffee, but the way he had all through that night.

The hospital lights were harshly bright, activating the hot-pink vinyl upholstery of the chairs that lined the walls. The television staring down from one corner had ceased transmitting long ago, and now ran the same lazy test pattern over and over. Nick sat down again, holding his fresh cup in both hands, and crushed the empty one with the heel of his shoe. There were now six styrofoam pancakes by his feet. No one else was in the room.

The arrival of the radio-dispatched taxi that Nick called from the corner phone had been mercifully quick; quick enough that its blinking taillights were disappearing around the corner just as Father Angustia, carrying a large black satchel, turned onto the block. They had reached the emergency room after a silent ride punctuated by blown red lights and the driver's curious glances via the rearview mirror. The line that stretched from the receiving nurse's desk was comprised of the San Franciscans that tourists rarely see: gashed and bleeding drunks, battered wives, punctual nightly overdosers; scattered among these were the stray hallucinating paranoid with a broken arm, the elderly transvestite who took a razor to himself. Nick and Judith had stood quietly at the end of the line, adding two more names to the list of victims.

Finally they had reached the desk. The nurse had peered up through her own cigarette smoke as Judith's head cradled on Nick's shoulder, eyes closed, strips of shirt wrapped tightly around her wrists.

"What's her problem?"

After Nick had answered for her, the nurse had looked at Judith once more with barely concealed contempt, and Nick had almost blurted out no, it was me, don't look at her that way.

"Then why don't you fill out these forms for her." And a tired old black man had taken her from his arms, placed her on a bed, and disappeared through a set of blue doors.

Taking another sip of coffee, he tried to face the fact that he had destroyed what little he had in San Francisco. Not only had he lost the only respectable job he was likely to get, he had also broken the law three times in the space of five hours. The possible morals charge involving Amanda paled next to the break-in at the plant store and the assault on its owner. From there he had gone home and driven Judith to try to kill herself.

All because of vampires, he said to himself. Who were they, if Judith wasn't one of them? He wanted to forget them, to leave the question of their aims and existence to others. And yet . . .

"Judy."

What luckless quirk in either of their natures had led him to view her as a vampire? Judith Harper, on her own and not yet twenty, so fiery, so devouring, had almost become a martyr for their love. The vampish, aggressive sexuality had merely been a cover for a girl still young enough to be infatuated with him. Why couldn't he have seen in time that the eater wanted to be eaten, the lover loved?

Maybe, he thought, recrossing his legs and gazing blankly at the clock on the wall, the reason was that he *wanted* a vampire in his waking life as badly as in his dreams. He had loved the delirious feeling of being possessed. Was that what love meant to him—a blazing, obsessed grappling atop a funeral pyre? Could he see himself merging only with death-in-love—a vampire?

It no longer mattered, he admitted. There was nothing left now. The clock opposite him read eight o'clock, and he stood up; visiting hours had commenced. He thought about washing up in a bathroom and combing his hair, then decided there was no point. He would apologize, explain as best he could, and leave.

The door to her room was open, and he slipped in. She was still sleeping, and he paused to gaze at her. Her hands and face were almost as white as the sheets, an illusion augmented by the lustrous black hair that spilled on the pillow. A tear rolled down his cheek, and she opened her eyes. The fire was a faint glow now.

"Judy."

But she shook her head, smiling weakly, the embers in her eyes flickering. She extended one slender hand, bandaged at the wrist.

"It was stupid. We were both stupid."

He hesitated; the words cut sweetly, razor blades in his heart. Then they both spoke, the same words, the same moment, Judith's voice quieter yet stronger: "I love you."

They held hands for most of the bus ride, saying little as the scenery north of the Golden Gate became more and more rustic, weaving brown and green over their troubles. The quiet also grew, in rhythmic succession, like waves; by the time the bus' wheels rolled into Mendocino County, the peace of silence was all there was.

Nick and Judith got off about a half-mile from the Sea Foam Lodge, on a stretch of road that looked down on the afternoon sea. He walked slowly, so as not to tire her, and they spoke only about the taste of salt and pine in the air. At the hospital she had refused to hear his guilt-ridden self-recriminations, or any of the strange, fateful circumstances that led to . . . what almost happened. Later, she said, there would be time to talk about those things.

Judith had checked out of the hospital at ten-thirty that morning. As far as they knew, her probation officer had not yet been informed of her attempted suicide; Judith felt sure that once he found out, the image of the suspected arsonist would acquire slashes on its wrists and she would be detained in the hospital's psychiatric ward. Nick agreed, and they decided to continue her convalescence in the country, where they could not be traced.

Before leaving, he tried to reach Father Angustia once more and inform him of what had happened, but the sexton who answered the phone said that the priest was neither at the archives nor at the rectory.

After registering as Mr. and Mrs. Richard Morsch, they were shown to their room by the old man at the desk. It was a simple log cabin straight out of a Technicolor western, but the large windows faced the ocean and the fireplace was well-stocked with logs. The old man smiled and left, and they kissed for a long time.

The kisses moved them nearer and nearer the four-poster in one corner, and Nick mustered the discipline to stop. She had to know what he was, and how it had all started, before they made love again.

"You don't have to," she said softly, holding his hand. "Not for me."

"I know," he smiled sadly. "It's for me."

He started at the beginning, with Lourdes and Ambrose; Judith interrupted almost immediately. "Wait," she said incredulously. "Don't tell me you *still* believe in vampires."

Nick let go of her hand and looked down at the Indian-print rug. "One of them attacked me three nights ago." He told her of the Siphon's sixty hours of vampirism, from his disappearance at the morgue to his death in front of the porno theater. "I don't know how else to explain all of that."

Judith moved away to one of the windows, and looked out at the Pacific. Faint lines formed between her brows and on the corners of her mouth. Ten minutes passed, and still Nick didn't dare look up and witness her torment. It's not fair to her, he decided. "Judy—"

"Wait." Her tone was commanding; it would accept no compromise. He realized with deep feelings of love and unworthiness that she was trying to save him from the nightmare that had almost killed her. "Let's just start by assuming that the . . . the Siphon . . . isn't a vampire, but a human being whose brain

has been turned into a sponge by alcohol and who-knows-what-
else. When you first saw him after he was supposedly dead—
when he followed you home that night—he never actually
attacked you. All he did is walk half a block behind you, and
try your door a couple of times. Maybe he just wanted some
company! Now the next night . . . you saw him kill a dog. All
right, he's crazy, he was hungry, and he could have used a
knife. That wouldn't be the first disemboweled dog found in
the Tenderloin."

Nick started to interrupt, but Judith raised her hand. "Let
me finish. You and that . . . *that crazy priest* . . . follow him back
to his door, bar the way in, and pull out weapons when he
complains. So the poor man runs away! He runs, and you two
follow him, right into a porno theater, where he thinks he finally
lost you. But you track him into the rest room—and how often
does *that* happen—and sic the manager and his assistant on
him. And they beat him up, and turn him out on the street to
who else but his two original tormentors! So the poor old alkie
has a coronary right there on the street—just like the theater
manager said."

She looked at Nick as if she were daring him to raise any
objections to her interpretation. He wanted to believe her more
than anything, but there was something she had forgotten. "If
the Siphon wasn't a vampire, how did he get out of his slab
at the morgue?"

"Because it wasn't the Siphon you saw get knifed to death."
She was ready for that one. "The man with the mask stabbed
someone else in the Siphon's room. Considering the fact that
you were splitting your time those days between a fifth-grade
nymphet with some very serious problems and a priest who's
built a hundred-year conspiracy out of one old diary, it's not
surprising that you made a mistake. Somebody else died that
day—not the Siphon. And the receptionist at the morgue wasn't
very surprised by the missing body. He said it happens all the
time."

He was silent for a long while, a time he spent refusing to
meet the eyes that awaited a response. He wanted to agree with
her so badly. When he finally spoke, it was with a sheepish,
cracking voice.

"Do you really believe that?"

Judith turned her palms to him, and he moved slowly toward her. Is it really over, he asked himself, and read the answer in her shining face. Yes, it was: he had been wrong about her, and he had been wrong about this. Her hand touched his hips, and then he lifted her blouse over her arms. It might be all right, he prayed, it really might be all right. Then her arms snaked over his shoulders and joined behind his neck; her nipples grew hard brushing against the hair on his chest. He kissed her on the neck, that beautiful vulnerable stretch, and begged forgiveness in her ear. She brought him down on her, led him in, and forgave.

The sun was beginning to set a few hours later as they sat in front of the window, eating the old man's roast duck in orange sauce. They had declined his offer of wine; they were drunk enough.

"I wish the ocean would always be as red as it is now," Judith said. "It's on fire."

"It always is, at this hour," Nick said softly. "Up here."

She licked the orange sauce from her lips. "Do you want to stay up here?"

Her question squeezed his heart painfully. He had to face the reality of his situation sooner or later. "Yes . . . I want to stay here. Next to you, by this window, with the sun sinking just as it is now. But there's a lot of trouble waiting for me in the city, and it's not vampires. I broke into a store last night and clubbed a man senseless. I almost—you know what I almost did to you. There's something wrong with me, Judy, even if we forget the vampires. And I don't think you should be involved with me until I . . . straighten all this out."

Judith slid her hand over the tabletop and rested her fingers over his. Her voice was preternaturally calm. "We all make mistakes—God knows I have—and you've made your share here, I'm not going to deny it. You're going to have to find out why you became involved in this . . . nightmare. Why you helped *create* it by succumbing to that priest's paranoia. But don't be too hard on yourself. Who knows how anybody would have responded in your situation? I mean, once you believed that crazy vampire plot that stretched back a hundred years, what *should* you have done?" She lowered her lashes. "I'm glad I didn't have to decide."

Nick turned his hand over and gripped her fingers. Judith had changed since her suicide attempt. She was more mature, as if she had successfully undergone a very personal rite of passage. Or had she always been that way, and he had just failed to see it?

Judith continued from another perspective. "You shouldn't forget that I can't go back to my nursing program either. Slashing my wrists and going *AWOL* are definitely violations of my probation. Believe me," leaning toward him with that wide-lipped smile he couldn't resist, "I didn't go through all this to end up a fugitive *without* you. Understand? I love you."

Nick started to laugh. He couldn't help it; things were turning out so well. Judith read his feelings and laughed too. With her advice and encouragement, Nick started a roaring fire so that they could make love in front of it. After they were satisfied, sweaty, and spent, they fell asleep before it, with their naked bodies serving as screens for the fire's dancing images. Nick was spared from his dreams that night.

The next morning they paid their bill at the Lodge and walked into the little seaside town to find the bus station. It turned out to be an airy, rather run-down country store with one long bench along the eastern wall, and a faded Greyhound decal on the vintage cash register. Nick bought the tickets and read the destination on them: CAMBRIDGE, MASS. They had decided over breakfast that staying in Mendocino, no matter how captivating, just wasn't practical for future professors or nurses. With the entire country as a possibility, they had decided to put as much distance between themselves and their memories of California as possible. And a pretty New England college town seemed like a good place to start.

Start over, Nick thought—a second chance. Then Judith touched his arm.

"I'm going to the bathroom before the bus arrives," she said.

"All right, but be careful," he kidded, and turned away from her toward the empty bench by the far wall. But the bench was no longer empty: seated on one end were a neatly dressed elderly couple and, between them, Amanda.

Nick, unbelieving, took a step back, his eyes riveted on the little girl. Her eyes, he noted with terror and dismay, were on *him*. How could she have found me, he thought, and tried to interpret the blankness in her gaze. Then she turned to the woman next to her, said something in an indistinct voice, and Nick realized that it wasn't Amanda after all, but another little girl with blonde braids on a country jaunt with her grandparents. He turned away, bracing himself against a coatrack, and wiped the perspiration on his forehead. Judith found him there.

"Nick! What's wrong?"

He turned to her, saw the worry in her young face, and tried to bluff a response, but he couldn't do it. Judith didn't repeat her question; she looked about the store for an explanation, and her eyes settled on the little girl.

"It's Amanda, isn't it?"

He knew what she meant: not the child on the bench, but the vampire in his psyche. He nodded, cheeks and ears aflame, even as he marveled at Judith's uncanny intuition.

Her expression sagged for a second, and he caught a glimpse of how she would look as an older woman; then it returned to the determined set of the incredible person intent on rescuing his life. "She's still a vampire to you. She feeds on your memory and your guilt. It's the only way you can stand what you feel." Judith took the two bus tickets from his hand and glanced at them. "We have to stop in San Francisco anyway to pick up our belongings. There's no reason why we can't stay a little longer at another hotel. I want to see this little girl. I want to see her in the playground, I want to see her walking home, I want to see her expression when her mother opens the front door and lets her in. I'm going to see her do all the normal sunlight things, and then we'll put a stake through her."

Nick blinked.

"Abstractly, of course," she added, smiling sternly. "When you see her, and see only a little girl, we'll leave San Francisco."

The day's golden weather made a mockery of their bus ride back to the city; there was little to look forward to except an indefinite period of detoxification in an unknown room. They parted at the Greyhound downtown terminal, from where Judith headed for the John Swett School, armed with the most objective description of Amanda that Nick could give her. After she disappeared around the corner, Nick started walking back to La Casa de Dolores.

Neither of them had noticed the woman watching them from the back of the bus.

Where is Amanda?

JESSIE REACHED THE playground just as Nick stepped into the lobby of the flophouse.

He had felt the emptiness as soon as he entered the building. The other roomers were barely visible, but the telltale noises of alcoholism and incapacitation had always filtered into the hallway. Perhaps Dolores had sent the rest of them away, he thought, and he felt deep down that they were all dead.

His room looked the same, and somehow this surprised him. He groaned in unison with the bed as he sat down on it, and ran stiff fingers through his hair. Then he saw it, lying under the dresser where it had rolled after he dropped it.

The stake. Its tip was pointed at him, like a severed, accusing finger. He no longer had the strength to deny it. He had used the specter of vampirism just as his beloved Victorians did: as a shroud over his stunted sexual psyche. The Cult of the Little Girl, graveyard of Lewis Carroll and Charles Dickens, had materialized in his life in the form of Amanda Westerhays; he had been no more successful in escaping its lure than they.

He still remembered Fred Olds's fatuous interpretation of his vampire fixation. "A vampire is a sucking monster stuck in the oral stage, a child whose feelings of love manifest with a desire to devour the beloved object." The bloodsucker image had fit in neatly with the fat psychiatrist's explanation of the central trauma in Nick's life. "Because you were never able to differentiate between the 'father' and 'mother' roles your mother played all your young life, you projected the typical, transitory Oedipal situation onto her. Your mind slowly synthesized the image of the desirable female with that of the castrator."

To love and devour: the words were indivisible, fatally al-
luring Siamese twins. They had waddled after him, grotesque
and implacable, through his innocent teens and promising twenties. He wished he could succumb to them, to be truly loved
for one bright moment, and then die. Instead, he was saddled
with the epithet *pervert,* and Fred's damning conclusion: "You
may experience pedophiliac impulses, where the extreme youth
of the desired female makes her less threatening . . . necrophiliac fantasies have similar roots."

So Fred had finally been proven right. Psychiatry could
explain anything, and it had *explained* him. But why stop where
Fred did? A vampire, after all, was the ultimate perversion of
a necrophiliac fantasy—the corpse turns on you. Or was *he*
the vampire? Did his obsession with ever-younger females im-
ply a desire to obtain eternal youth for himself?

It didn't matter anymore. He prayed that Judith with her
hungry mouth and giving heart would save him, but he felt
hope ebbing away. Amanda, he knew, would always haunt
him. Striding over to the dresser, he picked up the stake, and
miserably conceded to himself whom its ultimate target would
be.

Then, like an answer to a prayer, he heard Judith's footsteps
in the hall.

When Jessie Westerhays saw Nick and a young, black-haired
woman get on at one of the innumerable stops her city-bound
bus made, she first thought that her mind was playing tricks
on her. As the miles passed and the oblivious couple refused
to change appearance, however, disbelief gave way to anger
and, finally, fear.

That the man who had attacked her daughter was so close
to her, and in such an unlikely location, terrified her in a way
she could not explain. Jessie didn't have a paranoid nature; she
never considered that Nick may have been following her. It
was more a certainty . . . a dread . . . that now that he had entered
her life, he was never going to go away.

She waited a couple of minutes after they got off the bus
at the San Francisco Greyhound terminal before descending
herself. Despite this delay, Tod and Amanda were nowhere to
be seen when she finally stepped out onto Sixth Street. The

south-of-Market street life became increasingly curious of her lingering presence, however, and she was soon back inside the terminal, calling Tod's office from a phone booth.

To her surprise, he answered his extension.

"What are you doing there instead of here?"

"Writing a bio piece on Roman Polanski."

"What?"

"I can't believe it either," Tod agreed, "and I just finished it. A rumor's going around that Polanski's going to make a film of the Tate—LaBianca murders. The boss picked yours truly to cover it. Since there's no real story—the guy isn't *that* weird—I've basically strung together 800 words of bullshit."

"So how soon will you be here?"

Tod hesitated before answering. "Well, I'm still waiting to use the Xerox machine. Can you have a couple of cups of coffee?"

"Please come now, Tod. Nick Van Lo was on the same bus as me. He didn't see me, but—"

"Give me ten minutes. I'm leaving right now."

"Hurry."

Judith Harper had reached the playground just as Jessie dialed Tod. Forty minutes later, when Tod finally reached the terminal, Judith had entered another world.

"What the fuck happened?" Jessie exploded after she got into the Saab.

"What do you think happened?" Tod was clearly in no mood to be harassed. "What *could* happen in four blocks? A Muni bus hit a truck, and *nobody* moved for half an hour."

They drove in silence until Jessie realized they weren't heading home. "May I ask where we're going?"

"Amanda asked if she could spend the afternoon at—what's her name?—Polly Matthews's house. She lives out in the Richmond area, so resign yourself to some heavy traffic."

"She's never mentioned Polly Matthews before."

"Well, apparently she's her latest best friend. Mrs. Matthews was going to show them how to make tollhouse cookes in a Cuisinart, or something."

As they headed west, Jessie tried to recall the good feelings seeing Nick Van Lo had eclipsed. She had been coming home, after all, determined to bridge the gap between Amanda and herself. And while she wished that Amanda wouldn't have wanted to go visiting on the afternoon of her mother's return, Jessie could at least be glad that Amanda was seeing friends again.

Then Tod told her the good news. "Vic Varney says the Tenderloin property should be resold next week—two days after we take over. I thought we could celebrate by spending three weeks in Puerto Vallarta this Christmas."

"Oh, Tod," Jessie said softly, putting her arms around him. "You're so wonderful sometimes. Tell you what, I'll take complete responsibility for Thanksgiving."

"Then you've got about sixty hours to come up with something," he kidded, and stopped the Saab in the middle of a torn-up block that ran parallel to the ocean.

"This is no time to go parking," Jessie laughed, and nuzzled his ear.

"That's not why I stopped. This is where the address Amanda gave me should be."

Jessie turned in her seat, and peered out. It was pitch-dark, except for the streetlight on the corner. "You must have gotten it wrong, Tod. There are *no* houses on this street."

She watched, sensing the moment's clock slow, as Tod reached into his shirt pocket and pulled out a note. "This is it, all right. We're on the 2700 block, and this is the address Amanda gave me."

"Tod, you—"

His voice—sharp, loud, and ready—cut her off. "I had her repeat it *three* times, Jessie. There's no mistake!"

There was no doubt in her mind as to their next move. "Drive to a phone booth. We've got to call the police."

Tod turned to her as he switched on the ignition. "Okay. but what are we going to tell them?"

"That he's got her."

His voice was very quiet, almost hushed. "He couldn't."

Jessie lunged for his hand, dug her nails into his palm. *"I know he's got her."*

"Well, where should the police look? All over the Tenderloin? We've got to do better than that."

Jessie commanded her memory to replay their conversation on Halloween night. "He told me he lives right across the street from the Cathedral Arts store. I'm sure if we tell that to the police, they'll find him quickly enough."

Tod sagged in his seat, oblivious of the marks Jessie had left on his palm. "The hotel we bought. It's right across the street from Cathedral Arts."

They looked at each other, and Tod slipped the car into gear.

Nick was at the door in two strides. "Judy! I'm—"

His words died before her blanched countenance. For the first time since he had known her, he saw doubt and panic in her eyes.

"What's wrong, what's happened?"

"I got to the school just as it was letting out," she whispered, allowing her weight to sag against the doorsill. "I had no problem spotting her. Most of the other kids went to the playground, but she walked away from the school immediately. I kept behind her and—I sensed something too. There was a difference about her, something that wasn't . . . like a child. I didn't notice where we were going, I was so intent on watching her. It felt very natural. Then she turned into a building, and I saw why it had felt the way it did."

Judith paused and looked into his eyes; hers were round and glassy. "Nick—she came in here."

They Awake

SHE CAME IN HERE. It was as if a switch had been thrown in Nick's brain. All the whirling, clashing thoughts locked in place, and he felt no fear for the moment, only a renewed sense of purpose, and relief in the confirmation of his sanity.

"I want you to go now," he told her, taking both her hands in his. "Call the archives and the rectory, and find Father Angustia. Tell him everything that's happened." He paused. "And tell him I'll need him."

He pulled her to him and kissed her gravely on both eyes, on her lips. He knew where he was again, and Judith accepted it. If she had any qualms about her assignment, she stifled them.

He released her hands, and they moved to the door.

"I love you, Judy."

"I love you, Nick."

"Forever?"

"Forever."

She smiled to force back tears, turned, and left. Even as her footsteps faded away down the stairs, he was moving to his bed and picking up the stake. It felt comfortable in his left hand; he stepped out into the hall. Dusk was settling outside, but natural light never shone in that corridor. It was lit by four gas lamps, and the two at the other end were dark. Nick moved slowly, feeling the floorboards creak under his boots, sniffing for the same odor that had permeated Slater's room that night. But there was no scent of the undead in the hallway, and no sounds of activity behind the closed doors. He felt no different when he reached Dolores's door. She was the only one still alive, as far as he knew. He tried the knob, but it was locked.

Nick stepped back and laid his senses bare, trying to detect a counterweighing presence behind the door, a being he may not have been able to face. But it was early still; the sun hadn't quite set. He kicked savagely at the knob, and the door flew open.

As he had expected, the room was empty. There was a neatly made bed in the center of the room, but no other furniture. He was about to leave when he thought of the closet. His mind raced back to the time he had opened Slater's closet, empty save for one dead rat. Something told him there wasn't going to be a rat in this one. Before his suspicion could develop any further, he yanked open the door.

But there was no one hiding in this closet, either. It was a small one, no wider than the door and about three feet deep. Rising from the floor all the way to his sternum was a stack of mirrors, buried like treasure under decades of dust.

Nick smiled. It was all here. And he was going to find it all, one room at a time. Across the hall was Yo-yo's room. Nick didn't even try the doorknob; his boot lashed out and the door shuddered back.

The room seemed no different than it had the afternoon he and the Doctor had visited the old Japanese. Yo-yo was the only roomer at La Casa de Dolores who didn't drink; his stupors and outbursts came from premature senility. The smell was there, though, hinting of malice as well as decay. Nick peeked under the bed and found nothing. There was only one place he could be. Nick braced himself and opened the closet door.

A little yellow man stood before him, eyes open and unblinking, seeing nothing. He was wearing the same ratty bathrobe Nick had seen him in before; the maggot-infected bedsores the Doctor had examined were repulsively visible on his chest. Nick looked into the eyes again; they were silent. Then the scrawny vampire's lips trembled, and he saw the fangs.

"Yo-yo-yo," Nick mimicked, and plunged the stake into his heart.

Yo-yo's frail body quivered. A grunt escaped his lips, followed by a thin trickle of watery blood. More blood soaked the stake where it had torn through the robe. Then the vampire sagged to the floor.

A shudder ran through Nick; he knew he had to get out of
the room quickly. He put one foot on the dead vampire's chest
and pulled at the stake with both hands. He felt the cracking
of ribs under his heel—the stake was free.

His gait was less steady now, and this end of the hallway
seemed darker than before, if that were possible. He stopped
to calm himself, because next on his route was the Doctor's
room.

Nick tried the knob; the door was open. He wasn't surprised.
The papers were still in the little crate by the bed, the lone
chair was still swamped with clothes. Someone, however, had
tried to tear down the paper bags covering the window; Nick
could see the last rays of sunlight meekly filtering in.

The Doctor was in his closet also. Nick took in the open,
bloodshot eyes, the pomegranate of a nose. The tears welling
in his own eyes blurred the horror before him, and he remembered the last real conversation he and the Doctor had. The
poor devil, all he had managed were a few veiled hints about
the house's history. It had been a pitiful effort, Nick thought,
even though he may not have survived without it. And we all
want to survive; we are all afraid to die. Even this miserable
creature, who . . .

That was when the open, unblinking eyes shifted, fixing
him in their cold gaze. Those eyes told him the Doctor's survival meant his death. This is not the Doctor, he reminded
himself, and raised the bloody stake. The Doctor is waiting
for me to free him.

He drove the stake in with both hands, and held onto it
while the body went into convulsions. Blood poured out of the
mouth and nostrils, smelling like alcohol. Then the vampire
pitched forward, bumping into Nick before hitting the floor
belly-up.

Nick bit the first joint of his index finger and fought back
the urge to vomit. Turning away from the corpse by his feet,
he faced the other side of the room.

Father Angustia was standing in the doorway, a large steel
cross glinting on his chest. "He's finally been put to rest, I
see."

Nick looked back at the corpse as the priest entered the
room. "Looks like I'm a little late," Angustia said with a smile.

"I've been trying to reach you for the last two days."

The priest's radiating serenity soothed Nick; he smiled back. "Where did Judy—"

"She's here too, have no doubt," Angustia assured him. "We will get to her soon enough."

"Here?" Nick didn't understand. "Why? I—"

"Because she is Lourdes, queen of the vampires, my boy. She attacked me here last night; I barely escaped with my life. There's no longer any doubt."

A slow chill radiated through Nick. Was Angustia, his last hope, one of them too? He pointed at the corpse by his feet. "We have no time to lose, then. Stand back while I pull out the stake."

Angustia smiled, taking one step back, and Nick planted a foot on the Doctor's chest. It has to come loose on the first yank, he told himself, wrapping his fingers around the rosewood.

The stake jumped out with one superhuman pull, and Nick whirled—just in time to catch the swooping Angustia in the center of his chest. Angustia clutched the stake in both hands, howling with surprise and pain, his lips curled back over giant canines. He staggered back, crashing against the door, and reeled forward again like a vaudeville drunk. Finally he collapsed, face first, his blood oozing like an oil spill across the floor.

Nick closed his eyes and thought about the two bodies by his feet. The Doctor . . . and Angustia too. He must have come just after I left for the hospital with Judith. But how did the vampires trap him? And how could Nick hope to stop them when this monomaniacal priest had failed?

He hadn't reached an answer when the hand closed around his ankle.

Nick screamed and tried to shake his foot free, but the Doctor's grip was unshakable. Fighting the panic that clouded his thoughts, he tried to figure out what had brought the Doctor back to life. The answer came easily, now that it was too late— he had pulled out the stake.

Desperately he lurched toward Angustia, refusing to look down on the Doctor's famished features. When he reached him, however, Nick saw that Angustia's fall had put the tip of the stake right through the back of his cassock. He would never be able to pull it out.

There was only one thing to do. He reached down and lifted the priest's corpse by the armpits, then turned and dropped it, face up, on the Doctor. The vampire howled as the weight hit him, but he never let go of Nick's ankle. Nick gritted his teeth and squatted over the end of the stake still protruding from Angustia's chest. Putting all his weight on it, he drove the tip back into the Doctor.

He pushed long after the hand on his ankle relaxed for the last time, until the first clear thought stopped him dead: if the stake had to remain buried in a vampire to keep him still, how was he going to fix the rest of the vampires without more stakes? And—the fear was cold, colder than the corpses on the floor—what about Yo-yo?

The first question remained unanswered for a while longer; the answer to the second came like a bad joke with the sound of movement behind him: *Yo-yo-yo-yo-yo* . . .

Nick didn't want to look. They weren't giving him a chance to recover. They weren't giving him a chance. He was scared now—scared to death. But it wasn't a senile little Japanese coming up behind him, it was a vampire. When he finally turned around, Yo-yo was four feet away.

"Yo-yo-yo . . ."

Nick's eyes skipped over the gaping red hole in the vampire's chest, before smashing him just under the right eye with a fist. Yo-yo collapsed in a heap, and Nick hurdled over him and out of the room. Now that the sun had set and he had no stakes, he was powerless; it was time to make a tactical retreat. He would return in the morning with enough stakes to skewer them all.

Nick was halfway to the stairs when he realized he might not be going anywhere at all. Angustia was younger and fitter than the rest of them; it made sense that he would wake up first. But now the other doors began to open.

Mr. Slater emerged from his room, his eyes as glazed as those of the stuffed parrot clutched in his right hand. Then the door in front of him came ajar, and Charley the Tuna stepped into the hall. The only change in his syphilis-eaten visage was the rough gouge on his neck where they had taken him. And

there was Leatherface coming out behind Slater, the lower half
of his mask ripped off, slavering evilly when he saw Nick.
Nick stood frozen in his tracks, unable to tear his gaze away
from them.

His breath left him when a hand came down on his shoulder.
He spun around and found himself facing Uncle Bill, gaunt
and hungry now, no longer the drug-besotted former writer
holed up at the end of the hall. Their gazes swirled in a stew
of triumph and horror, and Nick almost gagged on the vampire's
fetid breath.

Uncle Bill lunged, clutching Nick by the throat, sending
them both sprawling to the floor. Nick landed on top and spiked
an elbow into the vampire's nose, crushing it. The creature
screamed and relaxed its hold on Nick's neck.

This time Nick didn't hesitate. Getting to his feet, he made
a dash for the stairs, knocking past Charley on the way. The
stairs were clear, and he reached the foot in four bounds, staggering at the end. The bright, live lights of Mason Street beck-
oned to him through the diamond-shaped glass on the front
door. He regained his balance and lurched forward when, as
if from nowhere, Slater and Leatherface materialized in front
of the door, blocking his way.

Nick stopped. He could never get past both of them without
getting bitten—not the way they were grouped together, awaiting his charge. Looking back up the stairs he saw Charley,
Bill, and Yo-yo coming down, mumbling and gurgling. That
was when the bilious nausea of horror almost overcame him,
swamping him with its noxious gases, surrounding, overwhelming, driving his resistance to its knees. He doubled over,
resigned, awaiting the eager fingers, the rancid breath that
preceded oblivion. This was fear, he thought: a hurricane of
the damned with its peaceful eye. He nestled in the calm of
its center, in the curious dreamlike paralysis it induced . . . and
remembered the door tucked away under the staircase.

He feinted at the pair by the door and darted behind the
stairs. There was the door to the cellar. He didn't know what
was waiting for him below, but it couldn't be worse than the
gang of decrepit vampires closing in on him. The moment's
hesitation passed; he descended the stairs.

There was no one in the basement, dark but for the strong

glow emanating from the ancient coal furnace on one end. After a hasty inspection of the window-less, rubbish-strewn room, Nick realized there was no way of getting out. He poked through rotted boxes containing drapes and fixtures, searching desperately for a weapon he could use against the vampires. He found it just as they began to make their way down the stairs, when he was starting to think a suicidal charge might be his only chance: a broom. Rushing over to the furnace, he opened its door and stuck in the bristle end, ignoring the tremendous heat. It ignited immediately.

When he faced the stairs again there were five of them milling about, grinning lewdly, waiting for him. He tried to avoid looking into their dead, cold, undersea eyes, eyes without a trace of warmth or lust or hate or any feeling Nick had ever experienced in himself or seen in another, at once cold and intense, impersonal and predatory. Holding his torch before him, he advanced slowly, hoping to God that vampires were afraid of fire.

The gambit worked. The vampires recoiled immediately, and Nick eased his way up the stairs, one step at a time, his torch illuminating the frustrated gnashing of their teeth. He was halfway to the top step when Uncle Bill, grinning evilly, grabbed Yo-yo and hurled him into the flame.

Nick reacted instinctively, using his broom like a bayonet, impaling the falling vampire on its burning end. Yo-yo gasped, a dry, scraping, hideous noise, and pitched forward. Nick lost his balance catching the corpse, and tumbled down the stairs as the other vampires pressed forward.

Lourdes's Story

HE DID NOT know what happened next, because the fall knocked out his wind, and then his consciousness. When he came to, his eyes focused on the golden, sparkling cross hanging from Dolores's neck. Ambrose's cross.

"Lourdes."

The ancient vampire nodded. "Yes, I was Lourdes."

She was seated before him in her wheelchair. Nick looked around. He was sprawled on a pile of refuse in a corner of the cellar. Behind Dolores the rest of the vampires stood around, two near the stairs, the other two by Yo-yo's transfixed corpse. Maybe they can't pull out the stakes themselves, he thought.

Then he turned back to Dolores. "Why did you wait until now to take me?"

Dolores's mutilated mouth twisted into a grin. "'Why' is a question we should only ask ourselves. Now as to 'how'...I shall explain it all to you, now that we're finally having our little talk. You are an important part of my plans, and I wouldn't want you to be confused as to your purpose."

She leaned closer to him, and he smelled the scent he was becoming so familiar with. "The Doctor and Angustia told you some things about me—they described my beauty, my power, even my lovers. They also told you that my influence deteriorated after Ambrose's suicide. They thought it was because I finally overstepped my bounds." Her cracking voice grew harsher. "They were fools to believe that. Ambrose's suicide would have presented no insurmountable problems for me. My power had no bounds. Or it had none until the evening his brother Emilio paid me a visit. Emilio: a miserable little eunuch married to chants and fasts. The eunuch fooled my servants, playing the fool, looking for his brother. He entered my bedroom just before nightfall, armed with a hammer and stake. I was immobile, but I could see him looking down at me, thinking of his bewitched brother, building his zealot's courage. He raised the stake over my heart, still hesitating . . . and I began to defend myself. Summoning all my will, I parted my lips. They were full, soft, red lips. I showed him my teeth, flicked out my tongue. The fire in my eyes was cold, so cold . . . and he hesitated, and the precious seconds ticked, and the time grew near when the sun would set and I could arise to claim him.

"He knew I was trying to seduce him, just as I had his brother, and still he wavered. The fangs had enchanted him, I thought, when he brought down the stake into my mouth. I bolted up with the setting sun, shrieking with pain.

"The servants burst in and dragged Emilio from the room. They kept their favorite implements in the hotel kitchen, and that was where they took him. Stripped of his stinking cassock, he was skinned alive, very slowly, very carefully, so that he would not die. It was only after his prayers and squeals faded into unconsciousness that they chopped him to bits and tossed him into the evening stew."

Lourdes paused. Her eyes bored into Nick's like slivers of dry ice. "Vampirism is the cure for hemophilia, Mr. Van Lo; unless the wound is fatal, our blood coagulates almost instantly. By the time the hotel's guests were supping on that cursed monk, I had dressed and was ready to go out.

"A vampire is all-powerful, but only when healthy, and only at night. A vampire is immortal, but its body can become an anchor, a prison, when it is not sustained. I found that I could not feed, not like before. Emilio's stake had cost me my right canine, and I could not make do with the left. In what became a vicious circle, I no longer had the speed or the strength to take the blood of the virile; so I withered with only the blood of the weak for sustenance.

"Christian disgust, vengeance, impotence destroyed me! That sexless monk! I began to grow ugly, grow old. My lovers deserted me and, with the loss of their influence, so did my servants. I no longer had the energy to run the hotel by myself, let alone go out, and fewer and fewer people spent the night there. The hotel was no longer my larder, it was my millstone."

Dolores's lips shifted; Nick was never really sure what each grimace meant. "Until the fire. Your priest upstairs, he thought the fire had finished me. Instead, it saved me. Lourdes disappeared in the fire, to come back as Dolores. The grand hotel became a cheap rooming house, and no one paid any attention to the gap-toothed hag that owned it. As a new class of roomers appeared, I thought, so would some of my vitality. But a pensioner's blood is of little use to a vampire; neither is the blood of filthy addicts and diseased drunks. It's a shame, because they were so easy to . . . drain. I sat down in a wheelchair for the first time in 1922. I have not risen from one under my own strength since.

"But fifty years mean little to a vampire. When the good Doctor moved into the house with his addiction to alcohol and a history of questionable transfusions, I began to plot my escape from this chair."

"He provided you with . . ." Nick could barely say it. "Transfusions?"

"A vampire is an ancient creature, Mr. Van Lo. It is a denizen of what you call the supernatural. Our organism works in ways even we do not understand. The act of feeding . . . it is a holy ritual, a sacred ceremony. Transfusions"—she spat the words contemptuously—"just wouldn't be the same."

"Then why did you want the Doctor?"

"Because I need a new body, a young, vital one, healthy and attractive enough to prey. The Doctor could bring me a young whore, he could drain her blood, and transfuse mine into her veins. This was my plan, even though the whores the Doctor brought me were soiled pieces of trash, unfit to be the vessel of my spirit."

The sheer loathsomeness of Dolores's plan paled for Nick in the face of the Doctor's apparent complicity. "He was your procurer?"

Dolores cackled malevolently. "Don't be too self-righteous, Mr. Van Lo, we all know of your weaknesses. The Doctor was an addict, like all of us are here." Another cackle. "He was addicted to alcohol—an addiction, you may be interested to learn, he considered more harmful than my own. I provided him with his ludicrous Scotch, paid him to be my rent collector, and made him completely dependent on me in little more than a year. Finally, one day, I cut him off. Only then did he realize that he was no longer capable of scrounging the ten dollars a day he needed. When I revealed myself to him—and my intentions—he never hesitated."

Nick still did not want to believe. "But something happened; he became a vampire himself."

Dolores slowly nodded her head. "Something did happen, Mr. Van Lo. Two rather unscrupulous speculators tried to extort my rooming house, and then you came along. So I altered my plans."

Nick felt his own blood ice. "Amanda."

"The realtor had a daughter. So did his partner, but *that* little girl had received too many intimacies from her boyfriend to be of any use to me. And by the time I found that out, she wasn't of much use to anyone." Dolores giggled at the memory, then grew serious. "Your Amanda, on the other hand, was perfect. The Doctor brought her to me for the ritual bite—the one that contaminates, that elects. The elect is under its master vampire's influence until it dies. Then it also becomes a vampire."

Which was why Amanda could move about in the daytime, Nick thought, and why Davey never became a vampire himself. He had been killed by a thirsty, possessed child.

"The tax and property laws have delivered this building to Mr. Westerhays, but the code of the night has granted me his daughter."

Dolores laughed weakly. "Your arrival marked the end of the Doctor's usefulness to me, which is just as well, since he was acting a bit too *paternal* with you. One by one, I turned all these buzzards"—she waved behind her—"into vampires. I fed them the Doctor. I fed them Angustia when he came here with his pitiful tool kit two nights ago. And tonight they will feed on you."

Dolores stopped, letting the words sink in. There was more. "They have already smothered the child Amanda. When she awakes as a vampire, they will suck her dry. And then . . . then the vampire Nicholas will drink my life blood, only to pump it back into the vampire Amanda's empty veins. The vampire

Nicholas will wean Amanda into adulthood, at which time he will cease to be regent and become consort to the queen of the vampires."

It was beyond belief. "Amanda will be . . . *you?*"

Dolores nodded. "It is a simple process, although a slow one. These creatures"—another backward wave of the hand— "are a little long in the tooth. If they drink too much of your young, rich blood, they are likely to go into a stupor. They have only just recovered from the feasting they had on Angustia." She giggled obscenely. "These boys never could handle their liquor, though. That is why I'll need you."

Nick shuddered at the horrible joke, then considered the role Dolores had outlined for him. She had forgotten something. "What makes you think I'm going to follow through on any of that once I'm a vampire?"

Nick waited a long time for an answer, all the while trying to recognize the expression on her riverbed features. The word he was searching for was *maternal*, and he never found it.

"How do I know you will do exactly as I say, Mr. Van Lo? Because you will be a vampire, a creature that can flourish for centuries. But it takes time to learn how to conquer time— time and a never-ending rabble of mortal fanatics, pests like the priest upstairs. Who can teach you the wisdom of the centuries? Not these buffoons. Certainly not the vampire Angustia, whom you disposed of so easily.

"No, I shall teach you. Through me you will realize the full extent of the power you have been selected to share. And with your help, I shall regenerate myself. It is a fair bargain. I have no doubts that you will keep your end of it."

Nick flushed. "What are you waiting for, then? Why not get on with it?"

"Patience, young man. A vampire must always have patience. We are waiting for the vampire Amanda to awake. Her fangs must be virgin for me to enter her body, so I'm afraid she won't be able to join the others when they initiate you, but I'm sure you will appreciate the irony of her presence."

Love at Stake

LEATHERFACE WHEELED DOLORES to another part of the cellar, leaving Nick alone amidst the refuse. There were empty paint cans scattered over a pile of dirty rags, a couple of crates full of broken furniture, an odd piece of molding here and there. Over to one side, scattered like a collection of fur pieces, were seven or eight rat carcasses on a mound of coal dust. Behind the mound he could just make out the stakes that Angustia had come armed with, poking out of a satchel crammed with garlic and crucifixes. The discovery wasn't worth much, outnumbered as he was, but it offered the hope of a small measure of vengeance before they killed him.

Except they weren't going to "kill" him. They were going to feed on him, contaminate him, make him elect. A vampire. He wondered how it would be, and could not imagine it. All he could sense now was the relentlessness, the inevitability, of the thorned garland of events that had woven itself about him. Because it couldn't have been just coincidence that brought a weak man like the Doctor into this house, placing him in a situation where he would have to relive the incident that ruined his life, nor was it coincidence that Tod Westerhays, who had sought to exploit a seventy-five-year-old bureaucratic oversight for his own profit, sent his daughter to the John Swett School. Nick forced himself to complete the thought: it also couldn't have been coincidence that had brought him here, and to Room 14, with his secret weakness that Dolores had so effortlessly uncovered and exploited.

Perhaps she was clairvoyant, with a telepathic ability these surprisingly mortal vampires were not known to possess. How else to explain those flashes (memories?) of Lourdes's world that he had experienced throughout the fall? *The ritual was an excuse for the blood:* it was as if they'd offered a glimpse into his future as well as the past. Had he been approaching the cellar of this house all his life?

His deliberations were brought to a halt by the sound of the cellar door being hesitantly opened. The vampires turned to face the staircase, and Nick craned his neck to watch the descent of the vampire Amanda, the locus of his undoing.

A ballet slipper appeared on the top step. "Nick?"

The voice was tentative, fearful; it belonged to Judith. Nick scrambled to his feet as Leatherface and Charley crept silently toward the stairs. "Run, Judy! Run!"

"Nick, is that you?" Now he could see the hem of her white skirt, her thin black belt, the simple white blouse she had put on that morning. He was moving to her as Leatherface's hand reached up from one side of the staircase and clamped on her ankle.

Judith screamed just as Bill and Slater intercepted Nick fifteen feet from the stairs. Nick lost sight of her as the three of them fell to the floor in a straining tangle of knees, snarls, and fingers. Their struggle was brutally brief; Nick was sitting on Slater, about to cave in his face with a lethal elbow, when he felt Bill's foul breath on his neck. He froze instantly. "That's right, laddie," the vampire whispered in his ear. "It's not your time yet."

Keeping his lips close to Nick's jugular, Bill rolled him off Slater and onto his back on the damp stone floor. Then the vampire sunk his knee into Nick's groin. Nick buckled on the floor, the air rushed out of him, and his eyes rolled up. A wave of nausea washed over him; he turned on his side, gasping, in the fetal position. It took all his strength to fight off the urge to retch, and to watch the horror before him.

Leatherface was holding Judith from behind, grinning evilly, while Charley ran his fingers up her arms and onto the soft material covering her shoulders. Nick could sense her almost imperceptible trembling, like the beating of a hummingbird's wings, as that horrible, cancerous face leaned closer to hers.

Nick tried to rise once more, but the pain and nausea overcame him instantly, leaving him crumpled and gagging on the floor.

"Oh, Judy," he whispered; it emerged a moan, a funeral cry from his broken soul. And she heard him. Her dark eyes homed in on his, and he felt her fear and confusion as if they were his own. There wasn't much time left, and they both knew it. Charley's fingers tilted her chin up, exposing her neck. She said good-bye to Nick, a final declaration of love saddened by its incomprehensible end. We tried.

"Take her," Dolores said.

Charley gripped her by the shoulders, brought down his head . . . and Judith's eyes snapped up as Leatherface sank his teeth into her, beating his brother to the mark. Charley growled with displeasure, and his knotted fingers tore Judith's blouse from her shoulders, exposing her breasts. The vampire's thick, loose lips rose up his gums, revealing four wicked yellow fangs. Nick shut his eyes as he fell on her.

Dolores ordered Bill and Slater to take Nick back to the refuse pile. They dragged him away by the armpits. Nick struggled weakly with them, but his strength had not yet returned. It was too late, he realized, to save Judith now from her fatal rape. All that was left to him was to bide his time atop the curtains and stakes, and hope that her martyrdom would gain him one moment of vengeance.

Judith also put up no resistance. Her body swayed, eyes closed, as Charley ravished her, as Leatherface guzzled the life from her. When Slater left his position over Nick and tore Charley from her to take his place, consciousness mercifully left her in the shadow of a giant bird's slowly flapping wing.

Charley staggered back toward Nick; there was blood all over his mouth, all over his sores. Bill caught him contemptuously, and leaned him against an empty crate.

"Take Leatherface's place, Bill," Dolores urged. "You haven't had your turn, and he's had enough."

But the tall vampire with the dead eyes and skin like parchment shook his head. "Someone," he croaked, gesturing toward Nick, "has to take *him.*"

Just then Leatherface's head lolled back, and blood trickled from the corners of his mouth. A gurgling sound came from somewhere in his throat, and a stream of blood poured from his mouth as he reeled away from Judith and crashed into a wall.

Dolores understood immediately, even though Nick did not. "Leave her now, Mr. Slater," she commanded. "Leave her!"

Judith had fallen to the floor as soon as Leatherface had released her, and Slater had sprawled over her softly breathing form like an iguana atop a desert rock. He paused for a moment, looking back uncertainly at Dolores, and Nick could see the unabated desire in his face.

"No more," she rasped. But the blood was pounding past Slater's temples in an orgasmic roar that blocked out his queen's voice. He went down on her again in a frenzy of ripping and drinking.

"Bill!" shrieked Dolores. "Stop him!"

Bill moved toward the blood-crazed vampire on the floor, and Nick seized his chance. Reaching back into Angustia's satchel, he gripped a stake and leaped after the only vampire still thirsty enough to be truly dangerous. Bill never knew what hit him; his already lifeless eyes rolled up as the stake's point peeked out through the breast pocket of his shirt, and he pitched forward, dead once more.

"Get him, Charley," Dolores exhorted, but Nick was already by the satchel, taking another stake. The vampire managed only to turn in Nick's direction, so that the flashing stake bayoneted past him just left of the sternum.

Nick didn't wait to witness the monster's death spasms; there were two more left, and he had no time to waste. One careless move, a single pricking of his skin by those fangs, and he was lost. A third stake was in his hands when he turned to face them.

Leatherface, he quickly saw, lay face down by the far wall in a blood-soaked stupor. But Slater was beginning to pick himself up from Judith's violated corpse, a drunken, leering grin befouling his features. He was on his feet, wavering, when Nick charged.

Slater raised his claws and spread his lips, revealing the fangs of a viper. His fingernails clawed Nick's face, his thirsty tongue snaked out, and the blood gushed forth from his gaping mouth, from the fatal wreck of his chest cavity. The avenging fury of Nick's impulse carried them into the wall, where the point protruding from Slater's back tore through the plaster, leaving the lifeless vampire pinned on the wall like a ruptured, pestilent insect.

"Mr. Van Lo." Dolores had regained her calm. "It is already too late for you."

Nick smiled grimly at her and went back to the satchel for yet another stake, then returned to the spot where Leatherface had collapsed on his face. Nick turned him over with one foot. The odor of blood and decay rose to his face, making Nick gag. When he tapped Leatherface's cheek with a boot tip, the vampire opened his eyes.

"Leatherface." You took her blood first.

The vampire grinned senselessly, and Nick rammed the stake into his chest. Blood gushed from the hole, from the vampire's mouth and nose and ears. He gave the stake a final stir, and Leatherface lay quiet.

Dolores seemed somewhere else, as if she were waiting for something, when Nick straightened up, pointed a finger at her, and walked back to get another stake. It was in his hands when he heard the voice.

"Hello, Nicholas." How could he have missed her coming down those stairs? He squeezed the stake for reassurance.

"Look." Nick looked. Amanda was in the center of the room, dressed in a white gown, smiling with teeth that could tear. Her skin was very white.

"It is time to choose," Dolores said from the other side of the room. "I am offering you immortality. The body of this child, only imbued with my wisdom. It won't take long. And it will be forever."

Amanda ignored the crippled vampire's words, looking only at Nick. "I need you, Nicholas. I'm immortal too, but I'm still a little girl. I'll die if you don't take care of me. Don't you see, we were always meant for each other. I always knew it, even before." She paused. "Come to me. I'll let you kiss me all you want, and then I'll kiss you on your neck. You'll be my daddy, Nicholas. And I'll be your favorite little girl."

"Don't be a fool, Van Lo." Nick could hear the desperation in Dolores's tone. "She'll be a millstone around your neck; what do you know about being a vampire? You saw how long these worthless derelicts lasted on their own. Come to me. I will bless you, and then you can help me enter her body. And don't forget the girl." Her hand pointed in Judith's direction. "You can have her also, if you want."

Nick closed his eyes. The stake felt slippery in his sweaty palms. Amanda stretched out her arms to him. He could hear the whine of the drill over his shoulder, but it didn't stop his advance. Hadn't he always wanted to be bitten? The kiss of death, the little death, the kiss of little Amanda. Her eyes flickered smokily, like dry ice. The drill grew louder, higher, his mother warned him to stay back. But now Amanda was in his arms, laughing happily, playfully offering her throat to him before her turn came. Nick breathed in the little-girl scent and the death scent, the scent of sweet decay. Amanda's mouth opened. Her breath was foul, vampire breath. He was growing warmer by the moment, his blood racing to a boil, ready for the offering. Now, she whispered. Now, Nicholas. And he planted his lips on her slender throat, bringing up her blood through the pores, before baring his own neck. He saw her smile spread, saw the inhuman hunger he craved to slake, saw the lip curl in anticipation . . . then surprise . . . and finally pain as blood dribbled from her rose-petal lips, as the stake ripped into her again and again, tearing her open, killing it, forever.

Her weightless little body leaned against his for only a moment before slipping to the floor. Nick looked down on her, and heard the whining dissipate. She sounded like a wraith robbed of its roost. He was exorcised; he was strong.

The last two stakes were where he had left them, stuck like markers in the coal dust. He withdrew one and passed a finger over a tip. There was no doubt where this one was going. "Do you have anything more to offer, Dolores? Or are you ready to join the rest of your kind?"

The old woman grinned, reminding Nick of an emaciated monkey. "You dare to mock me, you pitiful human? *This* is your finest hour, here, in this stinking cellar, with your two lovers transformed into what you fear and lust for. What do you have ahead of you? A hounded life, dogs snapping at your heels and inside your guts. I am a queen; I have drunk so much blood . . . so many throats . . . Finish me now. I am tired of this

wheelchair, otherwise I would never have considered such a
pathetic specimen to be my consort."

Nick's grin was demonic; the glow around him was blinding.
"Death would be too easy, Dolores. Death is what we all crave."

She looked at him, uncomprehending, as the stake came
down on her mouth just as it had one hundred years before,
tearing the wrinkled skin like rice paper, destroying what was
left of her gums, and shattering the queen vampire's last canine.

She howled like the timeless being she was, howled with
pain and hate, unable to block out what Nick had done to her.
He had condemned her to an eternity of bloodless existence.
She could no longer feed, and she could not die.

"Kill me! Kill me, you bastard!" He could barely make out
the words. Ignoring her shrieks, he went over to get the last
stake. This was the one that was going to hurt. It was going
to prove his love. It was for Judith.

He stood over her white, still form, feeling the tears course
down his cheeks. She had sacrificed her love for him again.
Bending down, he passed a hand over her bloodied skin. Here
had been his life, if things had only gone differently. He gripped
the stake tighter. *I'd do it again for you, Nick.* It was his duty
to this sweet girl who had loved him, to free her from the curse
of vampirism.

But he couldn't do it right then. There were too many memories he had to create, memories of the future they had been
deprived of, a future that could no longer be shared in the warm
sunlight. Love and death had always come together for him;
now they were united in the beautiful woman at his feet. And
this love would last forever. That they couldn't take from him.

The stake clattered to the floor. He put his arms around her,
holding her close, and dreamt of Snow White waking and
faraway warmth, while the last embers of Judith's humanity
flickered, faded, and died.

PART FIVE

LIFE AFTER DEATH

The grave's a fine and private place,
But none, I think, do there embrace.

—*Andrew Marvell*

Aftermath

SOMEWHERE ALONG THEIR desperate race from the Pacific Highway to the Tenderloin, Tod had the presence of mind to stop at a phone booth and call the police. The squad cars had arrived at La Casa de Dolores just before them, and it took Tod a few minutes to explain who they were, and be allowed through.

Jessie remembered having noticed the building before.

The homicide inspector had led them past the barriers and flashbulbs, and down a narrow flight of stairs to the building's basement. The room was dank and low ceilinged; teams of crime-lab technicians swarmed busily beneath pools of lantern light. There, among the smells of age and chemicals and violent death, they found Amanda. The stake that killed her no longer protruded from her chest, and she lay covered by a policeman's jacket. Later, Tod and Jessie remarked on the heartbreaking serenity of the moment, how quiet she looked.

They were driving in their own car for the first time since that night, driving back from the cemetery where Amanda had been buried, driving even though protocol called for them to sit behind the tinted windows of a limousine. Their families and friends had been notified about the tragedy, but all had been firmly requested to pay their respects by staying away. Tod and Jessie had no doubt that the shame of Amanda's death belonged only to them, and they had no desire to share their sorrow with their friends, or with the media.

They turned onto their own street then, and Jessie felt she was returning to the scene of the crime as they saw the TV crews camped out on their lawn. Tod cursed softly, but said nothing otherwise. They hadn't talked very much to each other since that night.

The cameramen and reporters were on them as soon as they stepped out of the Saab, firing the questions each of them had been answering to themselves every waking moment of the last three days. Jessie wished belatedly that she had worn a veil, and ducked her head while clinging to Tod's arm. The videotape touched her skin, probed for exposed feelings, and slid off. In twenty seconds they were back inside.

"It's like being inside a bell jar," Jessie said aloud, hoping that the sound of her voice would slow her runaway heartbeat.

Tod turned away, unable to witness his wife's pain, and looked down at the three rolled-up newspapers on the coffee table. Until this morning, they had lain scattered on their lawn, untouched since the paper boy had thrown them from the saddlebag of his moped. Each one had part of its front page inked with the blood of their daughter, and Jessie and Tod had had no desire to wake up and have their hands stained anew.

Now he picked up the most recent one, and held it before her. "This is the only way out," he said flatly.

Jessie nodded as he settled into the leather chair by the fireplace. She came up behind him, and Tod held the newspaper up so they both could read it.

"The Exorcist Massacre"

by Mark J. Dunau

To the list headed by the Zebra killings and the assassinations of George Moscone and Harvey Milk, San Francisco must now add the eight fatalities that took place during an exorcism ritual gone horribly wrong.

The Archdiocese of San Francisco and the Police Department will not discuss why a Roman Catholic priest was in the rooming house the night of the most gruesome mass murder in the history of the city, nor how the priest came to know Nicholas Van Lo—now missing, and the police's only official suspect. What they cannot deny is that Father Lawrence Angustia was found with a sharp wooden stake through his heart—one of eight victims in what is becoming known as "The Exorcist Massacre."

Was Father Angustia engaged in an unauthorized exorcism rite? Did he lose control of the situation . . .

Tod folded the paper over impatiently, and silently pointed to another article.

"Pervert . . . or Ghoul?"

by Leonard Kornberg

Nicholas Van Lo arrived in San Francisco not quite three months ago, and quickly got a job as a fifth-grade teacher at the John Swett School. He was fired last Friday, after John Swett principal Calvin Shanker witnessed Van Lo allegedly molesting Amanda Westerhays, one of his students. Three days later, Amanda Westerhays died with a stake through her heart, the most poignant of eight victims in a crime that has only one suspect. Nicholas Van Lo.

Who is Nicholas Van Lo: a pathetic child molester, or San Francisco's answer to Charles Manson? Is his disappearance explainable after his alleged assault on Amanda Westerhays last week, or is it proof positive that he murdered every inhabitant of a Tenderloin flophouse? The police . . .

Jessie turned away, remembering what Tod's reporter friend Schlackman had revealed: that the crime-lab technicians had sawn off the stake in Amanda's chest to skin level after dusting it for prints, just moments before she and Tod had arrived. They could not have borne to look at her otherwise.

When she looked back to the newspaper, Tod had turned to a third report.

"Did the Exorcist Have Other Victims?"

by Craig Zarley

Nicholas Van Lo, who attempted to exorcise eight innocent people by driving stakes through their hearts, may have had other victims.

Everyone in San Francisco, if not the country, knows

by now that the sexually warped elementary school teacher
ritually murdered six as-yet-unidentified down-and-outers
in the flophouse where he and they lived, as well as a
mysterious Roman Catholic priest named Lawrence Angustia.

And everyone knows the name of his eighth victim:
Amanda Westerhays, ten years old, bright and vivacious,
with two blonde braids and the misfortune to be the apple
of her educator's eye . . .

"Bastards," Tod muttered, and forced himself to read on.

. . . But few of us remember Davey Schwimmer. Davey
was Amanda Westerhays's best friend, and another of
Van Lo's unfortunate "pets." Davey was found with his
throat ripped out on the Westerhayses' lawn this Halloween night.

The first person on the scene, police have revealed,
was Nicholas Van Lo.

Then there was Lisa Varney, the daughter of the
Westerhayses' attorney . . .

"That's enough for now," Tod said quietly, and dropped the
paper to the floor.

Jessie walked around from behind the chair, and placed one
hand lightly on her husband's graying head. "What would you
like for lunch?" she asked softly.

Tod looked up at her, his eyes revealing the extent of the
pain he was mercilessly inflicting on himself. "Today's
Thanksgiving, isn't it?" The handsome lips curled for a moment. "How about turkey?"

She sat on his lap then, and he put his arms around her,
and they cried together until it didn't hurt quite so badly.

Before long, he felt Judith stirring in his arms.

The gestation period—that alien time when her soul wandered away from her body, lost itself amid stunted trees and
sluggish, syrupy streams, and learned the word *undead* from
a faceless teacher at the bottom of a well—lasted only a few
minutes with her. In that time, there was a perfect silence in

the basement, in which Nick could only hear his memories and his pulse.

Dolores watched it all from her wheelchair with a turtle's calm and patient gaze. She had immediately sensed Nick's change of heart, and wisely stifled the moans from her tortured mouth. There was no need to involve herself in the scene before her. Her moment would come last, and would only come once. She had to be ready for it.

And Dolores did recede from Nick's consciousness. For him, there was only the weight in his arms, growing oddly lighter with each moment even as his arms became more tired. He had made his decision, he was selling his soul for love, and whatever uneasiness he felt was due to anticipation rather than fear. The residue of doubt that still survived knew it had lost the day's battle, and was quietly marshaling its forces for another field, on another day.

The first movement Nick saw could have easily been an illusion, an indication of his eagerness, the mirage of a dark wine lake in a desert of bleached bone. The corners of Judith's mouth—not her lips, so full and pale, nor the tongue lying in wait like an adder inside—crinkled for the length of a wink. It was a flicker, a mild test pattern of electricity at some private joke. When she opened her eyes, Nick knew she was about to share it with him.

They were Judith's eyes, dark and almond shaped, seeing him for the first time, aware they'd known him forever. They probed him effortlessly even as he sank into them, told him everything he wanted to hear in a tongue he didn't understand. And when the tongue peeked out, when her thin arms snaked up his sides and her mouth opened like Dorothy waking from Oz, Nick met her lips with his.

They kissed shyly for a while, because Judith was learning, Judith was drinking in knowledge even before she would taste blood, Judith was sucking in human essence from his pores and it tasted good, it made her feel like a goddess. Only slowly did the lips slide off his, wetting the corner of his mouth, tracing the line of his jaw, finally coming home to roost over the thrilling arteries in his neck. And then the goddess took her due.

Nick felt the skin break, and moaned softly in release. There was a little pain, sudden and sharp, quickly dissipating into a dull ache. But the knowledge that he was hers now was stronger; even as he felt himself being drained, slowly being left with nothing at all, he was surprised by the satisfaction of it, the passive worth of the used. His body grew light, his bones soft, his skin dry, his smile set. Soon he had no form, could no longer feel her coursing fingers. There was only the wound, and the teeth, and the life being exchanged at such a rapid rate.

Finally, he was empty. There was only blackness, and he was the blackness. And as his personality disintegrated in the freezing silent winds of space, one last sensation was discharged. It was a shudder, the final coming apart of his natural core. It was a fearful shudder, the shudder of horror, proving by its very occurrence that he had been a man, and not a beast. Evanescent, like his humanity, it confirmed the wayward eternity of his now-soulless spirit.

Nicholas Van Lo, with his dying breath, had found religion.

William Powell & Myrna Loy

TOD AND JESSIE walked out of the York theater holding hands, and breathed in the cool Mission District night. In the two weeks since Amanda had died, they had spent many evenings in the beautiful Art Deco movie palace, watching films like *Annie Hall* and *Casablanca*. The hours spent before the theater's giant screen were an important part of the healing process they had begun.

They were still quite fragile, of course. Jessie cried about half as often as the Valium she was taking made her giggle; and Tod, while refusing any sedatives, drank more and more each day to dilute his sourceless restiveness. Nevertheless, starting with the Monday after the funeral, he had returned to the newspaper, and Jessie also forced herself to spend half-days at her studio. If they were going to dwell on their pain, they had vowed, it would only be in the evening, arm in arm before the fireplace.

"If they ever do a remake of that movie," Tod whispered in her ear as they neared their car, "they should cast us for the leads."

Jessie sat on the Saab's sloping hood and pulled him down to her. She, too, had felt a connection with *The Thin Man*'s quick-witted stars, William Powell and Myrna Loy; not only were she and Tod getting high as often as the celluloid couple, they were also pursuing a mystery of their own.

Ever since the fingerprints on every wooden stake had matched those in Nick Van Lo's room, the police had a suspect etched in stone. From his divorced wife in Palo Alto the investigators had learned that Van Lo lost his university teaching job after having a series of affairs with his students. Linking this with Davey Schwimmer's and Amanda's murders, they had pigeonholed the case as the work of a sexual psychopath. The fact that seven other bodies had been found near Amanda, all with stakes through their hearts, did not seem to shake the investigators' belief in their perspective.

Those seven bodies, however, were not the only reasons why Jessie and Tod could not go along with the police theory. There was also the one crucial fact they had withheld from the detectives, the one they never mentioned to each other, the undeniable: Amanda had intended to meet with Nick Van Lo on her last night alive. She had given Tod a phony story and a phony address in order to insure that her plans weren't upset. Her attachment to her teacher—to her killer—had been stronger than the one to her parents.

Tod and Jessie could live with that knowledge tonight, if they pretended they were William Powell and Myrna Loy; they had done it so far by pretending they were Humphrey Bogart and Ingrid Bergman, Woody Allen and Diane Keaton. But believing that someone had stolen their daughter's soul would eventually destroy them. They had to save her memory, by proving that *something else* had been going on, that Amanda had not willingly abandoned them. Both of them knew, without ever saying it aloud, that restoring Amanda's innocence was the only way they could save themselves.

"I spoke with Vic Varney today," Tod mentioned casually as he pulled out of their parking space and onto a deserted Twenty-fourth Street. "I told him to hold off selling the property until the investigation's over."

"Did he object? I know how Vic hates to sit on money like that."

"I don't give a shit what Vic hates. If he wasn't always looking for a scam, both our daughters . . ."

They drove in silence until Tod swung onto 101. "That's a crock, too. The police didn't find Van Lo's fingerprints on Lisa. And nobody forced me to go along with the deal. All I could think of was how much *money* I was going to make."

"Tod."

"I know we've discussed it. I know we've rationalized it. We can twist it into a fucking pretzel, but it'll still be true."

Jessie said nothing the rest of the way home. Last week she would have protested, trying to spare him the guilt she herself felt for having gone to Mendocino the last two weeks of Amanda's life. She would have waved her absence before him like a red cape, and Tod would have charged dutifully to her defense. But that stratagem no longer had any effect; they had lost the ability to lick each other's wounds. From now on, she knew, the healing process would be an internal affair.

Once they were home, Tod poured himself a double brandy while Jessie sipped white wine. She also felt like something stronger, but was worried about the effect the alcohol might have on her with all the Valium in her system.

Besides, she kidded herself, Myrna Loy didn't mix *her* poisons.

"So where do we go from here, Mr. Powell?"

Tod smiled, and clinked glasses. "Back to the source, I think. That's why I told Vic to hold off selling the hotel. I went back there the other day, and—"

"You did?"

"Just to . . . get a feel, do you know what I mean? Van Lo's room, for instance—you can sense him in there, think his thoughts, almost. It also gave me an idea of what to do next."

"What's that?" Knowing that Tod had returned to the site of the murders made her feel uneasy.

"I'm going to contact that Stanford psychologist, Fred Olds. Apparently they were friends before Van Lo left Palo Alto. He might know a side of the bastard that the police don't."

"Don't you think the police have already thought of that?"

"Maybe. But they aren't telling us about it if they have. And I want to know."

Jessie didn't like the grimness in Tod's tone, but knew he was right. At times it seemed to her that understanding Nick Van Lo was more important than capturing him. If they didn't have much to go on, well . . . what would William Powell and Myrna Loy have done?

"I'm going to visit whoever replaced him at the John Swett School," she finally said. "If he really did have a fixation on the children in that class, maybe this new teacher will have noticed if some of the other kids are acting like—"

"That's a good idea," Tod cut in, sparing Jessie the mention of their daughter's name. "Now come here." He stretched out his arms. "You ought to go to bed. Anyone taking as much Valium as you needs their sleep."

Jessie bit his ear in retaliation, then put her face close to his. "Aren't you coming up with me?"

"Nah," he shrugged. "I want to let all this settle a little more." He tapped the side of his head. "Awful lot of silt in there."

Jessie hesitated, then gave in and began to pull away, when Tod gripped her by the elbows. He was looking intently at her upper lip.

"What's the matter?"

"You know, you've even got a little moustache like Myrna Loy."

"And you're going to have a voice higher than William Powell's if you don't cut it out," she warned lightly, and went upstairs.

Taking off her clothes, she prepared herself mentally to find Tod asleep on the living room couch the next morning. He slept down there as often as not these days, passing out from the brandy after hours of fighting off sleep, and the dreams that came with it.

They came to him almost every night now, no matter how tired he got or how much he drank: nightmares where geeks bit off the heads of rats, and evil dwarfs violated Jessie and Amanda while he watched, powerless.

They made her afraid of him, and even a little guilty that the sedatives erased any awareness of her own dreams. But she knew herself well enough to admit that, without the pills, she would still be incapacitated in her waking life. It was a fair trade for the moment, a way to buy some time; until her real dreams returned, she could always go to the movies.

The Rules of the Game

WITH THE SETTING of the sun over San Francisco's Chinatown, its sweatshops poured out thousands of women rushing home to make dinner for their families; the narrow alleys, already crowded with tourists, darkened with the flood of humanity. The weight of all that flesh could be felt thirty feet beneath the pavement, beneath the packed earth, in a tunnel that had been sealed off since the ground shifted in 1906. It sent a tremor of longing to the three beings who had recently made it their home: a longing that would need to be slaked before tomorrow's sun arose.

The tunnel opened into a rectangular dugout forty feet long and twenty-five feet wide, with a ceiling low enough to prevent Nick from standing up to his full height. The walls, roughly carved out of the earth, leaked moisture and an occasional, surprised earthworm onto a dirt floor barren save for two spread blankets.

In the dim light provided by a single Coleman lantern, Nick and Judith dressed silently out of two canvas suitcases propped on orange crates, while Dolores repeated their instructions.

"You will only have one chance, so there can't be any mistakes tonight. Above all, the man must not be found drained of blood. We don't want the newspapers writing about a recurrence of the . . . Exorcist massacre."

Nick ignored Dolores's jibe, as well as the lovely, mocking eyes across the room from him. "Let Judith handle this one, Nicholas," the old vampire advised, "at least until she gets him into his car. Dump his body in the bay, down by Hunters Point, or even farther south. Drive the car back to the city, if you must, but abandon it far from here, and drop the license plates into a sewer drain. Even so, they will find it eventually. That means you must wear gloves tonight, Nicholas."

Nick dangled a wrapper containing a pair of clear plastic gloves before her. "I got these last night. Just after we went over the operation for the tenth time. Maybe you aren't getting enough to drink," he pondered wickedly. "Your memory's evaporating before our eyes."

Dolores stretched her lips and formed a toothless grin. "So long as I can wet my whistle, you'll always be my favorite."

Judith came up behind Nick and poked him in the kidneys. "You're wasting my time. Let's go."

Nick nodded, and they moved silently toward the entrance to the tunnel. As they ducked beneath the overhang, Dolores reminded them not to forget her dinner.

The entrance to the tunnel, hidden behind a pile of refuse in the boiler room of a Chinatown apartment building, was similar to the one behind the furnace in the flophouse's basement, which Dolores had revealed to Judith moments before the police had burst in upstairs. After wheeling Dolores through the camouflaged entrance, Judith had rushed back to the basement and dragged Nick's body into the passageway. The two women then, waited for Nick to awaken while, on the other side of the door, the crime-lab technicians catalogued the dead.

So it was thanks to Dolores that Nick and Judith survived their first night as vampires. During that night, in the first of a series of tunnels that had served as their lairs, the crippled old woman made it clear to them that they would need her knowledge as much as she required their surrogate foraging. The decision to remain together, however, had not come about smoothly.

After waking from a deep and refreshing sleep, Nick had quickly remembered how it was that he came to his newborn state; along with the joy of being reunited with Judith had come a rekindling of the hatred he felt for Dolores. He had responded quickly to her suggestion of a banding together.

"Do you really believe I'd choose you as a teacher? What would the chances be of my ending up any differently than you? I'd rather take my chances alone than risk that."

He had turned to Judith for the support he would need to

leave the old woman behind in the tunnel. But Judith only smiled enigmatically, and it was Dolores who finally answered his tacit question.

"You'll have to forgive Judith for her excessive caution, Nicholas, since it *is* her first night. But while you lay here at our feet, she suggested that we abandon you before you woke up. After all, it's you the police will be after. No one knows we even exist." Dolores paused, letting her words sink in. "But experience has taught me that there is strength in numbers, and that three is a much better number for a family. I insisted that we at least wait for you to awake, and ask you what you wanted to do."

Nick had looked at Judith for a confirmation of Dolores's words, but the cool smile never wavered. And with the swell of betrayal, hurt, and confusion had come the awareness that he could not abandon in the first hour of his new life what he had sacrificed his old one for.

So he stood next to Judith at the corner, waiting for the bus to come and take them to their target. With Judith refusing to talk about either the past or their relationship, he had decided for the moment that silence and patience were his best tactics. It allowed him to hope that, some night, she would forgive him for introducing her to a world that had only one way out.

When the bus finally came, they walked back to the seat immediately behind the rear door. From there they could watch everyone who came aboard, and escape quickly if Nick were recognized. Anyway, as Dolores had told them, reading faces was good practice. To a vampire, humanity was divided into two classes: victims and victimizers. While both were vulnerable, there was little percentage in continually gambling with prey that wanted to live.

Nick pulled the cord when the bus turned onto Bryant Street, and followed Judith down the back steps. They found themselves before the steps of the Hall of Justice, an ugly granite building that contained the City Jail. Across the street were a row of bail-bonds establishments, lights blazing behind their glass storefronts, waiting for the evening business to heat up. ELKIN'S E-Z BAIL was the second door from the right.

Stanley Elkin was fifty-two years old, married, a grandfather, and in good health. Since buying out his partner Al

Main in 1973, his net worth had tripled, allowing him to indu
in a small rooftop apartment downtown. It was the bail bon
man's only vice; he kept its existence secret from even his w
of twenty-nine years, and visited it only when the fringe bene
of his trade required it.

Tonight would be one of those times.

"Wait here until we come out," Judith instructed calm
"Then follow behind. Don't let him see you until we're in
car."

Nick nodded, and Judith crossed the street. After makin
show of reading the sign in his window, she entered the offi

The traffic was light this early in the evening, but N
decided to wait by the bus stop to avoid being conspicuo
The art of disappearing into the background—any ba
ground—was one of the first things Dolores had taught h
Invisibility was second only to a secure resting place in
survival of a vampire pack. That was where Stanley Elkin ca
in. He had made the mistake of renting his trysting spot i
building whose basement connected to one of the old Chinatc
tunnels. Nick didn't know how, but Dolores had known
Elkin, his apartment, and its purpose, the fact that the r
notices were mailed there, that no one in the building it
knew who was renting it. Dolores had told them they owe
great debt to Stanley Elkin.

Even from this distance, Nick could see Judith swiftly p
ing the leaves of the bail bondsman's heart. It would only
a few minutes more before Elkin offered to solve Judith's p
dicament by covering her kid brother's bail himself, in
change for a friendly drink in his cozy North Beach penthou
Nick wondered how she intended to dispose of him. As fa
he knew, she had never actually *killed* a victim.

Vampires, he had learned, didn't have to kill. One pin
blood a night—or seven pints, say, once a week—was all t
needed to survive. A pint, Dolores had pointed out humorou
was what people regularly donated at blood banks. Losing
pint per month was perfectly safe; even one per week, ov
six-month period, would not wreck the health of a nor
person. After six months, she had explained, the advanced s
of anemia would have thinned the victim's blood to suc

point as to make it unsatisfactory to a vampire, and the donor
would have won a reprieve by default.

Dolores had told them this because building a stable of
victims to drink from once every week or so was the preferable
way for vampires to exist. If many of their victims were to die
at once, the resultant vampire epidemic would inevitably mul-
tiply into a world of the undead, where blood would be scarcer
than gold.

"But we all overindulge occasionally," Dolores had conceded. She outlined several remedies to prevent an increase in
the number of their elite: throwing them in front of streetcars,
cutting off their heads gangland style, or securing their corpses
where the murderous sun would be sure to find them. "It's our
right and our duty," she had solemnly assured them, "to preserve our aristocratic privileges."

Then the lights went off in ELKIN'S E-Z BAIL, and Judith
walked out holding the bail bondsman's hand. Nick reached
into his jacket pocket and opened the wrapper that held the
plastic gloves. He waited until they were a half-block down
the street, then hurried across the intersection.

Elkin had a metallic-blue Cadillac Seville with a white vinyl
roof. After unlocking the passenger door and guiding Judith
into her seat with a firmly helpful hand, he trotted briskly
around the car and settled in behind the wheel. Nick, walking
up from the rear, could already see Judith throwing her arms
around him. He was going to have to hurry.

His gloved hand gripped the handle of the driver's door as
Judith slid past the stubble on Elkin's neck and found the carotid
artery. The bright blood shot across the interior like a geyser,
and the bail bondsman began to thrash all over the front seat.
Nick quickly opened the door, shoved Elkin's legs over, and
turned the key.

The engine started immediately, and the Cadillac roared out
onto Bryant Street. Nick made the light at the corner and turned
right, toward the entrance to the southbound freeway. By the
time he reached the ramp, Elkin was still.

Nick swallowed, and glanced to his right.

Blood was spattered on the seat, the passenger door, the
dashboard, the ceiling, and the windshield; most of it had

landed on Judith. She looked as if someone had doused her with a bucket of red paint.

"Are you crazy?" he finally shouted.

"Why?" Already she had begun to lick herself, like a cat finished giving birth to a litter.

"What if someone sees the blood on the windshield? What if someone sees *you?*"

Her words were slow, slurred. "You know how the Spanish drink wine from one of those . . . one of those . . . whatever. I caught a good bit of Stanley, just like that."

"You're talking like you *enjoyed* killing him. It doesn't have to be this way, Judith."

Rather than respond, she leaned over to him and ran a bloody finger across his mouth. Nick hesitated for a moment before loosening his lips and sucking the only taste he could remember.

After he was finished, she examined her finger, and giggled drunkenly. "So it doesn't have to be this way, huh?"

She laughed a few more times after they parked by the water; while Nick washed the inside of the windshield with Stanley Elkin's shirt, and just after the bail bondsman's body disappeared beneath the surface.

So the young family found a home above the streets of San Francisco. The tunnel was still there, hidden behind the boiler in their building's basement, the escape route their fugitive status demanded. But now, when the moon came up, they could rise from their beds, go to the windows, and look into an endless night, an endless panorama in which to circle, and swoop, and drink.

For Nick, the establishment of a stable from which he could safely feed became the focus of the last weeks of autumn. Most of his victims, he soon realized, were unsuitable for one reason or another: they lived too far away, they succumbed to anemia far too quickly, their personalities were too visibly altered by the contamination of their blood. Yet, for reasons Judith couldn't begin to understand, he persisted.

There was little she understood of him anymore, he admitted one cool, drizzly night, and followed her into the Balboa Cafe. Squeezing past the trolling patrons like two piranhas in a bursting can of sardines, they breathed in the overwhelming odor of blood escaping from a million pores, and ordered a couple of Cape Codders.

Nick looked about idly, in no hurry to end the mating rites of one unlucky woman in the bar. Unlike Judith, he had yet to develop an appetite for the seduction, for the kill that left its victim living. It was much easier to return to an earlier victim—they were broken, they wanted him, they had no other purpose. (It's like having a relationship, Dolores had joked once, to Judith's delight.)

The faces before him were in their twenties, in their forties; male, female, white, drunk, horny. They came through the door in groups that fanned out, or singly, like Eileen Morris.

It was she, just past the bouncer now, bright blue eyes hopeful, right hand running through her red hair for reassurance. Nick squeezed Judith's wrist, and wondered why it had taken so long to see another face he knew, that knew him.

"We have to go. There's someone here that knows me."

He saw the tension harden Judith's face, and felt her annoyance at being linked to a wanted man. She took a sip from her drink and surveyed the crowd.

"Who is it?"

"The girl with the red hair in the fisherman's sweater. She's a substitute teacher at John Swett."

Curiosity softened the set of Judith's shoulders as she spotted Eileen, and she nodded. "I'll distract her for a moment. Just walk behind me and out the door. I won't be long."

Judith made her way to Eileen, and set herself so that Nick could slip past unnoticed. A moment later he was safe on the sidewalk, looking from the outside in through the bar's plate-glass facade. They were still talking, almost as if they were old friends. When Judith laughed at something Eileen said, she passed a hand lightly over Eileen's hair.

She was going to take her.

Nick turned his back on the seduction, not really sure why he was incapable of watching. Was what was happening any more horrible because he once cared for the victim? Could he still claim the right to feel, to regret?

Pointless questions, Dolores would say, and he nodded in agreement. The man on the opposite corner smiled, and Nick crossed the street.

It was always like this, he thought as he approached the well-built homosexual in the orange Lacoste, as he calculated the encounter: a nod, a smile, and they're yours. They all want it so bad, it hurts.

The man smiled, crinkling his moustache, revealing a gap between his two front teeth. "What are you doing all the way up here?" he asked inquisitively.

Nick spread his legs and planted his hands on his hips. "Looking for something different, I guess."

"I think you found it."

"I think *you* found it," Nick teased, and pushed the man lightly into a doorway. Even as the man's arms wrapped about him, his mouth clamped onto the waiting throat.

The blood entered his body like a sluggish chocolate river, and he pressed against the sagging man, holding him up with the help of the wall behind him. It was always like this: the victim consenting, allowing the blood to flow, effecting a transfer of energy as natural as drawing vitamins from the juice of a crushed and mangled fruit. Coming alive with each surge from the vein, Nick could catch a fleeting taste of death. But the tingle it created, that promise of a magical transformation, was only a tease. He would never have the real thing—that was reserved for his victims, who were paying the price. There was no deliverance for the vampire, just process; and each time was like every other time.

Like the first time.

He had seen the woman as he and Judith left their tunnel that first night. She was a round little Filipino in her early fifties, the building's cleaning woman. While Judith waited impatiently outside, he had gone back in and asked her the time.

Her eyes never left the bucket by her feet as she extended the watch on her left wrist to him. Nick took the hand and held it, hesitating. He could feel a soft pull of resistance, but nothing overt; the woman had already consented, and was only waiting for the moment to end. Unsure he even wanted her, he circled her waist with his left arm and brought her to him. "It's not going to hurt," he whispered, and she nodded, crossing herself with her free hand.

Afterward, he had told Judith that the woman, alone and

available four nights of the week, would be the first member of his stable.

"Dolores had an archbishop," she had responded contemptuously. "And you look for floorscrubbers."

The man in his arms was gasping for air as the sudden blood loss caused him to black out. Nick had drunk enough. He let the man down gently against the doorway and turned back toward the Balboa Cafe.

Judith was standing there, scarcely ten feet away.

"Pretty chancy, taking somebody in plain sight of the bar," she mocked, and glanced down at the victim. "A faggot, huh? We're pretty desperate tonight."

Nick ignored her taunts. "Did you kill her?"

Her lips spread teasingly, displaying her weapons. "Why would I do that?"

"Because you like to kill. You've liked it since that first time, with the bail bondsman."

"No, I didn't kill her," she confessed. "I don't want her empty little body found in the Balboa Cafe's john." A pause. "That's where I took her, by the way. In one of the stalls. Just enough blood to get me through the night, because I want her for my stable. I think she's just my type."

"I think you're just trying to hurt me." There was no sense in holding any of it back. "You blame me for what happened to us, and now you want vengeance. You knew I cared for Eileen, and so you purposely destroyed her. Everything you've done since that night has been a denial of whatever humanity we still have. Of who you really are."

Her hand stroked his cheek mockingly. "Don't flatter yourself by thinking I blame you for anything. I was pathetic in my earlier life, and deserved everything I got. But now I know who I am. I've known it since I woke up in your arms and could only see your throat. I killed you, Nick, drinking your blood. And I loved it."

He remembered her kiss, and the choice that preceded it. "I'm going to get you back some day. I've got all the time in the world."

"Don't you know you disgust me?" Judith asked incredulously. *"All* victims disgust me. If Dolores hadn't insisted on keeping you, I would have left with her long ago. But she knows you're weak, she still thinks she can tempt you to help her get out of that chair. Because you can't accept what you really are."

"I'll never accept it."

"You're digging your own grave," she shrugged, and turned away. "I'm going back now. It's late."

The apartment was dark when they returned to it; the light bothered Dolores's eyes. Turning on a lamp, Nick noticed that she hadn't moved from her corner. They hadn't fed her much the last two nights, and she was hungry.

"What did you bring me tonight?" she asked crabbily, but Nick saw her eyes brighten when she noticed the squirming bag in Judith's hand.

They ignored her question, just as they ignored everything she said that was not related to their own existence. It was true that, for the moment, they needed her alive; but life, they had learned, was a matter of degree. Nick sat down in a rocking chair across the room from Dolores, while Judith dramatically pulled a live kitten from the bag by its tail.

"It's a little Felix, Dolores," she teased, watching the old woman's tongue extend just past her lips. "A little surprise for Granny from Nicky and me. Just so Granny doesn't feel she's not appreciated."

Dolores was always willing to play along; her pride had become selective, submerged. "Thank you, children. Now would you please serve your old grandmother?"

Judith looked over her shoulder at Nick, and slammed the cat like a wet rag against the wall. It died instantly, even before Judith slit its throat with the switchblade she always carried, and pressed it to Dolores's mouth.

Nick turned away, but Dolores was oblivious to the particulars of her meal. Somehow, even without her eyeteeth, her gums managed to draw in sustenance from whatever they fed her: rats, usually, with an occasional pigeon or cat. And, as long as they didn't willfully starve her, she never complained.

Nick undressed while Dolores finished the cat. When she was finally through, Judith dropped the remains back into the bag, and went into her own room. Nick, naked, picked up the dirty blanket behind Dolores's wheelchair and draped it over her head, as if she were some monstrous canary in a cage.

"Good night, Dolores," he said softly, and padded back to his empty bed. This night was over, after revealing a few more of its rules. There were many more to learn, because it was a game without end.

The Sun Over Her Shoulder

JESSIE GLANCED AT her watch as she hurried up the steps of Opera Plaza. She was late for her lunch with Eileen Morris.

It had taken her two weeks to set up the date; Eileen had not been very eager to see her. In fact, if Jessie hadn't called Calvin Shanker and asked the principal to intercede, she didn't think Eileen would ever have agreed to the meeting. Walking into Max's Son, the fancy delicatessen they had finally settled on, Jessie felt very much like a pariah.

Following the hostess to the table, she conceded that few people would look forward to lunch with the mother of a murdered child, and fewer still would have agreed had they understood her purpose. Then she saw the teacher, and knew she was right for persisting.

Jessie offered her hand before sitting down. "Hello, I'm Jessie Westerhays. Didn't we meet once at a parents-teachers get-together?"

"I can't recall."

Eileen Morris's handshake was limp, and her already-fair Irish complexion seemed more wan than Jessie remembered it, but there was no doubt in her mind that this was the lively red-haired girl who had been with Nicholas Van Lo just before Jessie introduced herself to him that first night.

"I'm sorry I'm late. Have you ordered yet?"

Eileen nodded, and Jessie turned to the waitress who had appeared by her side. "I'll have the tuna plate and a Perrier."

Settling back in her seat, Jessie launched into her well-rehearsed explanation of why she had requested this meeting. "You may think this morbid, but I worry that Mr. Van Lo— or whoever killed David Schwimmer and my daughter—may not be through with the children in your class. As Amanda's mother, I noticed certain changes in her manner prior to her death that . . . that may have come about through exposure to the killer." Jessie discreetly detailed Amanda's erratic behavior. "It seems logical that if the killer is threatening any of the other children, you may have noticed some early sign of it."

As Jessie spoke, a dreamy smile had slowly warmed Eileen's pale features; it took a few seconds of silence for her to realize that a response was called for.

"Aren't children wonderful?" She hesitated. "I mean, they all seem fine. They're only children."

This wasn't the sort of response Jessie sought, and she paused to reconsider her strategy while their lunch arrived. Eileen had ordered a small steak, rare, an order of chicken livers, and a spinach salad. That explains her coloring, Jessie thought: the poor thing's anemic.

She decided to try a different tack. "You knew Nicholas Van Lo, didn't you?"

Eileen nodded.

"The police have probably asked you all this before, but . . ." A pause, with no response. "Was there anything about him that would lead you to believe he could have done what he's accused of?"

"Oh, he didn't do it."

There was a certainty in the response, and an openness in the smile that accompanied it, that shocked Jessie. "Why do you think that?"

The smile faded to that foggy way station where it had been for most of their conversation. "I don't know," she shrugged. "I just—intuition or something, I guess."

Jessie looked at her unbelievingly, but received only a bland stare in return. Perry Mason I'm not, she finally conceded, and concentrated on her tuna salad until the waitress returned to their table.

"Taxi for Miss Morris."

It took Eileen a moment to respond. Until she did, she continued to aimlessly soak a piece of bread in the juice her steak had left.

"Okay, I'll . . . be right there."

Jessie forced a smile and extended her hand; it hung in midair while Eileen dreamily put the soggy bread in her mouth and rolled it about, as if it were a wine she were tasting for the first time.

Finally, she took Jessie's hand; Jessie could feel the bread's dampness on her fingers. Eileen left without a word, and Jessie watched her walk away toward the young cab driver before taking a napkin and drying her hand.

Later that afternoon, the cryptic lunch temporarily forgotten, Jessie sat by one of the windows in Amanda's room and waited for Tod to return home.

When she first began to frequent her daughter's room, Jessie had worried about being discovered by Tod, as if the habit were a sign of mental or emotional deterioration. But Tod had never found her there, and as the weeks passed, Jessie came to view it as the locus of her rebirth.

She could still see, very faintly, the aura of death in Amanda's mirror, and her memory still greeted her with soft shoots of pain whenever she squeezed into the little rocker by the window. When she went to a workshop in Mendocino and let Tod assume responsibility for their daughter, Jessie had admitted to herself, she ceased to be a mother. This was her true failure; this was where her guilt finally came to rest. But in this room, with the ghost of Amanda looking over her shoulder like the sun, the teary mist of her complicity was slowly evaporating into understanding, and acceptance.

The window, long since fogged by her steady breathing, clouded Tod's arrival; Jessie only knew he was there by the familiar thud of the closing car door. Putting her weight on the rocker's arms, she rose to her feet and intuitively made the decision she had been postponing all afternoon.

She would not tell Tod about Eileen Morris.

Their pursuit of Nicholas Van Lo, modest and ineffectual as it was, had become an obsession for Tod. She had gently used that word—obsession—to him three nights before, when he had come home with a dead rat wrapped in a baggie. It's like they go to that flophouse to die, he had explained to her: there's more every day, just like this one, dried up.

You went back to that place, she accused him. After you told me—

I'm going to find that man, he told her simply. I am *committed* to finding him.

No, she corrected. You're *obsessed*.

Maybe she hadn't been fair to him then; maybe, if the police had agreed with Tod that Nicholas Van Lo was a vampire, she would have stopped worrying about her husband's sanity, and simply been proud of him instead. But the police were sticking obstinately to their "Charles Manson" theory. To them, the fact that Van Lo had told his former psychiatrist that Amanda was a vampire who had killed Davey Schwimmer only added grist to their mill; the same went for his lifelong vampire dreams.

Tod thought differently. To him, the only truth greater than Amanda's death was Nicholas Van Lo's continued existence. That fact dominated his waking life, and it haunted his dreams. It made grotesque nightmares about vaginas with teeth as real and meaningful as the deaths of seven other people in a Tenderloin basement. And it made it impossible for Jessie to tell him that Eileen Morris' absent-minded soaking of a piece of bread had reminded her . . . clearly, jarringly . . . of the night she caught Amanda licking the blood off that plate.

"Hi, babe."

She kissed him lightly on the cheek, and noticed that he hadn't shaved that morning. "How was work today?"

"Real good," he answered promptly, and she sensed that his enthusiasm was genuine.

"Oh yeah? Tell me about it."

"Let me get a drink first."

She followed him into the living room, where he poured himself two fingers of Stolichnaya over ice.

"Want one?"

She shook her head and sat down on the carpet. It would take a few minutes, she knew, for him to unwind, to finish the pacing he was already starting, and talk to her. So she waited.

"I got together with Rich Schlackman today." A pregnant pause, masked by the grin she rarely saw. "He's going to do an article on the case."

Jessie said nothing, and Tod continued. "It's an interview, actually. I told him everything Fred Olds told me. I told him about all those dried-up rats. And I told him about the stakes. The stakes really got him."

"But . . . everyone knows about the stakes."

Tod swallowed a good bit of the vodka, and crouched down before her. "Everyone knows about the Exorcist massacre. Everyone knows about Charles Manson. That makes the stakes part of a ritual . . . but not the kind they thought."

His eyes, so close to hers, so painfully bright, made her want to turn away; but she resisted the impulse, and listened to his sermon. "Do you know what I saw that night, when the cops took us down there? The words that ran through my mind, looking at all those bodies with a piece of wood through them? This is like the end of a Hammer film, I thought, this is just like Dracula's castle, with all of the vampires at peace. *Except Christopher Lee got away.*"

Jessie barely succeeded in controlling her voice. "Tod, is Schlackman going to write all this?"

"He already wrote it. Second section, tomorrow morning. We couldn't get Haynes to run my picture, but what the hell."

"Do you know what you're doing?" There was no longer any point in disguising her feelings. "If Van Lo is still around . . . if he has any accomplices . . . he's going to come looking for you, Tod. You're asking him to!"

Tod smiled smugly and rose to get another drink. "That's the idea."

"You can't do it!" She was on her feet now, too. "If you're right . . . even if you're wrong . . . he'll kill you!"

"He killed me a few weeks ago, Jess. That's my ace in the hole. He's a vampire, and I'm a ghost."

The grin was fixed, blind. There was no point in contradicting him. He would never believe that the only ghost in this house was Amanda's. He would never consider what Jessie knew: that the wound in their daughter's chest had miraculously healed, and would now heal those who touched its unblemished, forgiving skin. Tod did not want the light Amanda was shedding on them, because it dispersed the darkness where his quarry hid.

Fearing the darkness, fearing for his sanity and his life, Jessie started to cry. And Tod, who loved her deeply, comforted her with soft and meaningless words.

A Crack in the Wall

THE WALL THAT supported the Westerhayses' life had a crack that made itself visible three days before Thanksgiving, when it swallowed up their daughter like a movie earthquake. Perhaps Tod knew that it was only a matter of time before the wall would collapse and come crashing down on him. Every day, every night, he would jab his fingers into the fissure, a blind man searching for meaning, daring the opening to close on his hand before he found what he was looking for. And Jessie, no longer able to see the man she had married, leaned against the other side, listening to the code of her husband's frantic touch.

The lesson only Jessie would live to learn, however, was that the wall had not only held up their happiness, it had kept out the world of grief. Why it had cracked wasn't as important as an awareness of its essential fragility. It was a membrane, a living thing, and it had been asked to do something beyond its ability. In supporting their wealth, it had shut out the poor, and in providing a dozen years of light, it had denied the reality of darkness. Strained beyond reason, it could no longer keep the demons out.

Across the city, on another side of the wall, Dolores listened to Judith's steady voice as she read aloud the article on Tod Westerhays. It told them that a human being had found one of them out. As minor as the problem seemed, it left them just one step from exposure, and disaster.

Judith tossed the paper on a table when she was finished, and turned to Dolores. "You and I better leave this city. Without him."

She didn't even glance in my direction, Nick thought, and

listened disinterestedly to Dolores's response.

"My dear, if you hadn't stumbled into my basement a few weeks ago and upset all my plans, Nicholas's little Amanda would be alive tonight, and I would be out of this chair. If you walked out the door tonight and never came back, we both know that our poor romantic would replace you soon enough, and maybe, just maybe, if Granny played her cards just right, she'd get another chance."

The two women looked briefly over at Nick. Satisfied, as if their glance confirmed her words, Dolores continued. "With you, alas, it's quite different."

"But I'm the one who keeps you alive," Judith protested. "I find those kittens you like so much. *He* knocked your tooth out—and he would have left you back in that basement if it hadn't been for me!"

"And you would have left him, and I would have left you," Dolores added sweetly. "But now, no one's leaving. We're becoming a real family, we three."

After one short cackle, she again grew serious. "And we'll remain a family, my dear, until you decide you've learned all you can from me. What bargain can I strike with you then? That will be the end of the little creatures you feed me, I'm afraid, let alone any chance of my escaping this chair. That's why I need our Nicholas. That's why I'll never abandon him."

Judith gazed at her uncomprehending. "Do you know how much he hates you? Do you really think he'd ever help you?"

"Don't answer, Dolores." Nick knew Dolores was about to say *Yes;* he suspected the old vampire understood him better than he did himself. He couldn't bear to find out *why* he would help her.

"Do that for her," Judith warned, "and never again dream of turning your back on me."

Nick shrugged, and Dolores waved her rake-like hands. "Children, children, we are drifting. We are forgetting about the legal owner of La Casa de Dolores."

"I'll kill him," Judith said simply. "I'll do it tomorrow night. I'll take his wife too, while I'm at it." A pause, and a tiny, wicked smile. "Nick had a crush on her, I think."

Dolores turned to Nick. "Isn't she wonderful?" Then, back to Judith: "No, we cannot *kill* Mr. Westerhays—not after the way his daughter died. The heat would really come down on poor Nicholas then. Mr. Westerhays will simply have to expire.

"Nicholas, do you recall tasting lips so . . . so ripe, they had the odor of . . ."

Judith gazed at him curiously, and for a moment Nick thought they were words he had whispered to her during sex. Then he felt them again, on his tongue: *like slightly rotting fruit.*

"And a ritual that was only an excuse for the sipping of blood?"

Yes, he remembered now. Before Judith, when he first arrived. He had thought they were the flotsam of his dreams.

Dolores smiled, showing him what he had done to her mouth. "Of course you remember, I only gave you those memories a few weeks ago! They came from my past, those memories of swollen lips, but weren't they also part of your dreams, long before we met? I could never have shared them with you, otherwise.

"Every person in this city dreams. All of them think they're safe from those dreams as soon as they awake. They think daylight is a wall, and they're safe behind it. But it's not a wall, is it, Nick? It's more like a membrane, isn't it, my dream lover? You fell in love peering through that membrane in the middle of the day, while I slept like the dead down the hall from you!"

Dolores laughed, the sound of two rusty knives scraping together. "Mr. Westerhays is spending quite a bit of time in his new property. I think it reminds him of his dreams. I wouldn't be at all surprised if, one of these nights, his dreams step out from behind that wall, and —how do you young people put it?

"Walk up and shake his hand."

By the next night, Tod Westerhays's dreams were waiting for him in the rooms of La Casa de Dolores. As the old vampire foresaw, they didn't have to wait long.

To officially end her period of mourning, Jessie had decided to attend the opening of Ellen Dimsdale's one-woman gallery show. Ellen was her friend as well as the person she shared her studio with, and helping to celebrate her art seemed to be an ideal way for Jessie to rejoin society.

By the time Tod pulled up in front of the south-of-Market gallery to drop her off, however, Jessie was about to change her mind.

"This is your last chance, Tod. Or I'm not going either. And we can *both* go to the movies."

Tod laughed at her anger. "She's *your* friend—I don't care what you do. If you want to see *Beverly Hills Cop* tonight, you're welcome to join me."

"Your taste in movies has really gone to pot, you know?"

"Write a letter to the editor. We love the controversy."

Jessie kept her eyes on the moving windshield wipers as she spoke. "You know, your self-pity is really starting to grate on me. I can't forget what happened either, but I also haven't forgotten that we had a life together before Amanda, and outside of Amanda. Feeling good for our friends was part of that life. If we want to get it back, we have to try, even when it hurts, even when neither of us really feels it. Like tonight."

Tod passed his hand softly down her cheek. "You're right, Jess. But I can't do it tonight. Give me a little more time. Okay?"

Jessie turned, and playfully bit his fingers. "You're not only self-pitying, you're also morbid, rude, and a couple of other insults you'd probably take as compliments."

She leaned over and kissed him. "Pick me up as soon as the movie's over. I'll be looking for you from the window."

Nick was also looking for him, but from another window. It was the one next to Mr. Slater's empty bed, in La Casa de Dolores. When he saw the rain-spattered Saab pass by slowly and pull into a parking space, he lowered the shade and smiled.

Dolores had been right, as usual.

They had been waiting for him here for three nights now. That had meant transporting Dolores from their North Beach apartment back to the tunnel behind the flophouse's furnace, and all three of them sleeping in conditions they had already forgotten. But they had to be close by for it all to work, she had insisted; they had to be close by to make Tod Westerhays's dreams come true.

Nick heard a key turning downstairs, and quickly left Slater's room. He was at the top of the landing when Tod closed the door behind him and flicked the light switch on the wall. Nothing happened, because Nick had disconnected the fuses three nights before.

"Mr. Westerhays will see," Dolores assured them, "all he needs to see."

Tod hesitated, then lit a match. After getting his bearings, he started to climb the stairs.

Certain now that their prey wasn't going to change his mind and leave, Nick moved back into the darkness at one end of the hall. He could feel Judith and Dolores, three levels below, eyes shut in the tunnel.

He could feel it all coming alive.

Tod paused at the top of the stairs, unsure which way to turn, before deciding in Nick's direction. Feeling along the walls with his hands, he advanced slowly until he came to the first door. A soft green glow, no stronger than a night-light, emanated from its keyhole. Tod's hand closed around the knob, and he opened the door.

The sourceless green light illuminated a silence broken only by the measured creaking of Amanda's rocking chair. Its curved back was facing Tod. He moved around it and looked down at the dwarf that was cradling his daughter.

He was old and wrinkled, with open sores leaking the corners of his mouth, from the sides of his nostrils. A dirty red stocking cap crowned his massive head.

Tod began to speak, then hesitated when he noticed that one of the dwarf's hands was moving furtively beneath the folds of Amanda's skirt. His fists clenched even as he sensed the powerlessness that came with dreams.

"What are you doing to her?"

The dwarf ran a tongue the shape of a sausage over the sores on his lips before answering in a high-pitched, child's voice.

"I'm stroking her. I'm stroking my little pet."

Tod took a half-step forward. His legs felt like bags of sand. "I want her back."

The dwarf's tongue waggled in midair, as if it were deliberating Tod's request, and he noticed the hard, knobby growths that marred its surface.

"Then take her," the dwarf decided, and pulled his hand out

from beneath her skirt. Tod saw the brown rat squirming in the dwarf's grasp, as Amanda fell to the floor with a hollow thud.

Laughing at Tod's horrified expression, the dwarf rocked furiously until one of the chair's rockers came down on Amanda's wrist. It broke off with a sharp, cracking sound, and Tod realized that the dwarf had only been playing with a ceramic replica of his daughter.

Tod backed out of the room and into the darkness of the corridor. Leaning against a wall, he listened to the dwarf's shrieking laughter while it smashed the doll to pieces on the floor.

It's not quite like you dreamed it, is it, Tod? Nick asked silently, and saw the beads of perspiration breaking across the face of his pursuer. *You pass through a dream door by door, room by room . . . but are you still sure you will wake from this one? There was no doll in your dreams, Tod. And now that you've come this far, now that there's no turning back, you're afraid. Because you're sleepwalking, but you know this is no dream.*

Suddenly a green mist poured from the doorsill by Tod's feet. His shaking fingers pushed the door open, and he entered the room.

There was no rocker in this one: only a little table, a chair, and a bed. Lying on the bed was a bare-chested man with bulging eyes and no chin. When he saw Tod, the chinless man sat up and grinned a demented, saw-toothed grin.

Tod addressed him in a quiet, pleading tone. "Where's my little girl?"

The chinless man shook his head from shoulder to shoulder.

Tod's head tipped to one side. "Please let me have her back."

The man hesitated, then reached behind the bed and pulled up another of the dolls that eerily resembled his daughter.

"That's not her," Tod explained. "That's not Amanda."

The chinless man nodded, and bit off the doll's head. After a moment, a rat crawled out over the jagged edges of the neck.

Tod staggered out of the room, a hand cupped over his mouth. He did not look up until he ran into Nick in the shadows at the end of the hall. Nick could smell the rancid odor of sweat and adrenaline, the bubbles of fear Westerhays was expelling with every breath.

"Where's my little girl?"

You don't even recognize me anymore, Nick thought, and tilted his head to the right. Tod opened the door, and stepped inside. He never noticed that Nick had followed him in.

"I found you, Amanda."

Amanda was seated on the floor, holding a Raggedy Ann doll. She looked pink and healthy, dressed in a red-and-white bibbed dress and black buckled shoes. But when Tod spoke to her, she only smiled demurely, and rocked her doll.

Tod knelt down before her. "Do you know who I am, honey?"

Amanda nodded absently, never looking away from her doll.

Tod felt one blonde braid, almost as if to make sure it were real. "Do you know who . . . you are?"

"I'm daddy's little girl," she answered. Then she raised the doll's neck to her mouth and tore off its head.

Tod straightened up from his crouch as if a puppeteer overhead had suddenly yanked his strings. But only sawdust spilled out from the headless doll's neck.

Amanda looked down at the grains, then up again at Tod. He could see the confusion in her face. Gently, he took the headless doll from her hands and tossed it into the darkness along the walls of the room.

"It's okay, honey," he soothed, fighting back the pounding of his own runaway heart. "It's going to be all right. You're not really one of them, you see? You're . . . one of us."

Amanda gritted her teeth and shook her head wildly. When Tod leaned down and touched her shoulder, she twitched spasmodically and he almost missed the shadow that emerged from the folds of Amanda's skirt.

It was a rat.

"Amanda!" Tod picked her up by the shoulders, and felt them . . . shift.

"Mandy, are you . . ."

Amanda looked at him wildly, and spread her jaws. A rat leaped on him from her mouth.

Tod dropped her instinctively, and Amanda fell to the floor. She could have been a sawdust doll herself, jerking violently as rats leaped from her mouth, as tails waggled from her ears, as her eyeballs fell in and were replaced by snarling rat heads.

Tod whirled around, but Nick was no longer behind him;

he was by the door, at the perimeter of a space that was swiftly turning into a churning, shrieking sea of rats.

"Help me!"

Nick shook his head, and closed the door.

Tod breathed in faster and faster, listening to the screaming of his oxygen-choked veins, to the adrenaline burning through his pores, his hair, the pupils of his eyes. He looked back down at what had been his daughter, and felt his heart leap just before he did. After her. Into them.

He was changing with her; changing fast, from blonde, to red, to black.

Requiem

BY THE TIME the gallery closed its doors that night and a very tipsy Ellen Dimsdale offered her a ride home, Jessie already suspected the worst. Ignoring Ellen's suggestion that she give Tod until midnight to sober up and come home, Jessie insisted that her friend take her past La Casa de Dolores. The request unsettled Ellen so much that she drove across Market to the Tenderloin without saying another word.

"It's that building up there on the right," Jessie pointed.

"Okay," Ellen said sleepily, and brought the BMW to a jerky stop.

"Jessie, isn't that Tod sitting on the doorstep?"

But Jessie was already out of the car.

Even as she approached, Jessie could see that Tod was very pale. Crouching next to him, she touched his forehead. The skin was cold and clammy. When she cupped his chin and turned his face to hers, his eyes failed to focus.

"Is he all right?" Ellen called from the car.

"I think he's in shock," Jessie answered in a faraway voice. "Help me carry him into the car."

Jessie held Tod in her arms in the back seat until they reached the U.C. Med Center. Very quietly, so that Ellen wouldn't hear, she asked him to tell her exactly what had happened. She listened carefully to his silence until the emergency room staff gently lifted him from her lap. The doctor in charge explained to her that Tod had died from terminal shock shortly after she found him on the doorstep.

Jessie woke up the next morning just before noon. She had no memory of getting home from the hospital, or how the Saab came to be parked in her driveway; what had been left in her bottle of Valium had gotten her through the night. Now, fighting a champagne-and-sedative hangover, she stumbled down to the kitchen in her nightgown and made herself some coffee. Twenty minutes later, her mind had cleared sufficiently; she was finally about to put her face in her hands, and cry.

She cried until the striations in her throat begged her to cease, until the headache caused by trying to squeeze tears from her depleted ducts finally stunned her into silence. She went upstairs then, drew a bath, and used the water's hermetic pressure to seal in what was left of her pain. She had lost too much already, what sorrow and anger remained, she was determined to keep.

The water calmed her, helped her feel at home with the awareness that she had known, known as the gallery crowd had thinned and Tod still didn't arrive, known as she had in Mendocino that her daughter was doomed. In the bath's warmth, the urge to pluck out her own eyes from grief and frustration dissipated as the muscles in her fingers relaxed, as her heart and mind came to terms with the curse of second sight and blinding impotence.

Late that afternoon, after initiating the interminable process of funeral and burial arrangements, of repetitive calls to relatives whose closeness in blood and law meant nothing as far as sharing an understanding of what had really happened, she received a call from the inspector in charge of the basement massacre investigation.

He read her the autopsy report over the phone. Tod had died from a combination of an overexuberant oxygen-consuming reflex, and overactivity of the sympatho-adrenal system leading to a state of shock caused by a sudden release of adrenaline. "In layman's terms, they believe your husband suffered a massive heart attack."

"That's impossible," Jessie blurted. "Tad was only forty-two, his blood pressure was normal, he had no history . . ."

The inspector respectfully let the silence linger before responding. "The responses of your husband's system, Mrs. Westerhays, are common signs of . . . of fear. What happened to him could happen to anyone, given the unusual circumstances. It's certainly not unheard of."

Jessie thought about what the inspector was implying. "So his death is no longer in your hands?"

Another pause. "That's correct. But if there's—"

Jessie thanked him for his courtesy, and hung up the phone. There was nothing they could do, she conceded, to investigate how an otherwise sane man could be . . .

Scared to death. That's what the man on the phone had tried to tell her.

Glancing at the kitchen clock, she dialed Vic Varney's law office, and told the attorney of Tod's death.

"Oh Christ, Jess—what is happening to this world?" His voice broke, and he had to pause before continuing. "I'm so sorry."

"I want that property out of my portfolio as soon as possible, Vic."

"It'll be gone in forty-eight hours. I don't know why Tod wanted to keep it."

"The buyer has to agree to tear it down. And turn it into a parking lot."

"I know how you feel, Jess. When they showed me Lisa's body . . ." Vic's voice trailed off. "Frankly, I won't be able to get you half as much as it's worth."

"That's all right. I won't be needing as much money as I used to." She didn't have time for delays. "Are there . . . papers I have to sign?"

"There's no hurry on any of this, Jessie. I can mail them to you, if you'd like."

"I'll be down at your office in half an hour. I know it's late, but wait for me."

Jessie dressed quickly, and chose an unfashionably large purse. Before leaving the house, she sorted through her collection of Henckels kitchen utensils and picked out a boning knife with a four-and-a-half-inch blade. It fit comfortably along the bottom of her purse.

The bank of fog settled over the city on the morning of Tod's burial. It didn't lift until long after the invisible sun had set.

The black veil covering Jessie's face filtered out the minister's eulogy, allowing her to focus on her own thoughts. Although she had put on the veil just that morning for the funeral, Jessie felt she had been looking through it ever since Tod died.

During the two days prior to the funeral, she had been politely distant to the friends who called or came by with Tupperware containers and sympathy; her manner did not change for the relatives that arrived from different parts of the country. She knew she had frightened away many of the people who had been a part of her life, and conceded that perhaps a psychiatrist would agree with some of them in considering her temporarily insane. It was the price she had to pay to preserve her precious focus.

Insane or not, her mind had wisely warded off all of the incapacitating questions that survivors always ask themselves. It allowed no distractions while she began to plot her revenge.

Revenge was the alchemical solution transforming her mind into the filtering device that allowed her to feel only what she needed to feel, to see only what she had to see. It guided her from her bed each morning, and through the dizzying day. It was the voice telling her that *someone* had injected the fear that stopped Tod's heart.

The police's efforts at solving Amanda's murder had produced no more results than a reading of tea leaves, but Jessie already knew where she would begin her search: with another visit to Eileen Morris.

Then her friend Ellen touched her softly on the hand, and whispered that the service was over. It was time to go to the cemetery.

Jessie lifted her veil to thank her, and absentmindedly felt through her purse for her car keys. When her gloved fingers brushed over the boning knife, she smiled.

They had left her with nothing. She was living only for revenge, because only revenge was allowing her to live.

The last time Jessie looked at the sky that night before she went to bed, it was a brilliant, moonless indigo blue. Squinting hard, she thought she could see Tod's headstone, the relatives saying good-bye after the funeral, the policeman who had called to confirm what she already knew—all of the last three days— fading past the most distant star. After the services that afternoon, all of that was behind her. The next morning would bring on the commencement of what she had to do.

Peering at her reflection in the medicine-cabinet mirror, she noticed the whitehead that had appeared by the side of her mouth. She tried to recall the last time she had bought a tube of Clearasil, and remembered that she hadn't renewed her prescription of Valium since she emptied the bottle the night of Tod's death.

Vengeance and Valium don't mix, she joked to herself, and turned off the bathroom light.

Jessie slept soundly that night, as she had—with drugs, and then without—since Amanda's death. Her bloodstream, spared so far from the plague that had poisoned her family, coursed quietly, free of sedatives for the first time in almost a month. Her brain, freed of the blinders imposed on it for so long, snorted, kicked up on its hind legs, and galloped blindly into a waiting dream.

The dream was an indigo mare, with a mane like blowing curtains, and hooves as sharp as rain striking a windowpane. When it tossed her to the ground, and she sat up in her bed, Jessie could not believe that it was gone, or that the two figures outside the window had been left in its place.

But they *were* there, tapping patiently on the glass, waiting for her to come to them, as they had come for her.

Jessie felt a chill as she rose from the bed and slipped into Tod's old woolen robe. It felt right, putting that on, as she prepared to greet her lost family.

"Hi, mommy."

Amanda was pale, and strangely disembodied, as she and Tod floated just feet from where Jessie stood. But she was smiling, smiling like Jessie hadn't seen her smile in months: eagerly, lovingly, with her long white teeth.

"Hi, baby." Jessie looked over her daughter at Tod, and they exchanged an easy, comfortable glance.

He looked good, too.

"Aren't you going to let us in, hon?"

Jessie placed her hand on the latch, and thought about how good it would feel to hug them both again, to smell Amanda's hair and feel their kisses on her skin. She wrapped her fingers around the latch, and hesitated.

"Before I let you in, there are some things I have to tell

you. If you still want to come in after, I'll open the window."

She saw Tod squeeze Amanda's shoulder, and they both nodded.

"I've been a lousy mom, Amanda." Jessie expelled her breath, then wiped the window so that she could still see them. "I couldn't help you when you were in trouble. I didn't know how to fight, so I ran. I gave you up."

Jessie paused, and brushed a tear from her cheek. "All I can do now is promise that I'll never give you up again."

Amanda pressed her fingertips against the glass, and Jessie pressed hers from the inside. Ice formed instantly where they touched.

"I forgive you, mommy."

Jessie tried to laugh, but only a sob came out. She no longer tried to control her crying.

"Tod, I have a confession to make to you, too." She gazed into his cool gray eyes and knew already that, no matter what she said, she would be forgiven. "I let Nick Van Lo make love to me on the night that Davey died. I never did it before, and I'll never do it again. It happened only because I was afraid, because . . . I wanted to let it all go."

Tod pressed his lips together, so that only his canines protruded over the soft flesh, and Jessie thought about how much her revelation must have hurt him.

"I left you both, and now you've left me. But I want you to understand that I've learned from . . . the pain I've caused. That's all I can say. If you stay with me, if your memories keep me warm and safe at night, I'll find that man and drive him from our lives forever."

Jessie looked through the glass as they spread their arms and opened their mouths. Their tongues were the color of black grapes, but she never noticed.

They wanted her.

She pressed down on the latch and flung open the window, welcoming the relief of the night: and in it came on hooves of glass, forcing her to cling to its mane while it carried her back to her bed.

Relief was an indigo mare.

PART SIX

LAST RITES

Why speak of rapture
And eternity possessed
When what you call love
Is colder than death

—*J.M. Kundry*

Nero's Fiddle

WHEN EILEEN MORRIS emerged from her apartment building and hailed a taxi, Jessie checked her watch. She had been waiting in her car, half a block away, for almost two hours.

The hunt had begun.

She noticed another taxi rounding the corner as she switched on the ignition. After only a moment of hesitation, she jumped out of her own car and flagged down the second cab. After instructing the young driver to follow her friend in the taxi in front of them, she settled back in the seat and smiled with satisfaction.

Jessie sensed the strange looks the driver was giving her via the mirror, and ignored them. It had been a snap judgment, deciding to follow Eileen in this cab, but she was sure it was the correct one. Nicholas Van Lo was familiar with the Saab, and she had a strong hunch it was to Van Lo that they were heading.

Even though hunches were all she had to go on, Jessie felt confident of her eventual success. Van Lo had made a mistake leaving her alive and with nothing left to lose. The strange, exorcising dream of the previous night had served to strengthen this perspective, clearing the decks for her while she slept: there were no loose pins for her to trip over anymore. Van Lo could still kill her, but he could no longer hurt.

"Have a good time, lady."

Jessie looked up into the driver's young, freckled face, and wondered if he had picked her up once before. Then she turned to the Folsom Street address they had stopped at, and blushed as she read the name painted over a discreet entrance.

They were at Nero's Fiddle.

Jessie tipped him generously, and hesitated before the heavy black door. Nero's Fiddle was San Francisco's most notorious omnisexual bathhouse, frequented by middle-aged spouses getting away from the kids for a night as well as a bevy of sex-seeking singles and couples, both gay and straight. Jessie knew all this, because she'd read an article on it in Tod's paper. And it was all she thought she'd ever have to know.

What is Eileen Morris doing here, she asked herself, and laughed aloud at the possible encyclopedia of answers. The laugh gave her the encouragement she needed; she opened the door, handed the cashier ten dollars, and stepped inside.

No satyr jumped on her in the first thirty seconds; no one even told her she had to exchange her jumpsuit for a towel. Relaxing a bit, she saw that the room she was in had a long, mirrored, ornately Victorian bar running along one wall. People were talking, more or less intimately, all along it. Some sported only towels, but most—including Eileen and the black-haired woman she was whispering to—were fully dressed. Jessie recognized her as the woman she had seen with Nicholas Van Lo on the bus, the day that Amanda died.

Jessie moved to the other end of the crowded bar, where she could keep an eye on them without being noticed. She ordered an Alvaro margarita from the bare-chested bartender, and gloated briefly on her luck. At this rate, she would be calling the police with Van Lo's whereabouts before the night was over.

Already imagining the moment, she turned her head to see if there were a public telephone close by. There was, not more than twenty feet to her left, tucked away in the shadows between two walls. Standing before it was the taxi driver who had driven her here.

No wonder it seemed so easy, she scolded herself. They were watching you the entire time, just as they always watched Eileen Morris. Because now Jessie remembered where she had seen the young cabbie before: he had picked up Eileen after their lunch in Opera Plaza.

Jessie looked back at the young man; his gaze was still on her.

If they had been shadowing her every move all this time,

she conceded, there was no point in her watching Eileen, no point in anything, because she was as good as dead. She may as well go see what the man by the phone wanted to do next.

Draining her margarita in one long swallow, she walked directly up to him. Her right hand rested nervously near the bottom of her purse.

Jessie could tell immediately that he was surprised by her approach. She decided to press her momentary advantage. "I can call the police from the phone right behind you. They'd be here in five minutes, and your girlfriend would be under-going some very serious questioning inside half an hour."

She saw the tendons in his neck quiver angrily. "There's no law in this city against being a dyke, lady. As I'm sure you know."

Jessie dismissed his words as a rather unimaginative insult, and tried again. "How long have you been following me?"

"About as long as you've been following Eileen," he snapped. "What's the matter, jealous that she dumped you for someone her own age?"

Jessie's hand relaxed around the knife handle, and she stepped back slightly. "Who are you?"

"I'm your cabbie, lady. The one you gave that big Pacific Heights tip to."

Jessie choked off a reflexive grin and noticed for the first time how very young her cab driver looked. "You're Eileen's boyfriend, aren't you?"

The hesitation gave him away, and Jessie removed her hand from her purse. Relief over not being exposed melted into sympathy for what she could already guess had been happening.

"My name is Jessie Westerhays. My daughter was in the class that Eileen took over from Nicholas Van Lo. She—"

"I know," the youth said quickly, sparing her the painful words. "Eileen told me about it."

He extended his hand shyly. "Matt Hemphill."

Jessie took his hand. "Are you old enough for me to buy you a drink, Matt?"

"My cab company thinks so." He grinned, and they moved back to the bar.

They squeezed in between two burly gay men and a tall, blonde woman, so that the women at the other end of the bar would be hard pressed to pick them out from the panorama of faces reflected on the bar mirror. After ordering a Miller and a second margarita, Jessie explained in very general terms the similarities in behavior she had noticed between Amanda and Eileen. She was careful to say nothing about Nicholas Van Lo beyond the fact that he was the police's only suspect.

Matt waggled his thumb toward the other end of the bar. "Do you know anything about her?"

"Just that she's a friend of Van Lo's."

Matt nodded. "Her name's Judith Harper. She's been vamping Eileen every few nights for the past two weeks. Or longer, for all I know."

Jessie touched the back of his hand lightly. "Do you want to tell me about it?"

Matt shrugged, and peered down the neck of his beer bottle. "I guess the thing is, she's older than I am. Four years only, but—I'm nineteen. We got together just after she got that job at John Swett and, well, it's been great. I don't want to come on like Mick Jagger or something to an older woman like you, but it's not like she's the only girlfriend I've ever had. She's just the best."

Jessie ignored the second reference to her advanced age, and nodded.

"Eileen comes across like a real party animal," he grinned briefly in recollection, "but there's so much more to her than someone who likes to have fun. She cares, all the time. Do you know what I mean?"

"I think so."

"You just had to know her before," he said urgently, and his voice cracked.

Jessie waited a moment before asking him how he thought Eileen had changed.

"Other than sailing over to the isle of Lesbos, you mean? It's hard to put into words, because . . . it's like she's dead. Like there's nothing inside. When she lost interest in me, she lost interest in everything."

He glanced quickly at Jessie. "Does that sound conceited? Cause believe me," flashing a quirky, gap-toothed grin, "there's not much for me to be conceited about. When I asked her if there was someone else, she told me, real matter-of-factly. Her name is Judith Harper, she said, and the sun rises and sets with her for me. And then she giggled. With me in tears almost, and—"

Matt gave her an open look. "No, with me in tears, period. Not that it meant much, because . . . it's like I never meant anything to her."

They finished their drinks in silence and watched Judith Harper nuzzle Eileen's neck in the mirror. Jessie couldn't begin to guess how the boy next to her could figure in her quest; yet, somehow, she was sure he would.

"Uh, Jessie, could I ask you something?"

She noticed that the rust-colored sideburns dipping before his ears grew down from his head, and not from his cheeks. He doesn't even shave yet, for God's sake.

"Sure, Matt."

"Are you divorced?"

Jessie acknowledged how reasonable the question was, considering her solitary presence here. "My husband died last week. I think that Nicholas Van Lo had something to do with it as well."

Matt looked away as if he'd been slapped. "Shit, I'm sorry. I mean . . ." Finally, he blurted it out. "Lady, you're unbelievable."

Jessie smiled and pinched his arm. "Another senior-citizen remark, kiddo, and I'll report you for being underage to the taxi company."

An embarrassed grin. "Oh, you mean what I said about Eileen dropping you for someone younger? I was just trying to ding you. You're a knockout, lady."

"Is that a pitch for another beer?"

"No, it just means you're a knockout. And before I blow this completely, maybe you ought to head home. They'll be less likely to spot me if I'm alone."

Jessie hesitated. "What about her friend?"

"Oh, I see what you mean. I'll follow her home, if you'd like. I've become a real pro at tailing people," he said, grinning. "I can call you afterward, if you'd like."

"That's okay. I think I'd rather have you come by tomorrow,

and we can consider our next move. If you want to, that is. I don't know if you really understand what you could be involving yourself with."

He looked at her frankly. "You're right, I don't. But I know who I'm doing it for, and that's good enough."

Jessie knew immediately that it was. She wrote her address and phone number on a napkin, and handed it to him. "Are you free tomorrow?"

"I've got a day shift tomorrow, but I can be at your place by four."

"Then tomorrow at four it is." Jessie stood up. "Are you sure you don't mind sitting here alone?"

"Are you kidding? Maybe I'll get lucky and meet some chick who wants to do more than talk," he joked. "Somebody who's been watching me talk to you all this time."

Jessie's lips moved briefly, and then she strode briskly toward the exit. Nick, who had been watching her talk to the red-haired boy all this time, decided to let her go for the time being. He knew where she could be found.

He had arrived at Nero's Fiddle shortly after Judith, but even she didn't know he was there, sitting at one of the small tables in the overhang that looked down on the bar. She didn't know he followed her every night after they left the apartment, that he observed her every move.

And now his observation had yielded very interesting fruit. He never would have suspected that Jessie Westerhays had the fanaticism of her husband, but her presence here suggested otherwise. She and the kid still nursing a beer down there would bear watching.

Then Judith and Eileen moved away from the bar, arm in arm, and Nick rose from his seat. When he saw what door they passed through, he dropped a five-dollar bill on his table and moved to the nearest exit.

Nero's Fiddle, like most of the other bathhouses in the city, catered to a variety of sexual tastes. Apart from standard amenities like private cubicles, showers, steam rooms, and Jacuzzi, it housed open rooms to satisfy every fetish. There were two dungeons, with very real manacles and whips hanging from its walls of papier-mâché stone. There was a gold-painted room shaped like the inside of an egg, with hot oil oozing from its curving walls. There was a rather elaborate labyrinth with mattresses tucked away in its corners, where wanderers could meet in darkness and disengage discreetly.

There was also the second floor, which cost an extra twenty dollars to enter. An open space of almost five thousand square feet, it was unfurnished except for the cushions strewn across the floor. No sexual activity was allowed there, and the drinks the ubiquitous waitresses served were twice the price of those downstairs. The attraction of the space—and there was usually a crowd one quarter the size of the one downstairs every night—were the two thousand panes of reinforced one-way glass embedded every four feet or so along the floor.

From there, one could theoretically watch anything on the first floor: every cubicle, every dungeon, every toilet. And if one knew his way around the second floor, as Nick did by now, one could swiftly move over the section covering the maze and find Judith and Eileen before one article of clothing was shed, before one drop of blood was spilled.

After buying a drink he would never touch, Nick dropped to the floor and placed a cushion under his chin. Judith, apparently satisfied with the intersection she had chosen, put her hand on Eileen's breastbone. Nick watched as Eileen began to undo the buttons on Judith's tunic.

Judith's arms hung loosely by her side with the regal bearing of a queen being undressed by a handmaiden, as Eileen lifted the tunic over her shoulders and allowed her hands to brush the tips of Judith's nipples. On her knees now, she lingered over the sound of each button popping free on Judith's jeans, then peeled the denim from her thighs. Her task completed, she gazed at her mistress with awe.

Undress yourself, Nick knew Judith was commanding beneath the glass. Eileen slowly removed her thin black belt and the loose thigh-length smock it girded. She was thinner than Judith, almost boyish in figure. Judith ran a finger from her navel to her throat, and Eileen turned her head to one side, offering her jugular.

In his mind, Nick heard Judith whisper, *Not yet*. They wrapped their arms around each other and sank to the floor.

Nick felt himself coming alive, just as he used to in the old days, when he and Judith could still make love. That was what put him under her spell from the beginning: the power of those hands and thighs to lead him up the thorny vines of lovemaking, until his lips could touch the petals of death. Just as she had once been the meaning of his life, so now she was a vampire, the mirror image of his soul. Watching her was the nearest he could come to accepting himself.

A hissing came through the glass and into his ears as the women's limbs stretched like snakes, and like snakes wrapped their fangs over the other's tail. There was no venom, only blood. Judith took far more than she gave, because this was a different life. When she had enough, she let her head loll back. Licking off the blood around her mouth, she smiled lazily up at Nick.

Nick averted his gaze for the brief moment he thought she had actually been looking at him through the glass. That was when his sideways glance first noticed the shadow moving just beyond the sweating women. Even before he moved to the next pane of glass and made sure, he knew it belonged to the boy who had been talking with Jessie Westerhays at the bar.

Nick raced across the room to the nearest staircase, hurdling a series of surprised voyeurs. There were two ways for the boy to leave the labyrinth from the spot where Nick had seen him; if Nick picked the right one, he could take him easily, pinning him against one of the sharply angled walls. And if he didn't, there was going to be hell to pay.

Picking his way through the corridors as if he were guiding himself from above, Nick homed in on the mouse that had wandered into his maze.

The Ambush

THE DIGITAL CLOCK over the Crocker bank read ten minutes until four as Jessie sped past it. She was going to get home just in time for her meeting with Matt Hemphill.

She had called Inspector Durning that morning and asked for an appointment with him. The inspector told her to come by that very afternoon, any time after two. Jessie was there promptly on the hour, and mentioned Judith Harper's name in the first few moments; she then spent the next forty-five minutes answering the inspector's curious questions. The interrogation would have been much quicker if she hadn't deleted Matt and Eileen's names from her story, but Jessie suspected that the last thing the red-haired schoolteacher needed was a visit from a homicide detective.

Instead, she simply told the inspector that the name of the woman she had seen on the bus with Nicholas Van Lo came to her in a dream the night before. The reason it had lodged in her subconscious, she now remembered, was because Van Lo had mentioned his girlfriend to her once in passing.

"Halloween night?"

Jessie nodded, and the inspector wearily began to scrape at the loose edges of her story. He spent as long as he did only because his experience told him there had to be more than Jessie was offering. But dreams and conveniently jarred memories, Jessie knew, are safe as pearls in an oyster. Durning finally closed his notebook and spoke into the intercom on his desk.

"McCarthy. Run a missing persons on a Judith Harper."

"Harper, like Paul Newman?"

Durning sighed. "Like Paul Newman, McCarthy. Anything interesting turns up, do a complete check on her."

The inspector asked Jessie if she would like to wait for the report, and she nodded. Half an hour later, a clerk brought in a long sheet of green computer paper.

Judith Harper, nineteen and the product of a broken home, had been enrolled in a nursing program in Daly City as part of her probation for the suspected arson of her mother's house. San Francisco General Hospital reported a visit she made to their emergency room after attempting to slit her wrists.

"She's been missing from the nursing program ever since," Durning concluded.

"And the dates?" Jessie asked.

The inspector nodded. "It all matches up."

Durning had thanked Jessie for the information, and promised to contact her as soon as they picked up Judith Harper. He also warned her to be careful.

Turning onto her street, Jessie argued with herself that she *was* trying to be careful. That was why she had gone to the police, even though she doubted they would "pick up" Judith Harper very soon. She had no desire to commit the fatal mistake that Tod had made: to have her sense of purpose mutate into an obsessive, hallucinatory crusade. If she wanted to capture the vengeance that had eluded Tod, she would have to recognize her limits.

Those limits also applied to Matt, her newly found young ally. Their conversation the previous night had muffled the pulse of her loneliness, and she had felt reassured by his quick mind and street-wise brashness. But now Jessie could only remember his goofy smile with the space between the two front teeth . . . and worried about where his lost Eileen would lead him.

Dancing with Nick Van Lo, she had caught a glimpse of his soul. That glimpse, she felt, revealed more than any psychiatric profile ever would. She had sensed who he was, and what he could do. Whether her knowledge would shield Matt any better than it had her own family, only time would tell.

Walking up to her door, she saw the letter peeking out from the doorsill, and bent to pick it up. It was from Matt.

Dear Jessie,

I'm writing this letter tonight, while what I saw is
still fresh in my mind, so that you'll understand why I
won't be at your house tomorrow at four.

I followed Eileen and Judith Harper into a section of
Nero's Fiddle called the Labyrinth. It's a sort of maze
with lots of turns and blind alleys where people do whatever in the dark. To make a long story short, I thought
I was watching them make love. But instead I saw a
vampire drink the blood of a human being.

I don't know how much you know, and how much
you kept back last night. I can guess, but I can't really
be sure—that's why I've got to be careful, even with
you. Calling somebody a vampire sounds crazy, I know.
If I were your age I'd probably run right to a shrink. But
I'm still a teenager, and I can't deny what my eyes saw.

It all boils down to my having to get some proof.
Tomorrow I'll visit Eileen at the school and get her to
tell me where she's going that night. One of my cabbie
buddies will pick her up and run her around long enough
for me to get there first. Judith Harper is going to get a
fair shot at my neck—but I'm going to get a better one
at hers.

This may be shitty to say, but even though I feel really
bad about what I think has happened to Eileen, it makes
me more comfortable with the whole thing. Because I
can get a grip on it now, I think.

One way or another, I'll call you tomorrow morning.
In the meantime, wish me luck.

                        —Matt

Jessie folded the letter and looked up at the unforgiving sky.
It was getting dark.

Matt shivered in his down jacket as he trudged up Mount
Davidson toward his rendezvous with Judith Harper, who was
waiting for Eileen by the giant cross at the top.

Wooded and desolate, it was the perfect place for an ambush, and he had come prepared. Pausing down by the base, he had checked the straps he had sewn into the inside of his jacket. They held the familiar tools of the trade: a rubber mallet, a surveyor's spike, and a knife.

He saw her as he reached the crest, and looked about to make sure they were alone. She was leaning against the cross, arms folded over the front of her shiny black Eisenhower jacket, her black hair curling over the upturned collar. Even in the darkness, the red swelling of her lips was plainly visible.

She didn't seem surprised by his approach. Matt nervously adjusted the scarf wrapped tightly around his neck, and nodded.

"How's it going?"

A glint of the tooth. "Nice night."

Matt blew smoke with his breath and grinned. "Yeah. Nice and cold."

Judith smiled, and raised one heel against the side of the cross. "Meeting someone up here?"

"Nah," he said, grinning again. "Who'd want to meet up here in the dark?"

"Someone who's not afraid of the dark."

"That counts me out. I'm scared shitless of the dark."

She looked at him quizzically. "Then why are you here?"

"I like to scare myself."

She laughed, and her tongue raced quickly around her lips. "Do I scare you?"

"Not yet."

Her arms uncrossed, and she touched the front of his parka. "Do you want me to scare you? Really scare you to death?"

Matt nodded, and Judith tangled her fingers in his hair as she brought his mouth down to hers. Wrapping his arms around her, he let her lips stray from his mouth, across his cheek, and to his left ear, where the edge of the scarf jutted stiffly.

"Do you want me to take off my scarf?" he asked hoarsely.

Judith nodded, smiling.

"Let me zip open my jacket while I'm at it," he suggested. "That way I can feel more of you."

Judith cupped Matt's ears with her hands while his fingers moved quickly inside his jacket; her fingertips flinched as they felt the concussive impact of the stone Nick brought down on Matt's head.

She was snarling even as the youth's knees buckled and he collapsed between them. "What the fuck are you doing? *What are you doing here?*"

"Saving your stupid life." Nick lifted the front of Matt's parka open with a boot tip and showed her the weapons he had been reaching for.

Judith gazed at the spike unbelievingly, then turned back to Nick. "How did you know..."

"Your cruelty's making you careless, Judith. There's no reason to lead them on like that before you take them."

But she didn't care about that. "You follow me around?"

"He follows you around. He was at Nero's Fiddle last night, having a drink with Tod Westerhays's widow at the other end of the bar from where you were nuzzling his girlfriend. After Jessie left, he followed you into the Labyrinth and watched while you sucked her up. I thought I'd better keep an eye on you tonight."

"Why didn't you tell me tonight when we woke?"

"Would you have believed me?"

Judith laughed at herself. "Okay. I owe you one. I'm not even going to ask how you know what he was watching in that maze."

"You don't owe me anything," Nick said quietly.

Judith ignored the sentiment behind his words, and pointed at Matt. "Tell you what. I like this kid's spirit, and my little schoolteacher's blood is getting damn thin. I'll trade you her for him, even up."

Nick said nothing, but Judith persisted. "Come on, you know you like her type. A real martyr. She'll follow a shit like you to the ends of the earth."

"Do what you want, Judith."

"Oh, I will," she agreed, sinking to her knees by Matt's body. "I always do."

Comfort from a Black Angel

JESSIE DROPPED MATT'S letter into her purse. It took her less than two minutes to decide what to do next.

The Veterans Cab Company was located on Army Street, at the other end of the city. Jessie arrived as the last of the night shift pulled away from the Quonset hut that served as headquarters.

She entered the ramshackle structure, and coughed as the atmosphere of stale air and cigar smoke wended up her nostrils. There was a desk in the center of the room, where a paunchy man in his forties with a headset over his ears barked instructions into a microphone. Wiping the irritation from her eyes, she strode up and stood before him.

"Can I help you, ma'am?"

"I hope so. Is Matt Hemphill working tonight?"

The dispatcher checked the duty sheet on his desk. "Hemphill checked out at three this afternoon. He's not due back until tomorrow evening."

"Oh dear." Jessie gripped her purse with both hands. "My name is Jessie Westerhays. I'm Matt's aunt. There's been a death in the family, and . . ."

She gave him an expression as winningly helpless as she could muster. "I live over in Walnut Creek, and I don't have Matt's address here in the city. I'm lucky I even remembered what taxi company he works for!"

The dispatcher eased back in his chair. "And you'd like me to give it to you?"

Jessie leaned forward eagerly. "I'm sure it's against all sorts of regulations, but if you could make an exception in this case," lowering her eyes, "we'd all be eternally grateful."

The dispatcher winked and copied the address onto a slip of paper. "I'll have the missus say a novena for the deceased."

Jessie read the address and thanked the man again before returning to her car.

The Mission District address had struck her immediately as strangely familiar; when she reached it, she realized why. Matt lived in a small two-story building across the street from the York theater, where she and Tod had seen so many movies. After parking, she walked up to the wrought-iron gate and pressed the buzzer by Matt's name. As she feared, there was no response. Matt had already gone out to get his proof.

It was going to be a long night, she admitted, maintaining a vigil on Matt's building from behind the locked doors of her car. She walked across the street to the York, bought a cup of coffee, and picked up one of their programs to read. It was only upon leaving the theater's lobby that she noticed the posters advertising that evening's double feature: *Daughters of Darkness* and *The Hunger*.

There was no getting away from them.

All of the corpses found in that basement had been staked as if they were vampires; her own husband had suspected it, and now Matt was telling her Tod had been right. But Matt had also been correct when he guessed that her three decades would prevent her from accepting the irrational. Her concepts of evil and possibility didn't have to change to accommodate the fact that Nick Van Lo had chosen to haunt her life. Jessie believed in Charles Manson much more than she did in Bela Lugosi.

That Van Lo and Judith Harper believed they were vampires, she was willing to concede; perhaps this was the best way to pursue them. But until she actually saw one of them spread both arms and change into a bat, she would reject the word *supernatural*, and believe that the night only brought sleep, and an end to her loneliness.

Jessie dozed intermittently until shortly after dawn, when the drunk who had spent the night sleeping on the hood of her car slipped off and the sudden lift of the front end jarred her awake. She rubbed her eyes groggily, then stepped out of the car to stretch the stiffness from her joints.

After ringing Matt's buzzer several times and getting no response, she decided to warm up inside the Mexican luncheonette next door to the theater. She crossed the street, and opened the mirrored door with its tinkling bells attached to the frame.

Matt was sitting in the last booth.

"Matt! What happened to you?"

"I cracked my head open."

Jessie took in the white bandage around his head, the freckled skin that seemed so pale, the fingers listlessly pushing a fork through a plate of *huevos rancheros* and blood sausage.

"What happened last night?"

"Picked up the wrong customer, I guess." The familiar gap-toothed grin showed no sign of life.

"But you didn't work last night."

"See what I mean?" He slowly rotated an index finger by his ear, and Jessie thought of a Buddy Holly forty-five playing at sixteen RPM. She looked away until the urge to cry subsided, then sat down across from him.

"Matt. You wrote me a letter yesterday that said you saw a woman drink Eileen's blood. You were going to confront her last night. What happened?"

Matt shrugged. "I didn't go. Eileen doesn't like me. She doesn't like men, period. I finally accepted it, before I made an even bigger fool of myself."

"I don't think you really believe that," Jessie said quietly. "You saw her drink her blood."

"Look, lady." He carefully set down his knife and fork. "Jessie. You're a sophisticated woman, you know where that blood came from. To each his own, is all I'm going to say about that. Now, I don't know what it's like to lose my entire family in two weeks—I hope to God I never do. But you can't count on me to help you through this shit. I'm fucking nineteen years old."

"Okay, Matt." Jessie looked at the clouded brown eyes, and tried to recall what made them so different before. "You have my number if you ever want to talk about it. If you want to talk about anything, please call me."

Jessie went home that day and cried harder than she had since Tod's death. The tears tried to blot out the memory of Matt

Hemphill, whose soul had gone the way of Amanda's and Eileen's. They succeeded only in washing clean the window to the barren future Jessie's vow of vengeance had exiled her to.

In the days and nights that followed, she resigned herself to tailing the movements of Eileen Morris. But Judith Harper never reappeared, and all that Jessie witnessed was the slow disintegration of a twenty-three-year-old girl. Eileen prowled the singles bars of San Francisco each night, drinking herself into a stupor when no man offered to take her home. As the clocks struck two and the bars closed, Jessie began to wonder how Eileen could teach a class in a matter of hours, and found out that she couldn't. Calvin Shanker confided to her over the phone that Eileen was one hearing away from being suspended.

On the days when she felt too depressed to follow Eileen, and too embarrassed to drive one more time past the little building across from the York, Jessie worked mechanically on her stained glass, trying to piece together the shards of her life. But the colors before her refused to come together in a design that justified the emptiness she had chosen; so the terrible loneliness that had visited her, the loneliness she could not bear to part with, continued.

It wasn't until the twenty-third of December, when Jessie came home with a Christmas tree and wondered if she could muster the courage to trim it, that the call came, and waited for her on the spools of her answering machine.

"Hi, Jessie. I like your recording."

There was a pause, the first of many to follow. "The reason I'm calling is . . . there's something wrong, and . . . my mind doesn't work so good anymore. I try to talk and—there's like words, and pictures, and a cloud comes. It's like there's something else in here with me, and I can't see it, because it hides in the cloud, and it rolls in with the cloud, and it takes over.

"I don't eat much. I just sleep, even though I'm scared to sleep, because . . . because . . . I'm afraid I won't be here when I wake up. The guy at work said I was crazy today . . . he fired me today . . . and I guess maybe it's true, I mean I know there's something wrong . . .

"But that's not why I'm . . . I'm calling. I'm calling because I still care for Eileen. I know she's gone, I know I'm gone, but . . . I care for her. I want you to know this because I can't think of the words . . . it's all bullshit. Everything I told you then was bullshit. Please believe me, I don't know how else to say it."

Jessie could hear his breathing in the long silence that ensued. "I'm going to go now, because . . . I don't want the cloud to come back anymore. I just . . . Jessie, I don't know how to say a joke anymore."

He hung up then.

Fighting back panic, Jessie drove as fast as she could to the Mission, and pressed every buzzer on the gate of Matt's building. When the Mexican superintendent finally buzzed her in, Jessie explained in her halting Spanish that the boy in 2B was trying to commit suicide.

The superintendent nodded and opened Matt's door with his passkey. They found him on the bathroom floor. His breathing was slow and ragged.

Jessie immediately called for an ambulance, then helped the man carry Matt to his bed. The paramedics were there in minutes; Jessie rode with them the seven blocks to San Francisco General. Before she left the tiny apartment, the superintendent's wife whispered that she was sure it was all the fault of the girl he'd been seeing the last two weeks.

"The girl he'd been seeing the last two weeks" finished feeding Dolores her dinner, then licked her own fingers clean.

"Hey, boy," she called out to Nick, who was standing by the window. "Dolores has been complaining that you don't keep the mirrors clean."

They both looked at Dolores, and broke into cold, mirthless laughter.

The first time Nick had entered a bar as a vampire, he had been surprised to see his own reflection in the mirror. Later that night, he and Judith had learned that the reason all the mirrors had been removed from La Casa de Dolores was that Dolores could not bear to witness her own decomposition.

Since then, over a dozen mirrors had come to hang in their apartment.

Dolores nodded patiently. "Feeling giddy this evening, children?"

"I got me a big, new boyfriend tonight," Judith offered smugly. "He should last me through the month."

The question drifted into Nick's consciousness on the coat-tails of his jealousy. "What happened to that kid—Eileen's boyfriend? I thought he was just your style."

"Nah, he was all fucked up. Took a bunch of pills tonight and ended up at San Francisco General." Then she remembered, and winked at Nick. "His landlady told me your old girlfriend saved his life."

Nick's voice dropped an octave. "What girlfriend, Judith?"

"Why, the Westerhays widow, Nicholas."

Nick's eyes locked on Dolores for a confirmation of his response; her eyes told him it could be as bad as he feared.

"You dumb, vicious bitch. You're going to expose us long before the police ever catch up with me."

"Watch what you say to me, Nick. I'll make you pay for every word."

"Nicholas has grounds to be upset," Dolores interjected. "We made a compact as a family, and as an aristocracy. Aristocracies are not meant to proliferate. We agreed to keep our number small by keeping stables—and by burying our dead. If that boy wakes up with a thirst for blood in a room full of doctors, you will have endangered our existence."

"*We* bury our dead?" Judith sneered, hands cocked on her hips. "Where did all this bullshit about precautions and aris-tocracies get you? A throne with two wheels, where you suck on rats so you don't lose consciousness . . . and a future with a child molester who wants to live in the past!"

"You think there's only one vampire in this room, my dear." Dolores spoke slowly. "But there are three, and you shouldn't ever forget it."

Finished with Judith, the ancient creature turned her chair to face Nick. "Something must be done about that boy right now, Nicholas. Before he becomes the fourth vampire in this city, or before Mrs. Westerhays has him released in her care. Do you know what to do, son?"

Nick hesitated, then shook his head.

"Well, you can't very easily spirit him out of the hospital, can you? And I certainly wouldn't recommend that you drive a stake through him, not with all the talk of *vampirism* you created in the press last month. You could set him on fire, of course, but smuggling a jerry can of gasoline into his room wouldn't be very practical."

Nick saw that Judith had caught the rhythm of what was happening, and waited for the inevitable, *practical* suggestion.

"No, I'm afraid you're going to have to put a pillow over the boy's head and smother him," Dolores continued conversationally. "He'll be no problem after that."

Judith knew there was more. "No problem for what?"

"Why, no problem for Nicholas to cut off his head."

The two women looked at him and laughed.

"I won't do it," he said quietly.

"But Nicholas, who else is there?" Dolores reasoned cruelly. "There's no sense in needlessly exposing Judith if anything were to go wrong."

"Oh, he'll do it," Judith assured Dolores. "That is, if he doesn't want me to walk out of here tonight. He'll do it, and he'll bring us the proof of the pudding. Won't you, lover?"

"Don't push me too far, Judith," Nick warned, and brushed past her into the kitchen. There was only one knife big enough for the job. He wrapped it in newspaper and stuck it inside his boot.

When he reached the door, he hesitated. "I don't know his name."

"Matt Hemphill," Judith offered instantly, and waved a mocking good-bye. "Tell him I sent my love."

Nick transferred onto the 47 Van Ness bus, and reached San Francisco General in forty minutes. Once inside, he ducked into a phone booth and called the hospital's information desk. After asking when visiting hours commenced the following morning, he received instructions on how to reach Matt's room.

Carefully wending his way to the fourth floor via deserted, unlighted corridors, Nick finally came across an unlocked supply closet. He took a green doctor's smock from one of the shelves, and put it on over his turtleneck.

Reaching Matt's ward, he nodded to the solitary nurse reading at her station. It wasn't until he was halfway across the waiting room that separated him from his quarry that Nick noticed Jessie Westerhays. She was asleep in her chair: a chair just like the one he had sat on, the night that Judith slit her wrists.

He slipped past her safely, but the feeling in the pit of his stomach was still there. It wasn't until he reached the door to Matt's room that he recognized it as doubt, rather than fear.

Nick knew how watching Judith commit her crimes had compromised him, and understood that to sever Matt's head was to sever all hope of redemption. But if he failed tonight, he knew he would lose her forever. Even though he wasn't sure he wanted the horror she had become, he couldn't bear to concede that there was no reason for all he had done, and no meaning to all he had lost.

There was no way out. After glancing back at the nurse on duty, he slipped into the room and wedged a chair against the doorknob.

Matt was alone in the dark room; as Nick drew nearer, he noticed that the boy was asleep. There was a tube taped to his arm.

Nick took off his smock, so that he was dressed all in black. He unwrapped the knife, but left it in his boot as he leaned over the bed.

"Hello, Matt."

Matt slowly lifted his lids, and Nick saw him struggling to focus. Then his dry, cracked lips moved, and Nick leaned closer.

"Who . . . are you?"

Nick smiled. "A black angel."

Matt tried to smile also, and Nick smelled the tiny drops of blood bubble and burst on the boy's lips.

"What's it . . . like?"

"It's very dark," Nick answered softly. "And very warm, like going back inside your mother. It's so close, you can touch it." He eased his hands under the boy's head, and lifted it. "It's like being covered with pillows."

The boy made an effort to balance himself on one elbow, so that Nick could pick up the pillow. "Thanks for telling me . . . who you are," he said weakly, and fell off the bed to the floor.

Nick caught the IV bag in midair as the tube on Matt's arm

yanked it free from its hook, but Matt's fall had sent the metal table next to the bed crashing down. Nick glanced over his shoulder instinctively and listened for approaching footsteps. By the time he looked back down on the floor, Matt had rolled under the bed.

Nick dropped to one knee and peered under the frame; Matt's eyes, wide and bright, met his. In the boy's hand was the emergency call device that had been on the table. His thumb was already turning white from pressing on the button.

"You son of a bitch." Nick considered dragging him out by the arm and slashing his windpipe with the knife. But with the light on the nurse's panel already blinking for the last fifteen seconds, he no longer had the time to saw off Judith's proof. He pulled the green smock over his head, kicked the chair out of his way, and ran out the door.

The nurse was in the room moments later, flicking on the lights. She gasped when she saw the wreckage.

"Child, what did you do?"

Then Jessie was kneeling by him, her frightened eyes swollen with sleep. "Who was it, Matt?"

"The angel of death," he whispered, and grinned his goofy gap-toothed grin.

Silent Night

WHILE JESSIE INSISTED to a young intern that she be allowed to spend the rest of the night in a chair by Matt's bed, Nick unlocked the door to the apartment, and braced himself for the onslaught that awaited him.

Judith was sitting in a chair by the corner where they kept Dolores. She finished whispering something to the old woman before turning to Nick.

"We were just talking about leaving the city and buying a motel somewhere," she explained. "Isn't that a great idea?"

Nick nodded, avoiding her eyes. "Why, is the Bates Motel up for sale?"

"Hey, that's good!" Judith laughed. "But we're going to call it the Roach Motel . . . cause the people that get in aren't going to get out!"

Nick smiled weakly, then gave up the pretense. "I didn't kill him."

Judith sobered immediately. "Let's hear what happened. And it better be good."

Nick shrugged, and leaned against a wall. "He buzzed the nurses before I could do anything."

"You could have slit his throat!"

"That would only have made it worse," Nick said quietly. "He would have turned into one of us while some doctor sewed up the wound."

Judith, ignoring his response, whirled back toward Dolores. "Sending that fool isn't so funny anymore, is it? You should have sent me. I had that boy eating out of the palm of my hand."

"And that's where he would still be," Dolores countered, "if you'd only watched over him more carefully. What's done is done. If Mrs. Westerhays didn't believe in our . . . *nature* before, she must now. So we shall pay them a visit on Christmas Eve. The widow will learn that her foundling still has one foot on the other side.

"But that is tomorrow. Tonight, we sleep in the tunnel. That is the price we have to pay for allowing ourselves to be exposed. Let it be a humiliation, and a lesson."

Judith stood up and moved behind her chair. "I'd rather die than live like a mole in those tunnels."

And, without warning, she threw the chair at the gilt-edged mirror across the room from her.

Dolores glanced at the shattered wood and glass as if it were a dust ball. "It's only for one night, my dear. Are you sure you never mentioned where you lived to that boy?"

When Judith didn't respond, Dolores continued. "Are you sure you never *thought* it? You are in his mind as much as you are in his blood. He will help us tomorrow night, but he could lead Mrs. Westerhays here during the day. I know I'll sleep much sounder with walls of rock surrounding me."

Judith hesitated, and Nick spoke for the first time in minutes. "Just for tonight, Judith. We'll take care of them and then . . ." A halfhearted smile. "That motel idea sounds good."

Judith stared at him unbelievingly. "It sounds *good* to you? What do you *see?* The two of us drinking the blood of tourists and living happily ever after?

"Let me show you something, Nick," she said softly, and unbuttoned her shirt so that he could see her breasts. "Do you remember the night those sweet old men sucked my tits while you watched from the floor? You've never seen them since then, have you?"

Judith strode up to him, cupping them with her hands. "They're all scarred up, Nick. Scarred by vampire fangs. I want you to hold them, so you can feel why I hate you."

Nick looked at the tiny white stitching crisscrossing the translucent skin, and turned away.

Judith spoke to his back as she buttoned her shirt. "I don't hate you for having let me die. I hate you for having let them scar me forever."

"My, but you're a petty little girl," Dolores commented.

Judith shot her a look of warning, then returned to Nick. "I'm going to sleep in that tunnel tonight, and one hour after I awake, Matt Hemphill is going to wish you'd killed him tonight. Then I'm getting on a bus to Palo Alto, so I can look up your little boy."

The muscles beneath Nick's ear fluttered. He turned around to confront her. "I'll find you, Judith."

The bridge that had connected them, that flimsy, condemned structure that Nick had patched with lies and blood, was finally swept away; they faced each other across a black river seething with hate. Judith smiled, then left the apartment.

Dolores allowed the charged air to dissipate before speaking. "Forget what she said, my boy. Her bark is worse than her bite." She suppressed a chuckle. "Anyway, we'd best get down to the tunnel ourselves."

Nick nodded and folded up the tarp they covered Dolores with. A few minutes later, when they were riding down in the elevator, Dolores continued.

"I've been thinking about that little schoolteacher who replaced you, Nicholas. Judith tells me she's abandoned her and, well, we don't want a repeat of tonight's fiasco, do we?"

"That's Judith's problem," Nick answered curtly.

"I think you should make her your problem, son. I think you should seriously consider making her your girlfriend."

The old woman let her words sink in while Nick pushed her out of the elevator and into the basement. When they reached the spot where the entrance to the tunnel was hidden, she raised her eyes to him again.

"There won't be the . . . history you and Judith had. It will be the way you always wanted it."

Nick paused after uncovering the entrance. "And if it's not, I can get rid of her, right? And maybe then I'll finally break down and do what you've wanted me to do all along—find another Amanda, and help you enter her body. *Then* I'll be happy, right, Dolores?"

The vampire shook her head slowly. "You don't want happiness, Nicholas. You want a very special kind of love. The kind you've dreamed of since you were a little boy. I've always known this. And only I can give it to you.

"But it won't happen now, because you don't believe me yet. When you do, I won't have to ask. You'll come to me."

Darkness was already falling as Jessie and Matt pulled into her driveway. It was almost five o'clock on Christmas Eve.

"Home at last," Jessie sighed, as she set the parking brake. Matt smiled back at her, then scratched the bandaged spot where the intravenous needle had been. You look so tired, she thought—almost as tired as me.

Jessie had finally spent the night in the chair by Matt's bed; she agreed to leave the room only when the hospital's daytime bustle convinced her that Matt was no longer in danger.

The rest of the morning was spent convincing the hospital's bureaucracy that, as Matt Hemphill's aunt and only local relative, she be allowed to have him released in her care. Her persistence got the papers completed just before noon, but the doctors decided to keep Matt until four, when the last of his tests came back from the lab.

Jessie took advantage of the delay to go back to Matt's apartment and pack most of his clothes. From there she drove to the supermarket near her house, where she bought a turkey. It was only after the bird was in her oven that she got around to making the call.

"Happy holidays from Pacific Security, Tony speaking."

"Hello, my name if Jessie Westerhays." She gave him her address. "Would it be possible for me to hire two security guards for the night on such short notice?"

"Sure it's possible, but tonight's Christmas Eve. That means double time. How long did you want them for?"

From sundown to sunrise, Jessie thought, and added the hours in her head. "Thirteen hours. Five-thirty to six-thirty."

Tony whistled. "That comes out to . . . six-fifty. Six hundred and fifty dollars, Mrs. Westerhays. Is that agreeable?"

Jessie blinked. "That's fine."

"Okay then. Would you like to pay by credit card over the phone?"

Jessie agreed, and read him her Amex number.

"That's it then. I'll put the job through as soon as I verify your credit. Any special instructions, Mrs. Westerhays?"

"Yes. Have them patrol the perimeter of the property. Thoroughly, but discreetly." She smiled. "We'd just like to have a safe, quiet Christmas Eve."

She could hear the man chuckling as he hung up.

The smell of the turkey roasting in the oven greeted them as they entered the house. But Matt detected another, cooler odor.

"Jessie, do you have a Christmas tree?"

She nodded and led him to the living room, where the tree leaned, unadorned, against the fireplace. Trimming the tree was the one thing she had neglected to do that afternoon.

"I thought you might want to help me do it up."

They hugged each other then, until their tears had finished setting the bond they both sought.

Before the day nurse had come into Matt's room that morning, Jessie had quietly asked him to explain what had happened the night before. When Matt described the man dressed in black, Jessie recognized him as Nicholas Van Lo.

"How did you know it was one of . . . them?"

Matt had smiled weakly. "I didn't. But when I talked to him, and he answered, I realized we were both *really* there . . . I remembered Judith Harper drinking Eileen's blood. And I knew I wasn't crazy."

Jessie had looked at the window then; Matt correctly interpreted the movement. "Your husband was right, Jessie. I know, because I'm one of them, too. That's why I'm so fucked up. That's why Eileen's fucked up. We've both been bitten."

"It's not true. I've watched Eileen Morris." Her voice trembled. "I lived with my daughter. They couldn't do what you did last night."

"That's because no one helped them." Matt squeezed her hand. "No one could, because no one knew. Not until now. You saved me last night, and now you know."

Yes, now she knew. It was true that there were such things as vampires in her cloistered world; it was true that her husband had died far saner than anyone suspected, trying to save their daughter, because she had become one of them. Even if Jessie had wanted to deny it, Matt's condition wouldn't have let her.

They stopped speaking of it then, and they didn't speak of it now, as they strung the lights and hung the ornaments and sprinkled it all with tinsel. There were lessons to be sifted from the pain of those thoughts; but this night, it was more important to remember that it was Christmas Eve.

After they finished trimming the tree, Jessie carved the turkey and served it with a quickly tossed salad. By the time Matt finished telling her how he made his way to the Bay Area from Lincoln, Nebraska the summer after he finished high school, they were both ready for bed.

"Oh, damn," Jessie exclaimed. "I forgot to get you a present."

Matt slapped his forehead. "Can you believe it? *I did too!*"

They laughed and climbed the stairs slowly, arm in arm. After she set him up in Amanda's room, Jessie paused by the door.

"You know we can't stay here tomorrow night, don't you?"

Matt finished tugging his pullover over his head and nodded.

"They're going to come after us every night until they get us or we get them. But nothing's going to happen tonight." She told him about the security guards outside. "So sleep well."

Jessie closed the door to her room and took off her clothes. Slipping beneath the cold sheets, she placed her fingers on the lips of her vagina, and thought of Tod.

Promise you'll keep me warm until this is over, she whispered to him. I know what I have to do. But I'd like to feel you inside me, until it ends.

Her thighs tightened around her wrist, then relaxed as the warmth and the comfort spread through her. Minutes passed before she heard the tapping on her door.

"Come in, Matt."

He hesitated by the door before coming over to the side of the bed.

"Are you afraid of what will happen after you fall asleep?"

He nodded; she saw him shiver in the darkness.

"Lay down next to me," she said, lifting the sheet.

She sensed the embarrassment he felt, and let him roll over so that his back was to her. When his breathing became more regular, she pressed softly against him and placed her hand over his heart.

"It's beating just like mine," she told him softly.

And so they slept, the rest of that last, silent night.

Auld Lang Syne

DOLORES SMILED AS she read the note Nick had found on Jessie's kitchen table earlier that night.

> *Keep missing each other. Back at sunrise. See you at your place soon.*

"So the hunted think they are becoming the hunters," the old woman mused.

The vampires had laughed when they encountered the security guards patrolling the house on Christmas Eve; they knew that time was on their side, since Jessie could not afford such elaborate precautions for long. But when they returned to the house on Christmas night, the only trace they found of their quarry was the note.

"Forget the house," Dolores decided. "I think they know they're safer sleeping in Mrs. Westerhays's automobile than in her bedroom. Since we cannot come to them, we must make them come to us."

Judith ran her finger along the moist stone face of the tunnel and shook her head disgustedly. "How do we do that—an ad in the personals column?"

"There's no need to go to such trouble," Dolores reasoned. "They found you easily enough before. Return to your usual haunts. Go together, and early enough in the evening that you give yourself time to maneuver afterward. Walk out when they see you, but let them follow you. Lead them to another of these tunnels. Once you have them trapped inside, they will be no problem. Don't forget that the boy is one of us."

Judith wasn't happy with the plan. "What if we don't run across them?"

Dolores answered bluntly, confident of her gradually building power. "Then you will spend New Year's Eve in this tunnel, my dear. Unless you greatly surprise me and carry out your threat to abandon us."

As Dolores had suspected, Judith came back to the tunnel the next night, and the four after that. She wasn't yet ready to abandon the security that even the most quarrelsome of families offer. But Judith refused to go out with Nick in search of their adversaries, and she stopped bringing Dolores her rats and kittens.

Providing sustenance for the old woman became the task of her wayward, prodigal son. It was also Nick alone who returned, night after night, to the bars and clubs that he and Judith had become so familiar with in the past month. As Dolores had predicted, he eventually encountered Matt and Jessie. But first he found someone who had been waiting for him even longer than they had.

He saw her in a Folsom Street dive frequented by punks and adventurous junior executives. When she stepped out of the john and entered the dimly lit corridor that led back to the bar, he appeared before her.

"I've been waiting for you, Eileen."

Her arms and legs wrapped about him like larva in the darkness; her blood leaped from her veins into his. In an instant he realized that if he didn't pull back, the force of her own pounding heart would leave her bloodless in minutes, but her system refused to stop pumping, to let go. Nick reeled with the onrushing waves of red and black, and punched her as hard as he could in the stomach.

Eileen crashed back against the wall, deathly pale, the wind knocked out of her. Nick held her up by the armpits before she could slide to the floor. He saw the whiteness of her gums and lips.

"Don't ever leave me," she whispered, and passed out in his arms.

He came to her the next night, at another bar. When he asked her if she wanted to go back to her place, she shook her head and pulled him to the toilet. He smelled the dry, chafing heat in her breath, the desire to have the burning damped forever by the soothing coldness of his touch, and drank her slowly, so that she wouldn't sense how little blood he was taking.

When he left, she made him promise that he'd kill her if he ever tired of her. He came back—the following night, and the one after that—even though her pitiful words had gutted all memory of the person she had once been. He came to her because he was a vampire, and the screaming need of her veins to be milked was irresistible.

And whenever he remembered Dolores's proposal during those first three nights, he put it out of his mind.

Jessie took her laundry out of the dryer and folded it in neat stacks. She could hear Matt playing Tod's Doors records in the living room. They still had an hour left before it got dark, when they would have to go out.

It was New Year's Eve.

Earlier in the week, Jessie had impressed Matt by deciding to trade in the Saab for a car the vampires wouldn't recognize; and then made him laugh by choosing a Volvo. Since they learned that Eileen Morris had disappeared, there had been no change in their routine. Every evening at about this time, they left the house and renewed their tour of the city's singles bars. And every night at closing time, they drove to the modest motel south of the city where they could sleep in peace.

Jessie walked over to the stereo and lowered the volume. "We should go soon, Matt. Are you all set?"

Matt was stretched out, eyes closed, on the couch. Although still technically anemic, the color had returned to his freckled cheeks.

"Not really," he answered quietly.

She could sense what was coming; she had been expecting it for days.

"Oh? Why not?"

The skin around his eyes tightened as he spoke. "Because it's New Year's Eve, and . . . I don't want to spend it looking for people who want to kill me."

"I see," she answered softly. She lifted the needle from the record.

Matt had been everything she could have hoped for since he moved in with her on Christmas Eve. It wasn't just the courage he exhibited each night that made her so happy with him. The jokes at breakfast in the motel cafeteria each morning, the blaring of the rock music that had been missing in her house since Tod's death: all this reminded her of what it meant to be alive, of what she was fighting for.

And he had taught her how to fight. His mind fitted together what it had learned at drive-ins and midnight movies with the images of Judith that his subconscious sent up to the surface. These vampires were about only at night, because they slept during the day; that meant that the sun was fatal to them. What Nick Van Lo had left behind in the flophouse basement confirmed that a stake would kill them. To this Matt's memory of Van Lo's visit added a knife through the heart, or across the throat.

But Matt, she knew, was fighting something else. He had been bitten; although his personality had yet to warp like Amanda's, or disintegrate like Eileen's, the constant fear that it might had to be taking its toll.

Jessie hesitated, then made the concession she had promised herself she wouldn't make. "We can take tonight off, if you'd like."

Matt shook his head slowly. "It's crazy, living like this."

"I know," Jessie said, sitting down next to him. "But it's suicide not to."

She let him lie there, saying nothing for the twenty minutes they still had left. She knew she had no right to press him on this—tonight, or any other night. Jessie had lost her family to the vampires; Matt was in danger of losing much more.

Finally, Matt sat up. "I guess I'm going out with an older woman this New Year's Eve."

Jessie laughed and hugged him. "This older woman's got to be careful. I've seen some of those secretaries making passes at you the last couple of nights."

Matt grinned. "Don't think I haven't taken down a few phone numbers, either."

Jessie tipped his chin and looked into his eyes. "You'll get a chance to call them."

The Glass Slipper

As a New Year's surprise, Jessie took Matt to dinner at the Hayes Street Grill, where they dallied over thresher shark covered with the restaurant's unique Szechuan peanut sauce. By the time they returned to the car, it was eleven-thirty.

The area they had chosen for their evening's search was North Beach, an old Italian neighborhood whose bookstores, coffeehouses, and strip joints made it the western capital of the Beat generation. Its heart beat somewhere near the intersection of Broadway and Columbus, from where a giant neon replica of Carol Doda winked southward at the City Lights bookstore.

On New Year's Eve, more than any other night, both the barkers outside the strip shows and the poets pushing sheets of verse on street corners promise something special. It could be the end of your frustration, or the end of the world; all you have to do is pay your money and step through the door.

Jessie slipped her arm through Matt's and pressed through the throngs milling past Big Al's. There were a hundred bars they could try that night; she had been waiting for the inspiration to choose the right one. It came just fifteen minutes after a cheer went up all around them and she'd impulsively kissed Matt on the lips. A young man wearing both diapers and long johns handed her a flyer that invited them to a private club three stories over where they stood. It was called The Glass Slipper.

The party the old elevator wearily lifted them to had begun a little after ten; by twelve-thirty, everyone inside was frantically attempting to burn brighter than the Chinese-red lacquer on the walls. The heat produced by all this supercharged blood made Nick dizzy, and he pressed his forehead against Eileen's cool, white shoulder.

Eileen had asked him to dance a while ago. They had shuffled together, arms draped over shoulders as if imaginary cigarettes smoked from their fingers, until midnight struck. *Kiss me,* Eileen whispered, and Nick moved his lips over hers, letting his tongue search for a way to tell her that even this could be called love. She squeezed his crotch as he withdrew the last touch of his lips.

"Kiss me, Nick." The sound of her voice was both a whimper and a growl. "Kiss me, or I'm going to fucking die."

There was no way to give her what she wanted, now that he understood what it was. He had already drained her of more than she could stand tonight, minutes after he'd met her. Sliding his hands up her shoulders and around her neck, he tried to get behind the uncomprehending blue eyes and ask, *do you really want to die?*

Eileen squeezed him again, harder, and his fingers tightened about her throat. His calluses felt the blood quicken, then slow and darken with the lack of oxygen; he saw her pupils dilate before the lids closed over them. He choked her within a breath of unconsciousness, relaxing his grip only when he was sure that her blood vessels knew they were dying and could no longer calculate why. She sagged against him, breathing painfully, and he raised his eyes to the mirrored ceiling as if to heaven.

Jessie Westerhays was looking at him.

Matt had sensed him as he emerged from the elevator, moments before Jessie sensed the boy's fear.

"They're here, aren't they?" she asked.

Matt nodded wordlessly. She gripped his hand.

They made their way through the party, unsmiling, eyes sweeping left to right and back again. When Jessie saw Eileen leaning against Nick by the bar, she stopped and nudged Matt. But he had already seen them.

"What do we do, Jessie?"

Jessie looked through the crowd that separated her from the

creature that had destroyed her family. She passed her arm around Matt's waist and answered, "Wait."

Waiting was all they had to do; Nick knew it even as his mind skipped across the crowd to the elevator just beyond. He had a bedtime, and they didn't. Dolores's plan—that he allow them to follow him back to a tunnel—meant little without Judith's help, and with Eileen leaning against his shoulder. He considered abandoning her and making a break for the stairs, but there was no way to pass quickly through the crowd.

He had to think of something else.

Jessie and Matt situated themselves as close to the exit as they could without losing sight of their quarry. Arms around each other's waists, they fixed smiles on their faces so as to avoid notice from the partyers around them. As the hours slowly passed, the body heat in the room combined with the adrenaline coursing through them to dry out their mouths even as their bodies broke into a sweat. But neither even considered going for a drink; instead they watched, with a mixture of envy and disgust, as Nick chased shot after shot of tequila down Eileen's throat with glasses of beer.

Jessie, feeling Matt tense as if to bolt forward, held him back. "What is that motherfucker doing to her?" he asked angrily, as he forced himself to stay back.

The answer came soon enough. Nick, cupping her chin, felt most of the beer he had nursed into her mouth spill over his fingers. He moved Eileen's head from side to side. Her eyes rolled back as she pitched forward into him. He caught her around the waist, then grabbed the shoulder of the man next to him with his free hand.

"The lady's sick, buddy. How about running interference for me before she rains on the whole party?"

The man tipped his party hat forward aggressively and made a circle with his thumb and index finger.

"Gangway!"

Nick slung Eileen over his shoulder; they were off.

It only took Jessie and Matt a moment to figure out that Van Lo was finally making his exit, but even as they pushed off the wall, the crowd pushed them back. Everyone was trying to outdo the other, shouting "Gangway" at the top of their lungs, clearing a path wide enough for a wheelbarrow. By the time they made their way through to the exit, they saw that they were too late.

"Hold the elevator!" Matt shouted to the man in the party hat, but it was too late. Nick looked at them impassively as the elevator doors closed with Eileen unconscious in his arms.

"If you can't wait, fella," the man in the party hat advised, "take the stairs." He pointed behind them.

Matt beat Jessie to the door and flung it open. Sure enough, there was a circular staircase winding down to the ground floor. After making sure Jessie was behind him, he took the stairs three at a time, using the banister for balance. They were in the lobby in less than half a minute, but Nick was nowhere in sight.

Matt spun around the first person he reached outside. "See a guy carrying a chick in his arms?"

The elderly man hesitated, so Matt improvised.

"She's dying!"

"He . . . went that way," the man stammered, pointing to his left. Jessie and Matt raced to the intersection. They caught a glimpse of them, rounding a corner two blocks west. He was heading toward Chinatown, Eileen draped over his shoulder.

"He's not a gorilla," Matt said hoarsely. "He can't carry her like that forever."

Jessie put a hand over her heart as Matt broke into a run, and followed as fast as her lungs would let her. She could hear him shout every fifty feet or so, as he sighted them in between the clusters of late-nighters that still rolled through the streets. By the time he stopped, Jessie had fallen more than a block behind.

She could see the frustration in Matt's face as, gasping for air, she reached him. "We . . . lost . . . them?"

Matt punched his palm with his fist. "Son of a *bitch!* She's got to weigh one-ten easy!"

Jessie waited for her breathing to calm before she spoke. "We followed them all the way to this block. So he's here someplace, inside a building, hiding behind some doorway. He either lives on this block, or he's hiding until we leave."

"So either way, we don't move until the sun comes up. And

if he doesn't show, we come back tomorrow at sundown." Matt nodded. "Okay. Let's spread ourselves out a little, so we can see the last building on either end as well as ourselves."

There were two hours to go until sunrise.

The Last Embrace

NICK LOOKED DOWN from the bail bondsman's apartment as Jessie and Matt moved cautiously toward opposite ends of the street. They're staking out the block, he mused, and moved away from the window.

There was no longer any danger for him, because they couldn't see him make his way down to the basement and into the tunnel. Tomorrow night, he and Judith could go out through any of a dozen exits. At worst, they would have to find themselves a new apartment.

Or a motel, he remembered bitterly, and opened the bathroom door.

Eileen lay naked in the salmon-colored bathtub, her hair plastered to her face as the shower sprayed ice-cold jets of water over her head and chest. Her clothes were heaped on top of the toilet, where Nick had dumped them. Nick adjusted the nozzle so that the jets centered on her belly. Eileen smiled briefly before closing her eyes again.

Eileen was a more difficult problem. She couldn't go, and she couldn't stay. He turned the shower off and watched the water run down the drain.

"I'm cold," she mumbled, and tried to grin through lips that had long since lost their natural color. Nick smiled patiently while he helped her to her feet. When he felt the shiver that ran through her, he offered to towel her dry.

"Say you'll never leave me," she asked, and her swollen blue eyes flickered with something he knew was irretrievable. He covered her head with a towel before her eyes could read his mind.

It will be the way you always wanted it, Dolores had promised: there won't be the history you and Judith had. Nick rubbed Eileen's back harder than he had to, and recalled their playground flirtations long ago. Yes, he admitted, the history was different. But what about the endless present that deprived the future of all meaning?

Eileen turned around, and rested her hands on his shoulders while he dried her ribs and belly. Resisting the shy call of her eyes, he focused on the cleft of her navel and told himself he loved her.

Not the girl, perhaps; she had always been too pallid for him. Before, in life, and now, as she staggered toward death with the outstretched arms of the blind. But she wouldn't be a girl when she woke up—she would be a vampire, just like him. He would suck her into the vortex that was drowning him, clutch her so she could feel the dark red pain he had felt and caused, and finally love her, with all the force of the black hole in his heart.

He let the towel drop to the floor.

"Eileen, do you want to live with me forever?"

She nodded happily, and he thought of the kittens Judith had brought Dolores. He ruffled the red hair over her vagina as he told her what he was. He reminded her of Judith, of the endless drought he had broken outside the toilet of a Folsom Street bar. He sat her down on his lap and related how Judith's kiss had sealed her off from everything that grows in the sun. When the confusion in her mind became evident, he pressed her against his chest, and explained how she would be just like them after he made love to her one more time.

Eileen wriggled free of his grasp, and took a step back. Nick saw what little blood she had left blush to the surface of her skin.

Rather than being accusatory, her tone was curious when she asked, "Why'd you do this to me?"

"I didn't." Nick's mouth spread in an involuntary, embarrassed grin; he brusquely scrubbed it away with his fist. "It was Judith . . . at the Balboa Cafe. I just told you about it. Can't you remember?"

Eileen shook her head. Nick turned away, wondering how the twilight life she was passing through could have erased her memories so thoroughly. When he looked back at her, however, and saw her lowered lids rise, he realized she was thinking about something other than the question he had put to her.

"Nick, why do you . . . why do *you* do it at all?"

Her words were spoken shyly, but the light behind the blue of her eyes had been rekindled. She wanted an answer; to dwell on the pain it would cause him . . . to speak of pain to her . . . was an insult.

"Let me see how I can answer you." He thought of fire, what it meant to the tribesman warding off the terrors of the night. "It's a light," he began, picturing lovers lying by a hearth, a Viking's funeral disappearing into the ocean mist. "It renews us," he continued, and imagined a blaze shriveling a forest and roaring through the little village sleeping by its side.

It cleanses, he wanted to say, and choked on the lie his mind was telling him. "I do it because I have to, not because I want to. I need it."

"Then you're with me . . . for my blood?"

"Of course not," he blurted, much too quick, and held back from taking her hands. She crossed her arms beneath her breasts like a child, waiting for him to continue.

"I can get . . . blood anywhere, from anyone. They never see me coming, if I don't want them to. I'm with you . . . I'm making you like me . . . because I want to be with you. I need blood, yes. But I also need you. No one else, Eileen. Just you."

The skin below her eyes—not so much dark as translucent, devoid of sunlight and substance—crinkled as her nostrils flared and the corners of her mouth lifted in that once-familiar expression of hers: that look of amusement and disbelief holding hands, ever so tentatively.

"When I'm like you . . . it'll be blood I care about—not you, right? I know what you said, but . . . I won't really, will I?"

Nick saw the luster return to her hair as it dried. Eileen was gathering the scattered pieces of her essence, restoring herself through an effort of sheer will. It was—*she* was—beautiful to behold, like the radiance of the terminally ill just before death.

"If I can care for you," he tried, hesitantly, "then perhaps you can care for me, too."

"We were good friends once, weren't we, Nick?" She smiled

wearily, a little sadly even; he knew she didn't expect any more answers. "We were never going to be great lovers or anything, but . . . we cared for each other, I remember. Just a little, just enough to think we'd never hurt each other."

A quick, bright laugh, with as much strength as she could muster. "That's not so little, is it? No, it's quite a lot."

Nick saw that she was aglow.

"I remember this crow." Her eyes blinked, as if in amazement at the resurfacing of a long-buried memory. "This crow that landed on my swing when I was little. Someone had trained him and . . . the crow would follow me to school, would eat out of my hand, would . . . Someone came for him one day, the person who'd trained it, and took it back. I missed the crow, but I understood the *process*. That was the way it was supposed to be. And—can you believe it?—that memory is a completely happy memory. A completely happy one. Isn't that incredible?"

Eileen moved toward the door, then turned around. "I don't think I want to be with you, Nick. I don't want to be like you forever."

He sensed the chill then, cutting through the fog he had generated. But she was already running; he heard the shattering of glass before he could rise from his seat.

Down on the street, Jessie saw how the passing of time can bring even the most innocent shadows to life. As her eyes strained to sift shapes from the depths of unlit doorways—as the minutes grew to an hour, and then more—she thought she saw Nick Van Lo floating away in the shadows between buildings more than once. But each wail of recognition proved to be a false alarm, only a few thoroughly soused revelers stumbling home an hour ahead of the dawn disturbed their vigil.

Jessie yawned and glanced at her watch. The sun would rise in less than an hour, according to the Weather Bureau tape recording she called each afternoon before leaving her house. Unless Van Lo was waiting for the last possible moment to make his escape, he had found a corner to hole up in until the next night. She was just beginning to think grouchily of the long early morning walk back to the car, when the window exploded above her.

The body hit the sidewalk forty feet from where she stood.

Even as she ran toward it, Jessie recognized Eileen's long red hair. She dropped to her knees, and instinctively cradled the girl's head in her lap. From the ease with which the neck adjusted to the shift, Jessie knew that it was broken. As Matt's footsteps drew near, her gaze shifted reflexively from Eileen's battered features to the window she had jumped from.

Nick Van Lo was looking down at her.

Jessie rose to her feet, never taking her eyes off the frozen face in the window, as Matt made a small noise in his throat and covered Eileen as best he could with his jacket. Later, she would remember walking toward the building's entrance, and thinking that it had to end that night.

Matt reached her side as she tried the door to the building's lobby. It was locked.

"Stand aside," he ordered gruffly, and kicked it open.

He saw her open her purse and withdraw the boning knife. "Do we go up for him?"

Jessie shook her head. "There's no need. He can't stay in that apartment—not with that broken window, and Eileen lying below it. Sunrise is in less than half an hour. All we have to do is seal off his exits."

Matt agreed, and quickly checked out the lobby.

"There's just three doors down here," he reported. "The one we came through, one leading down to the basement, and the fire stairs. The only other way down is the elevator."

"That's it, then. Go over by the elevator, and I'll watch the fire stairs. Are there floor lights over the elevator door?"

Matt nodded.

"Then call me if it starts coming down."

Jessie positioned herself next to the door by the fire stairs, so that she could plunge the knife into whatever opened the door from the other side. There were only two questions left to consider now. Could she do it? And if she did, would the knife have any effect?

Matt's voice interrupted her thoughts at that moment. The elevator was coming down.

Jessie joined him quickly. They stood before the elevator, watching the numbers descend. Matt leaned forward in a slight crouch as the first floor light came on; Jessie squeezed the handle of the boning knife . . . but the doors failed to open.

"What's happening?"

The answer awaited them at the left edge of the row of numbers over the elevator, where the letter *B* lit up. The elevator had gone all the way down to the basement.

Matt recovered first. "The stairs. Quick."

They ran over to the basement door, and opened it. After the third step down, all they could see was black.

"There's got to be a light switch," Matt said. "I'll feel along the wall as we go down."

"Wait a moment." She put her hand on his arm. "It'll be daylight in less than half an hour, and we've got him trapped in the basement. He's no better off than he was before, upstairs. Why don't we wait?"

"You mean, I take the elevator again, and you watch this door?"

It was obvious that Matt didn't agree. "I think something's up. Otherwise, there's no sense to what he did." He paused, then came up with the possibility they hadn't foreseen. "What if there's another way out of the basement?"

Jessie nodded; there was no other way but to go down.

Nick closed the opening behind him and disappeared into the darkness of the tunnel. Jessie Westerhays and the boy were forgotten: they would never find him now. Instead, he thought about Eileen.

They had slept together once . . . made love, in a way. She had given all that he had asked of her. Now that she was dead— now that she had hurled herself through a window to escape an eternity with him—he admitted that he'd never loved her.

He couldn't have loved her, because he had killed her. Eileen was a victim like all the rest, and nothing more. If he were ever to doubt it, he only had to recall the drained and broken thing lying on the pavement somewhere above him.

No, it was all over: for him, for his doubts, for everything. And, having admitted it, he knew what he had to do.

Matt found the light switch on the staircase wall as he reached the sixth step down. The basement was a rough square, with a boiler on one side and a collection of trash on the other. There were no doors to walk out of, and no windows to squeeze through. There was also no sign of Nick Van Lo.

"He couldn't have vanished into thin air," Jessie said quietly, and turned to Matt. "Could he?"

"If he could have, he would have done it the moment after Eileen jumped from that window. No, there's got to be a way out of here that we haven't found yet."

"A secret passageway?" Jessie offered uncertainly.

Matt smiled briefly. "Not really. This is an apartment building, not a castle. But a hidden door..."

He moved about in a circle, surveying the basement. "If there is one, it's got to be behind that boiler. Nobody's touched that pile of trash in months."

There was a wooden cabinet in the gap between the boiler and the wall; the space itself was less than two feet. Matt looked at Jessie, and leaned all of his weight against the cabinet. It slid easily into the wall, like a door.

Matt's eyes widened with surprise. "Like I said, this is an apartment building."

Jessie wiped the sweat from the handle of her knife. "Can you see anything inside?"

Matt peered in. "Not much . . . Bare rock walls. It's some kind of tunnel."

"We don't even have a flashlight on us," Jessie said disgustedly.

"And Van Lo's probably crawling out the other side. Let's go, before we think of any other reasons not to."

Jessie took his hand. "Be careful where you step. And . . . don't let go of my hand."

Matt felt the damp, packed earth beneath his sneaker, and moved forward. In the blackness that quickly enveloped them, the walls' proximity became their only sense of place or direction. The tunnel narrowed and widened without a pattern, so that sometimes they could only squeeze through the craggy rock, while at other moments the sudden expanses completely disoriented them. With every apparent dead end, with every sudden loss of direction, Jessie tried to convince herself to turn back, to return in the daylight with a flashlight and a gun and a crucifix and whatever else she and this boy could dream of. She gave up trying only after admitting the obvious: once she left this tunnel, she would never come back.

It was clear by now that the tunnel did not merely connect one basement with another in an adjoining building; it was leading them somewhere else. Neither of them spoke as they advanced. They didn't want to give themselves away, in case Van Lo was near; in any case, there was nothing left to say. Apart from an occasional echo and the brushing of their own feet, all they could hear was the furtive movement of rats.

After the initial shock and revulsion, Jessie hadn't been surprised by the presence of rats; it only made sense that they would inhabit a cave like this one. When one leaped from a crag above her and brushed her shoulder, squeaking with fright before scurrying away, she only closed her eyes momentarily and squeezed Matt's hand all the harder. But it seemed that the farther they penetrated into the tunnel, the more rodents they sensed. It was more than the periodic brushing against a foot, or the blending of tiny, scattered shrieks into one sustained note. There was a foulness in the air they were breathing, a congestion of evil and fear that had no room for them.

Matt hesitated; she felt his hot breath near her face. "Can you feel it," he whispered. Then the light came on, blinding them.

Jessie and Matt immediately braced for an assault. But none came, and when their eyes adjusted, only Judith Harper stood before them, her hip resting on the arm of a wheelchair covered with a blanket.

"Did you miss me, Matt? I sure miss you."

Jessie was surprised by the fragility of her voice. It was cold, brittle—like glass. Then Judith slipped off the wheelchair and folded her arms over her striped seaman's jersey. She certainly did not appear very threatening as she advanced slowly toward Matt.

"Now you know why it felt so good, don't you, Matt?" She giggled. "Now you know why it drove you crazy."

Jessie looked over at Matt; her stomach rolled queasily as she realized that he was wavering. She stepped in front of him, brandishing her knife at Judith.

"Get back—now!"

Judith smiled at Jessie, freezing her, but she moved back by the wheelchair.

Her eyes returned to Matt. "No housewife's ever going to make you feel like that, honey."

"Shut up!" Jessie gritted her teeth, and felt her fingers ache from the pressure she was applying on the handle; she couldn't make herself stab the beautiful young girl sweet-talking Matt over to her side.

"You know you're one of us, Matt. Sooner or later, for now and forever. You can let me kiss you here, or you can wait until you die of old age. Either way, you'll be one of us. It's up to you to decide if you want to join us looking like that"—pointing at him with a long mauve fingernail—"or like *this*."

She pulled the blanket off the wheelchair with a flourish. Jessie screamed when she saw Dolores's hideous, grinning skull. Her grip on the knife loosened momentarily, even as Nick Van Lo jumped on Matt from behind and sank his teeth into his neck.

"No," Jessie wailed—then her peripheral vision picked up Judith's onrushing form. She barely managed to raise her hand as Judith leaped, but the tip of the blade found the vampire's windpipe and slid through it.

Judith's eyes widened with shock, but she kept moving forward. Her outstretched hands knocked Jessie's arm to one side, and the knife ripped free out the side of her neck. Jessie caught her by the hair as Judith fell on her, splashing her with the bright red of her ruptured carotid. As the vampire crumpled lifelessly to the floor, the ripped skin on her neck began to tear in earnest. Jessie tasted the blood that stuck on her lips and slashed frenziedly at the few connecting strands, until the blade and the screams severed the head from its body.

Nick was bent over Matt, draining him in earnest, when he caught sight of the head hanging from Jessie's hand by its hair. He let go of Matt, and rose to his feet.

"You didn't have much choice, did you," he asked wearily, and wiped the blood from his mouth.

"My baby," Jessie answered. "You killed her."

Nick shook his head. "No, Jessie. *She* killed Amanda," he replied, pointing a finger at Dolores. "I spared her something

. . . worse. There's not enough time for me to explain everything that happened, and I couldn't expect you to believe it all. Let's just say that Amanda didn't have much choice, either."

Jessie was panting fiercely, just fifteen feet away from his teeth. The expression on her face, Nick thought, was scarcely more human than the one dangling from her hand.

"I cared for her, once," he continued, nodding at Judith. "For Eileen, too. I meant well, Jessie. We were on the same side once. If I'm guilty of anything, it's of wanting to become a victim. What happened . . . I had no say, no choice, in it. A lot of people have no choice in what they become."

Dolores spoke for the first time in Jessie's presence. "Shut up, you fool. Can't you feel the sun rising already?"

Nick glanced briefly at Dolores, then turned back to Jessie. "I just wanted you to understand, a little. If I were still the man you knew, I'd ask for your forgiveness. But I'm not." He smelled the moisture on the walls, the earth beneath it, the rankness that had become the confines of his life. "I've got nothing left from then—no lovers, no innocence, no excuses. I've finally learned to exist without any of that."

He shrugged, smiling sadly. "That's why I'm going to kill you."

His eyes homed in on the curve just above her collarbone, and he leaped forward.

Jessie, looking down at Judith's head as if for the first time, hurled it at Nick with a wrenching groan. It bounced off his chest, knocking him back, and she ran into the tunnel.

She ran, even though her mind had yet to figure out that it was her only hope, even though leaving Matt behind seemed the lowest betrayal imaginable. Lungs screaming, hands outstretched, she groped through the tunnel, blundering into the veering rock walls, ignoring the fear and the pain, never stopping. She couldn't stop, because Nick Van Lo was stronger, Nick Van Lo was faster, Nick Van Lo could see in the dark and would never stop until he blotted her life from the sky.

And Nick was gaining on Jessie. After stumbling blindly for thirty years, he had finally seen the red light in the blackness, and sprouted wings. The hollowness within him, the open grave that love could never fill, had burst from hunger and given birth to his future.

There was no love, only lies; and an endless race across a frozen steppe called survival.

Sighting her as she neared the end of the tunnel, he knew that he would catch her before she made the sun.

Jessie reached the lobby, and turned for the door that was only a moment away. She could see the sun's first rays glowing on the glass panes. She knew that if she got out, the vampires inside were doomed. Because she would come back in an hour as they slept, and avenge Matt, and—

She was ten feet from the door when Nick lunged. His hand came down on her shoulder. He had caught her.

Jessie never stopped moving as she let him spin her around. She threw her arms around him as his fangs closed in on her throat, and her embrace only tightened as the vampire realized that their impetus was carrying them through the door.

Nick only struggled for a moment as they crashed in a heap on the sidewalk. As the pitiless, warming rays of the sun cauterized his skin, a mirage of regret shimmered briefly in his mind before it was vaporized by fear. His fading gray eyes focused on Jessie's, inches away.

"Hold me," he whispered, in a voice like pouring sand.

And Death gently wrapped him in the folds of its cloak, until the burning light was replaced by the red, and the black.

Epilogue

WAITING FOR THE SUN

As the weight on her mysteriously lessened, Jessie disentangled herself from the corpse. Rising to her feet, she remembered that she had to go back to the tunnel. She wasn't really sure what she had just done, or how she had survived. All she could do was move her feet, one step at a time, through the lobby and down to the basement.

The old woman's eyes were on her as she emerged from the tunnel. When she spoke, Jessie thought of crumpling sheets of parchment.

"I'm not surprised to see you, Mrs. Westerhays. Nicholas wasn't like you at all. He didn't know what he wanted, until it was too late."

Instead of answering Dolores, Jessie moved to Matt's side. Cradling his head in her lap, she waited for him to regain consciousness. Matt was very pale. She didn't know how much blood Van Lo had taken from him, or what effect it would have on the boy's wavering humanity. She didn't know what would happen when she took him out into the sun. She only wanted for him to open his eyes and speak to her.

"He is one of us, Mrs. Westerhays. You must save me, or it will all have been for nothing."

Jessie ignored her, and bent over Matt. "Are you okay?"

The boy opened his eyes blankly. She asked him again and, after a moment, he shrugged.

Jessie tousled his hair. "Give me your hand. I'll help you up."

Matt stood slowly, and leaned against her until the dizziness went away. When he felt ready, he nodded. "Let's go."

Jessie braced herself as they approached the wheelchair. This was the old woman's last chance, and she knew it.

Dolores brought her fingers together and peered up at Matt. "Who's going to help you when you die, boy? Don't you want the secret of eternal sleep? *She* can't save you then."

Jessie gripped Matt's elbow as he wavered. He looked at her quickly, and they moved forward again.

Dolores turned to Jessie. "Aren't you curious about what happened to your daughter?"

She let her lips roll back in an evil smile. "I want you to sleep well at night, Mrs. Westerhays. Without any doubts as to how Amanda became what she was, or what she did afterwards . . ."

Matt hesitated only a moment before pulling out a handkerchief from his pocket and wadding it into a ball. He pushed Dolores's forehead back and forced open her mouth.

The old vampire jerked her head to one side, trying to avoid the gag. *"You don't know who I am!"*

Then she was silenced. Matt and Jessie looked at each other, and took their places behind the wheelchair. Pushing their load forward, they re-entered the tunnel.

As they made their way through the darkness, Jessie allowed herself to think of what was awaiting her, and what she had lost. Her family was gone, but now there was Matt. It wasn't the same: nothing ever would be, or was meant to be. Her love for Matt—her responsibility for him—couldn't ever extend as completely as it had for Tod and Amanda. And it shouldn't: she had learned that much from her mistakes.

Just four months before, she had been happier than she would ever be again. It was a happiness she hadn't earned, but the memory of it was hers to keep, hers to lean on as she grappled with the present, with all of the precarious tomorrows. Knowing how fragile life was made it all the more wondrous. It made her feel alive.

Finally they reached the basement. Jessie turned to Matt while they waited for the elevator to descend, and spoke as lightly as she could.

"I was thinking . . . in all those vampire movies, the victims are always all right after Dracula dies."

"That's the movies," he answered softly, and met her gaze. But then, instead of saying *this is real life*, he grinned: that goofy, gap-toothed grin. And they pushed the wheelchair into the elevator, and out to the waiting sun.